SHOO-FLY

On this June day, with the doors open to the garden, the house should have been filled with sunlight. But there was a chill.

'You know about my son, Mrs Blair?' Hubert Neville stood, hands in pockets, staring out at the rose-bed.

'Yes. I'm sorry.' The murder of Julian Neville had hogged the headlines for weeks. Nasty business, Elizabeth thought. A good-looking young man with everything to live for found lying in a pool of blood up on Beechen Cliff. Bludgeoned to death with a length of iron railing. No witnesses. No one charged. Most of the evidence washed away by a midnight thunderstorm.

'I want you to find out who killed him.'

About the author

Lizbie Brown was brought up in North Cornwall and read English at the University of Sheffield. She now lives with her husband near Bath. She has a grown-up son and daughter. Her earlier work includes many short stories and suspense serials for magazines. She has written two earlier novels in the series, *Broken Star* and *Turkey Tracks*. She is also the author of an historical novel, *Golden Dolly*, published in New York in 1988.

Shoo-Fly

Lizbie Brown

NEW ENGLISH LIBRARY
Hodder & Stoughton

First published in Great Britain in 1998
by Hodder and Stoughton
First published in paperback in 1999
by Hodder and Stoughton
A division of Hodder Headline PLC

A New English Library Paperback

10 9 8 7 6 5 4 3 2 1

A CIP catalogue record for this title
is available from the British Library.

ISBN 0 340 71750 5

Typeset by Hewer Text Ltd, Edinburgh
Printed and bound in Great Britain by
Mackays of Chatham PLC, Chatham, Kent

Hodder and Stoughton
A division of Hodder Headline PLC
338 Euston Road
London NW1 3BH

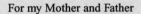

For my Mother and Father

CHAPTER ONE

On this June day, with the doors open to the garden, the house should have been filled with sunlight. But there was a chill.

'You know about my son, Mrs Blair?' Hubert Neville stood, hands in pockets, staring out at the rose-bed.

'Yes. I'm sorry.' The murder of Julian Neville had hogged the headlines for weeks. Nasty business, Elizabeth thought. A good-looking young man with everything to live for found lying in a pool of blood up on Beechen Cliff. Bludgeoned to death with a length of iron railing. No witnesses. No one charged. Most of the evidence washed away by a midnight thunderstorm.

'I want you to find out who killed him.' Neville seemed to be in some country of his own inside his head. Rather a handsome head, as it happened. Spare and lean, bushy eyebrows, the mottled, reddish cheeks of an outdoors man. 'He spent that last evening in town with friends. At The Bargepole. You know it?'

'Argyle Street.'

'That's it. They had a few drinks – nothing heavy, you understand – but youngsters today, well, they can't gossip without a glass in their hand. They were talking, horsing around, having a good time. One of Julian's schoolfriends, Toby Perrin, usually gave him a lift home, but he decided to walk. I wish to God he hadn't.'

'What time did he leave the pub?'

'Elevenish. Some of them were going on to eat, but Julian didn't bother. He was last seen down by the weir with a girl.'

'Do we have a description?'

'Blue jeans, long, dark hair. Only no one's been able to trace her. I thought you might try.'

Elizabeth studied him with her calm, green gaze. 'I'd need a list of his friends. Names and addresses.'

'That's no problem.'

'Were there any later sightings? If he walked home—'

'One brief glimpse. He was seen crossing the ring road at the lights. He must have taken the short-cut through the station. His usual route.'

'Was the girl with him?'

'No. He was alone. And that was the last anyone saw of him until – until his body was discovered next morning.'

'By whom?'

'By a woman walking her dog.'

'So when did you report him missing?'

'At lunchtime the following day. He sometimes crashed out on a friend's floor, you see. Then he'd ring in the morning. We go to bed quite early. He knew that. Wouldn't want to wake us.'

A clock ticked away in the drawing-room. Hubert Neville talked on in a harsh voice, filling in all the details that stuck like needles in his brain. 'He was beaten senseless. Died of head wounds in the alley that leads on to Beechen Cliff. It's a short-cut that he often takes. I don't know if this has any significance, but they've had a lot of trouble on the allotments that back on to the alley. Theft, vandalism. The police did wonder if he'd surprised someone up to no good.'

'And what do you think?' Outside, bees droned in the roses. The city lay pale yellow in the heat.

'I think it was someone he knew. A man called Gerard Dundy.'

'Who is . . . ?'

'Bloody nutcase. Dundy's married to a girl who worked with my son. He'd already attacked Julian once in public. Accused him of carrying on with his wife, which is ridiculous. I mean, good God, the boy didn't need to mess around with married women. Girls swarmed round him like bees. He was a young man of considerable charm.'

'Julian was your only child, I believe?' She had done her homework, looked the case up in back numbers of *The Chronicle*.

'Yes. We wanted more children, but my wife . . . she couldn't have more.' He removed his half-moon glasses with a shaking hand. 'Biggest regret of our life.'

Elizabeth flipped over a page in her notebook. 'And he worked . . . let me see . . . at the Ministry of Defence?'

'Yes. Up at Draycott. Hadn't been there long. Paper pushing. Nothing at all sinister.'

'And before that?'

'After he left Oxford, he knocked about the world for a year. Kids do these days. When he came back, well, he was broke, so he took the first job that was offered. The MoD was a stop-gap, until he could get into the career he wanted.'

'Which was?'

'Something in the media. Something more exciting. But it's hell these days. Too many of them fighting over too few places.'

Silence. Through the folding doors was a long dining-table and a jug with a pale splodge of honeysuckle. Beyond that, an Adam fireplace as big as a battleship.

'Was anything stolen in the attack?' Elizabeth asked. 'Money? Personal effects?'

'His wallet was missing. Never been found.'

It was at this point that her mobile bleeped. 'Excuse me,' said Elizabeth, foraging in her bag.

It was Max. The boy had a habit of calling at the wrong moment. 'Where are you, Betsey?'

'At the Neville house. Beechen Grove.'

'Nobs' Hill.' She heard the grin in his voice. 'Good.'

'What do you want, Max?'

'While you're up there . . .' He was munching his way through a mint, by the sound of it.

'Yes?'

'I wondered if you'd pop into the allotments.'

'Allotments?'

'Yeah. Halfway down the hill. They run parallel to the

3

Kennet and Avon. I had a call from a Squadron-Leader Jones. Says he's had his onions pinched.'

'You are joking?'

'No. He's hopping mad. Prepared to pay whatever it takes to catch the culprit. I said you'd meet him in the potting shed.'

'Thanks a bunch. What time?'

'Half an hour?'

'OK,' she sighed. 'Max—'

'Elizabeth—'

'Why can't you see to the Squadron-Leader's onions?'

'Too busy.'

'Doing what?'

'Standing in a cupboard.'

She ran a hand through her fair-to-greying hair. 'Any particular reason? Or is that a stupid question?'

'Pinhole camera job. The case of the slamming door.'

Now she remembered. The Council investigation in a small block of flats . . . Angola House. It had started as a noise complaint, but was probably rooted in something more sinister. The complainant being too scared to testify in court, the Council was paying Max to set up a time-lapse video to monitor a suspected drugs dealer who had visitors at all hours of the day and night.

'OK, Max.' A pause. 'There's just one thing.'

'What's that?'

'Check that you've got the right address this time. It sort of helps.' She cut him off before he could come back at her.

'Sorry about that,' she told Neville. 'My young partner, Max Shepard. His detective agency is above my quilt shop in Pierrepont Mews.'

Neville said abruptly, 'I don't quite see—'

'I have a finger in both pies,' Elizabeth told him. 'It works quite well.'

Sometimes she was in serious danger of being overworked, but it was better than being brain-dead. And plugging into one of the Shepard Agency cases kept boredom at bay and took you into corners of Bath that you would never otherwise have entered. It surely was a fascinating city. The kind of place that got a grip on you. She was for ever singing its praises to her folks back home in Turkey Creek, Virginia.

'So will you take the case?' Neville asked.

'We can turn over the ground that the police have covered. I can't promise results.'

'Just do what you can.' His voice was kind of flat and clapped-out. A door behind them clicked. Someone had come in through the panelled hallway. A woman . . . tall and elegant in a spare sort of way. Thick, grey hair twisted behind her longish neck and knotted with a silk scarf. Pearl stud earrings, white silk blouse, navy linen skirt.

'Diana!' Hubert looked at her with a kind of blustery surprise.

'Who's this?' Cool, grey eyes surveyed Elizabeth.

'Mrs Blair. This is my wife, Diana.' Hubert was startled. 'I . . . didn't expect you back.'

'Evidently.' Mrs Neville sounded like lemon juice. Tart and acid.

CHAPTER TWO

'Mrs Blair runs a detective agency.' He said it almost defiantly. 'I told you I was thinking of calling someone in.'

'And I told you it would be no utter use. Why don't you leave it alone, for God's sake? I hate deception, Hubert. I hate it when you do things behind my back.'

'Sometimes it's the only way.' Neville stared out at the heat waves shimmering and dancing down over the valley. There seemed to be a rumpled look about him, but it was hard to define exactly. 'I had no choice. You wouldn't listen. Someone has to find out what happened to the boy. I can't bear it sitting here day after day, not knowing. Nobody caring.'

'So you have a monopoly on caring. Is that it?'

'Of course not. But—'

'I mean, you didn't even have the wits to go down to her office!' Diana dumped her bag on the table and turned to face him with an irritated stab of the hand. 'You can't even call in a grubby little detective without being caught out. It's pathetic. You're pathetic.'

Grubby? thought Elizabeth. I've been called some things. 'Now hang on—'

'Stop that tape, would you? And clear out of my house.'

Elizabeth blinked at this female of the braying classes. Okey-doke, she thought. If that's how you want it. 'Are you talking to me?'

'You know I am.'

'Then I'd appreciate a little courtesy. If you could rustle some up.'

'Courtesy?' Diana spluttered.

A winning smile. 'It oils the wheels, I find.'

7

'Of all the cheek! Get out of my house. Just get out.'

'No. Stay where you are.' The colour had risen in Neville's already ruddy cheeks, but he held his ground.

Elizabeth had a good poker face when she needed it. She sat there on the edge of her chair, fascinated by this contest of wills.

'So what do you think she can do? Some nosing woman from some riff-raff little detective agency? The police are doing what they can. They've still got a team on the case.'

'Two men. Part time. In between all the other cases. Car theft, rapes, muggings and God knows what else.' His voice was weary. 'I'm sorry, Diana. It's not good enough.'

'So what can she do that they can't? Tell me.'

'She can follow Dundy day and night. Rattle his cage. Harass him. Kick start something or other . . .'

'Now hang on—' said Elizabeth. 'I don't do harassment.' Save your breath, she thought. The battle flowed on.

'You get these half-baked schemes in your head. It'll cost a fortune—'

Hubert's voice was unsteady, but militant. 'I don't care. Have you forgotten this . . . this . . . trash?' He pulled something from his pocket – a tightly folded, dog-eared tabloid newspaper with a lurid headline – and smacked it down on the coffee table.

'Dundy's story? A parcel of lies.'

'But lies that people read and believed. Lies that denigrated our son's name. And Dundy got paid handsomely for the exercise. I won't have it, Diana. I won't have him get away with murder and profit by it. It's an insult to Julian's memory.'

'I told you to set light to it.'

He was rigid with anger, his breath coming in short jerks. 'No way! I need it as evidence. I'm going to sue.'

'May I see?' Elizabeth said, taking her life in her hands.

'No.' Diana Neville snatched up the newspaper. 'It's nothing to do with you.'

'Let her read it.'

'Over my dead body.' Was that panic in her voice?

'Let her have it, damn you!' Hubert was advancing on his

wife, arm outstretched. He tried to grab the paper, but failed. His face went suddenly ashen. He's going to hit her, Elizabeth thought. But his right hand came down again, clutching the chair back. His left was on his chest.

'One of your attacks?' In a trice, Diana dropped the newspaper and had him by the shoulders. 'Calm down. Deep breaths. That's it.'

He stood there inhaling deeply; once, twice, three times. Gradually his colour came back. He began to look more normal.

'Want a pill? Had you better?'

'No.' Another long, deeply held breath. 'Not till teatime. I'm all right now.'

'Sure? Come on,' Diana said. 'Lie down. Forget it all for now. It's doing you no good.'

'Can't forget it.' He bit his lip as it trembled with emotion. 'Christ, woman, can't you see—?'

For a moment more, her hand rested on his shoulder. Something flashed in her eyes and was gone again. She straightened her back. Shrugged. 'No. Well, if your mind's set on it . . .' If there was emotion, it was once more hidden behind an expressionless mask.

'She seems hard, but it's a façade,' Hubert said after his wife had left the room. 'She's detached herself, do you see? Can't take any more. Underneath she's in as bad a state as I am. Can't concentrate. Can't work. All seems pointless you know?'

'I do know, actually.'

He shot her a quick glance.

'I lost my husband in a car crash in the States five years back. It's worse, losing a child. But—'

'You know something of it?' His eyes were tortured.

'I do. I came over here on vacation to get away from my grief. Liked it and stayed.'

'Do you miss the States?'

'I miss my family at times. But they come visit. Are you OK?'

'Fine now. Touch of angina, that's all.' Neville smoothed

the creased tabloid and folded it in two. 'What you don't know is that it's a double blow for my wife. She lost her favourite brother in a boating tragedy as a teenager. Julian looks just like him. Looked—' He agonised over the tense. 'If only we could find out why – or who – then maybe, eventually, we'll be able to put it behind us. No matter how awful. It's the not knowing . . .'

'I'm sure.'

'So will you have a go? Take the case?'

'I don't see why not. Though I can't promise anything.'

'I realise that. Just do your best.' There were sudden tears in his eyes and his voice turned gruff as he fought for control.

'May I borrow that?' She held out a hand towards the newspaper.

'If it helps.'

'And you'd better know our terms.' She folded the paper into her bag. 'It's not cheap, I'm afraid.'

'That's OK. I don't care about the money. What's it for now, anyway? There's no one to leave it to.' He walked stiffly with her to the front door. 'Just do what you can. That's all I ask.'

Pigeons circled over the city as Elizabeth ambled down the hill. She turned to gaze back at the Neville house. One of a terrace of graceful old Regency buildings with square-paned windows and traced ironwork balconies restored to an elegance that the original owners probably wouldn't have recognised. Shimmering heat over Palladian rooftops. Not a cloud in the sky. But here, under the green, wooded hill, there was a beechy smell. The trees were very still. Hard to imagine a pleasanter place to live. Or a more incongruous setting for a murder.

She stood in the shade of a high stone wall and tried to get a fix on the Neville household. Tortured father, grim-faced mother. Not a happy home. Well, you wouldn't expect it under the circumstances, but for all that, there was something a bit odd. She tried to pin it down. Diana Neville. Tense. Her emotions coiled as tightly as her hair. That sharp glance she had thrown at the tape recorder. Why on earth would she be scared about her husband calling in a detective? You'd think she would have been pleased. Doting mother, only son. But instead there had been – what? A certain watchfulness. Something that raised suspicion. Of course, you might be reading too much into it, she told herself. Have a fudge bar. Or two.

It was Friday noon and there was no way she was going to quiz the Squadron-Leader about his onions with a hole in her stomach. As she munched, she studied the A-Z. The allotments didn't seem to be marked, but the Kennet and Avon Canal was there. So if you took one of these left-hand alleys and kept heading downhill in that direction . . .

The alley turned itself at last into a zigzag track that went down through a wicker gate. Rough terraces now, directly below Beechen Cliff, baking hot and pin-drop still. There was a flower patch – roses and fat dahlias. The burnt-out shell of a car (how had they got that down here?). And then, straight in front of her, a double row of pea sticks that would somehow have to be circumvented.

As she took a short hike through a rhubarb patch, she cursed Max. Dirt was filtering into her sandals and sticking, grittily, between her toes. If I'd known, I'd have worn deck shoes. He never warns me. Never thinks ahead. Never thinks at all.

Elizabeth stood like a stork and shook the grit out of one sandal. Hopped sideways and tried to do the other one, which was how she came to topple sideways. Which was how she came to land one foot in the middle of a row of carrots. Which suddenly, and inexplicably, exploded with a flash of blue flame.

CHAPTER THREE

'What in hell's name—?' Elizabeth found herself stumbling backwards down the hillside. Slithering to a halt at the back of a garden hut.

'Well, that worked,' a voice said. A thin, compact man in navy ankle socks and baggy khaki shorts appeared like a genie through the acrid smoke. His pink face wore a satisfied grin.

Elizabeth glared at him. 'What worked? What the hell was that?'

'Trip wire fitted to an alarm gun. Nifty little construction, though I say it myself.'

Her ears were still popping from the explosion. 'You fired a gun at me?'

'Only blank twelve-bore cartridges. But they had the desired effect.'

Enough noise to waken the dead. He was dangerously disordered.

'You shouldn't have been trespassing,' said the genie. 'They thought you were an intruder.'

'They?'

'My carrots. They were primed to go off.'

Booby-trapped carrots? 'God damn it,' said Elizabeth. 'You could have killed me.'

'Not with a charge that small. Sit down a minute. Recover yourself.' Suddenly he held his hand out. 'I'd better introduce myself. Roland Jones. Squadron-Leader.'

Great, thought Elizabeth. That's all I need. For a crumpled dollar, I have to look on this nitwit as a valued customer. Be polite, instead of telling him to go boil his head.

'Elizabeth Blair. Shepard Detective Agency.' She found

13

herself, ridiculously, echoing his clipped speech.

'You're American.'

He was astute. 'Any objection?'

'Not really. Flew with a few during the war. Mouthy. But mustard when it came to the job in hand.'

'That's me,' she said, dropping into a battered garden chair. 'At your service. So . . . what's the problem? What can we do for you?'

'Petty theft. That's the problem. It's reaching epidemic proportions. Something has to be done.'

'So what have you lost?'

'What haven't I lost? You name it. They've nicked it. Mowers, tools, benches, tables, plants. Over two hundred thefts in the last eighteen months. I charted them, you see. A cowboy gang . . . that's what I think.'

'Clint Eastwood?'

The city dozed below them in the heat. Somewhere a dog barked. Scattered potting sheds, perched on strips of baked earth, gave the hillside a ramshackle air.

Jones said testily, 'Cowboy gardeners, that's my theory. There's a lot of them about these days, knocking on doors, toting for work. And when it comes to plants and trees . . . well, they're not going to cough up for the stuff, are they? They'll come up here and pinch it. Plant the stuff next day in some poor sucker's garden, Mrs Shepard.'

A zephyr breeze ruffled the grass. 'Blair,' Elizabeth murmured.

He wasn't listening. Too busy riding his high horse. 'What's it matter if the plants keel over a couple of days later? They've had the money and gone by then. A chap down on the next plot had his hedge stolen, would you believe? A little laurel hedge that he planted to shade the vegetable patch and make it more private, like.'

'Did he call the police?'

'Police? Of course he did! But all they say is, there's a lot of it going on. No time, that's the problem. So . . . when I lost my prize begonias, well, I'm mild-mannered as a rule. Polite as the next man. But we all have our limits. I started to take

14

my own preventive measures.' At Elizabeth's raised eyebrow, he said, 'I was in two minds about the alarm gun, but it's my last line of defence.'

'So what else did you try?'

'Security lights. Dummy cameras. Locks and bolts. But you can't rivet an onion into a socket, now, can you?'

A ticklish question, when you came to ponder it. Almost any answer you gave would lead to further horticultural, or even philosophical ramblings, so Elizabeth took him down different avenues. Explained her terms and conditions and finally parted from him with a promise to make enquiries and be in touch.

There was still a whiff of gunpowder and onion lingering about her as she walked through the front door of her shop, Martha Washington, in Pierrepont Mews. Caroline, polite as ever, pretended not to notice.

Caroline had worked in the shop since it opened three years back and Elizabeth had never seen her fazed. Had never heard the girl's little plum mouth give out anything except little plummy sounds. If the sky crashed on her meticulously groomed head, Caroline would simply find a compelling reason to make a fresh pot of Earl Grey and ring her aristocratic mother for a chat. ('Seriously,' Elizabeth had once heard her say, 'you'll have to knock the Duke's luncheon on the head.')

'Everything OK?' Elizabeth asked now.

'One awkward customer, I'm afraid.'

'Oh?'

'Wanted to borrow the Oregon Trail book instead of buying it.'

'Cheek! You didn't?'

'Of course not,' said Caroline, twiddling a pearl ear-ring.

'Is Max back?'

'Five minutes ago.'

'Then I'll just pop upstairs.'

As she got to the door, Caroline said, 'He was a bit odd, I thought.'

Now Caroline, on the whole, lived her life inside her elegant shell. She wasn't a natural observer. So if Max's behaviour had got through to her . . .

'What kind of odd?' Elizabeth asked.

On that, Caroline was hazy. 'Oh . . . you know.'

'No, I don't, my dear.'

'Well . . .' Caroline stood and thought. 'He came flying in to see if you were here and . . .'

'Yes?'

'He seemed . . . excited.'

What could have happened to the boy in the last hour? There was only one way to find out. Elizabeth climbed the creaking staircase that led up to the Shepard Agency office.

Max – floppy brown hair, turned-down blue eyes and almost matching shirt – was stretched out by the desk with his feet on the window sill. 'How did it go?' he asked.

'The Neville case? Interesting. We'll take it.'

'And Jones the Onion?' When he slung that live-wire grin at you, the whole effect was pretty attractive, which would be awful if he were aware of the fact. But thank God, the boy wasn't even remotely sure of himself in the charm stakes, though he would rather die than admit the fact.

'Nutter of the first order,' said Elizabeth. Caroline's right, she thought. You could see in an instant that Max was lit up. And there was a bottle of beer beside him. He rarely drank in office hours.

'Somebody's birthday?' she asked.

'Nope.'

'You won the lottery.'

'Better.'

Then it had to be the usual thing. Some female.

She was proved right. Max's voice was jubilant. 'Jess rang.'

'Jess, your ex-girlfriend?'

'Yep.'

'The one who dumped you?'

'That was in Manchester. A lifetime ago.'

'So?' said Elizabeth drily.

'So she needed space to build up her modelling career. She's done that. And now she's here in Bath. Her caravan has hit town. That's what she said on the phone. They're on a shoot.'

'Pheasants?' Elizabeth enjoyed needling the boy. She wished Max would learn some sense about women. He always fell for the wrapping paper instead of what was inside the package and she was tired of seeing him get let down.

'So how did she get your number?'

'Not sure.' His face had gone all blank.

'Are you going to meet her?'

'I might.' Max, having stared at the beer bottle for some time, picked it up and took a long swig. A vague flicker of consciousness seemed to have returned. 'Well, actually, I'm meeting her tomorrow night.'

'Where?'

'My place for drinks. Then a restaurant.'

'Who's paying?' At this time of the month, Max wouldn't have a bean. And the business was not over-remunerative and the rent was due.

'I am,' he said defiantly.

'With what? Buttons?'

'Look – I can hardly ask her to pay the bill.'

'Why not, if she's flourishing?'

'Oh, shut up, Betsey. Mind your own business for once in your life.'

It was her business, she told him, if he borrowed from petty cash. Max refused to discuss the matter. In the end, she didn't press it, but filled him in on the Neville case.

'It was a violent attack. The boy was struck repeatedly round the head and body while he was lying unconscious. He was facing down the alley towards the main road. Possibly, he'd attempted to run for it.'

'So whoever did it must have been covered in blood.'

'Unless he got hosed down by the heavy downpour just after midnight.'

'We're assuming the attacker was male?'

'Not necessarily.' It was odds-on, but a killer – even female – in that kind of frenzy could no doubt summon up extra strength.

'Time of death?' Max asked.

'Between 11.30 and 12.45 a.m., according to forensic.' She pulled a cutting from the folder that lay on the desk. Julian Neville's face gazed out from the front page of a *Daily Mail*. The face of a Botticelli angel, she'd thought on first viewing it. Thick, fair hair cut in a swept-back style that seemed to reveal rakish confidence. You could imagine him flicking a hand through it as he eyed the ladies. Self-assured blue eyes slanting towards the camera. One degree less and the smile would have been natural affection. One more, and it would be calculating. He was standing on somebody's lawn, wearing a blue denim shirt and cream shorts. A good-looking young man who was perfectly aware of the fact. Who was about to say something to the person behind the camera. Hurry up. Get on with it. The eyes had some rebellious emotion building up behind them. A charming impatience. Or was that fanciful? Elizabeth wondered who had taken the shot.

'He gained a reputation for drunken horseplay while at Oxford. Streaking down the High for a bet. Breaking up the contents of a rustic establishment called The Wooden Pig, deep in the Oxfordshire countryside.'

'Bloody hooray Henry,' Max said.

'Thoughtless, light-hearted fun, according to his mother. The dons said he had a brain, but didn't use it. Might have achieved more if he'd worked once in a while. Concentrated on his studies instead of batting off to London at weekends, treading the boards with OUDS, visiting racecourses and disc-jockeying at nightclubs.'

What else? Julian had come to Draycott with a poor Third in Politics and Economics and had done nothing in the ensuing months to alter his reputation as a charming layabout. A colleague called Hilary Russell had told the *Sun* reporter that she didn't believe the rumour that he'd been sleeping around with half the women in his department. Certain people might be eaten up with jealousy, but Julian had always been very respectful towards her. And just because a man was good at flirting, it didn't mean he was about to leap into your bed.

'Which is perfectly true,' Elizabeth said after reading out the relevant passage to Max. 'I thought I might pop up to Draycott. Nose around a bit. That OK with you?'

He turned his head and gazed at her for a minute as if she were an alien from Mars, before answering the question with a disturbing vagueness. 'Yeah. Right.'

It wasn't like Max to go in on himself – not in his nature – and Elizabeth found herself perturbed by the half-frown on his face. She was fond of the boy and she didn't relish the thought of seeing some pea-brained little floozie leading him by the nose. Though she didn't positively know it, she had a strong suspicion that this Jess was the wrong sort. However, for once, she held back from lecturing him on the subject of his love life.

'Right,' she said briskly. 'So we'll get the Neville stuff on the computer. Yes? Names, addresses, phone numbers.' The list of Julian's friends (largely female) that Hubert Neville had given her would no doubt keep them going for a while.

As she dropped her bag on the desk, there was a noise on the landing and a head popped round the door. 'Oops – sorry. Didn't mean to interrupt.'

'You're not,' said Elizabeth. 'Come on in.'

The girl had startlingly red hair, masses of it, drawn neatly back into a ruched silk band. 'This *is* the Shepard Agency?'

'It is. What can we do for you?'

'I'm the new temp. Sorry I'm late.'

CHAPTER FOUR

'I didn't order a temp.' Max was back in the present.

'No, but I did,' Elizabeth said. 'This place needs a good sorting out.'

'Over my dead body!'

'I hope not,' she told him. 'But if it's a choice between you and the mail backlog—'

'We'll catch up.'

'Not if you keep bunging things in that damned cupboard. It needs clearing.'

'Nobody touches that cupboard. I've got a system.'

'You could have fooled me.'

The girl coughed. 'I could come back later.' Grey eyes surveyed them from behind little granny frames. Her white arms had a smattering of freckles. She wasn't conventionally pretty, but there was something about her; something sturdy and energetic. She wore a green silk shirt and grey trousers and an air of competence which was already reassuring.

'Stay right where you are,' said Elizabeth. 'Tell us about yourself. Previous experience?'

'Three years with the RAC in Bristol. Two with Lloyds of London. I've just come back to Bath to live and I'm temping while I look for something permanent.'

'Sounds fine. We'll need references.'

'Of course.'

'Now hang on,' Max said.

'You'll thank me, Max, I promise you.'

'I'm the senior partner.'

'True. But as an organiser, you're semi-useless.' She beamed a smile at the little temp. 'Anything you want to ask us?'

The girl's gaze went all round the office, then came back to the look on Max's face. 'Does a flack jacket come with the job?'

A sense of humour. You'll do, Elizabeth thought. 'A hard hat and a bottle of aspirin,' she said crisply. 'So when can you start, Miss . . . ?'

'Dickinson. Jane. But everyone calls me Ginger,' the girl said with a resigned air. 'I'll start in the morning.'

The MoD establishment called Draycott stood on a hill overlooking the deep valley between Bath and Bristol. The ground behind and above its perimeter fence was sharply terraced and topped by a ridge of ancient beeches, bosky in summer, bleak when the leaves were down.

To the left of the main gates was the road down to town, lined with substantial properties hidden behind tall stone walls. On the right, open fields until you came, half a mile beyond the crossroads, to a pub called The Angel Gabriel. Formerly a Georgian farmhouse, it was said to be named after some ship. No one knew which vessel or when, but the naval connection was thought singularly appropriate for the MoD naval establishment alongside, the nerve centre of which was an old, grey-gabled building left over from the original manor house which had stood there until the Thirties. The kind of house that once held stags' antlers, but now was clogged with desks and filing cabinets and shipping maps and bank after bank of computers.

During the last war, these grand old rooms would have been manned by personnel in boiled shirts and gold-rimmed spectacles. Now it was a plain grey flannel place. Respectable, formal, a touch on the gloomy side. Draycott was known locally as a place where you had a job for life. As a repository for dead wood and the bone idle. Trailblazers might occasionally arrive, but they certainly didn't stay.

Around the main building, there still stood a rabbit warren of Nissen huts left over from wartime, when the site had been used as a transition camp for the Wessex Light Infantry.

'I'd like to speak with Hilary Russell,' said Elizabeth to the security man at the main gate. 'I'm sorry, I have no idea which department.'

He nodded. 'Do you have an appointment?'

'No, I don't.'

'And your name?'

'Elizabeth Blair. I was just hoping—'

The phone shrilled behind him. He leaned backwards to answer it, had a brief conversation, pressed a button and spoke to someone else. 'Wait there,' he said. 'She'll come down and get you.'

Squirrels scampered under the chestnuts, fed, on summer lunchtimes, on a diet of cake crumbs and the tail ends of ham sandwiches. Through a window opposite, Elizabeth could see a girl tapping at a keyboard on a desk that seemed to be knee deep in paper; in-trays and out-trays stacked high with forms made out in triplicate. If you lost something, she thought, it would lie hidden for months. Perhaps years.

'OK, George. I'll take it from here. Mrs Blair. Delighted to meet you. I expect you got held up in traffic. I said you wouldn't be long.' Hilary Russell turned out to be a baby-faced girl wearing a pink headband. Heavily built; top heavy, with breasts the size of water melons. She wore an Indian muslin tent affair, sandals and flesh-coloured tights. She didn't wait for Elizabeth to introduce herself, but jumped into the passenger seat with an enthusiastic speech of welcome. 'You can park just up there on the right. The admiral's already started his tour, but if we hurry we should catch him.'

'Actually—'

'The quickest way is for me to take you.' No sooner had Elizabeth switched off the engine than the girl was out of the car and guiding her visitor into the nearest Nissen hut by a side door. 'They don't like Press people wandering around on their own. Anyway, you'd never find him. This place is a labyrinth.'

Elizabeth almost decided to put the girl right. She opened her mouth to do so. But then she thought, it's more fun to go with the flow. You learn such interesting things by letting people rattle on. And besides, Hilary was well ahead of her down the corridor, talking ten to the dozen. She was a natural mother hen.

'We'll cut through the kitchen. Bernard doesn't like it, but what the heck!'

'Bernard?'

Hilary Russell giggled with just a quiver of her ample bosom. She was perhaps in her early twenties, but already there was more than a hint of the matronly. Her face seemed to have little shape. The floor tiles clacked beneath her weight as she lumbered along.

'We wouldn't dare call him that to his face. It's Mr Lucas most of the time. He's the big boss around here. He's all right, is Bernard. Mind you, he runs a tight ship. That's his favourite phrase. I'm running a tight ship here. You've all got to pull your weight. He won't let anyone take liberties. Isn't this heat a killer? Still, it's Sports Day tomorrow. We've got the afternoon off.'

'Sports Day?' Just like school, Elizabeth thought, bemused.

Hilary laughed. 'We have one every year, down at the Recreation Ground. Just a bit of fun. Track and field and an egg and spoon race.'

'End of term stuff?'

'That's it. We're lucky with holidays here. They give us loads. The Queen's birthday, which you don't have to take on the actual day. You can save it and take it in lieu. Plus we have Maundy Thursday. And gardening leave, if you're high enough up . . . so that you can sort of catch up on your delphiniums.'

Elizabeth dragged a hand through her hair as if to nudge her brain back into gear. Breathed in the faint odour of paint and ink and rusting paper clips. She noted the deep gully where Hilary's black bra strap cut into the ample flesh of her back.

'I say, you're from the States. Am I right?' The girl glanced around to make sure she was still following.

'Right.'

'Mummy has a sister in Florida. How long have you been working for *The Chronicle*? Is it fun? I suppose you're always out and about?'

'Well, actually—'

'I showed one of your colleagues around last year. When we raised all that money for leukaemia research. He kept asking about a day in the life of a normal civil servant. I told him, no one's normal at Draycott. They're all a bit mad. That's the first thing you learn. Some of them . . . the ones who've been here years and years . . . don't have a clue how mad they really are.'

'Was Julian Neville mad?' asked Elizabeth suddenly, carefully watching the girl's reaction. Hilary had stopped abruptly in her tracks. Silenced.

Well, now.

Without taking her eyes from her companion's face, Elizabeth went on, 'I'm afraid I have a confession to make. I'm not your press lady. I'm a private detective investigating a murder.'

CHAPTER FIVE

There was no mistaking the fear. One of Hilary's hands touched the wall behind her, as if for support. She couldn't work out what to do with the other one. It came down from her mouth, fidgeted with the silver cross around her neck.
'Julian's murder?'
'Who else?'
She looked at Elizabeth, then away. 'But I don't know anything. I can't help you.'
'No? I heard you were a friend of his.'
'I was.' She flushed a dark, shiny pink.
'Girlfriend?'
An involuntary giggle. 'Don't be silly.'
'Just good friends then?'
'Yes. Yes, I think so.'
'Only think?'
'Well, you could never quite tell with Julian.' Her voice was still shaky. 'But, yes . . . we were friends. I don't know why exactly. I'm not at all his type. Wasn't his type. I mean . . . if you'd seen him . . . He was like a pop star. You could have imagined him doing all that. He had the looks, the charisma. And I'm . . . well . . . look at me.'
You were flattered by his friendship, Elizabeth thought.
'I suppose we were friends because I looked after him when he first came to Draycott.'
'That would be about a year ago?'
'That's right. It was my job to show him how things worked . . . where everything was. The filing system and such . . .' She was talking in a rush, intermittently stopping to pick up a stray thought. 'He could be so sweet, when he

27

was in the right mood. He bought me a lovely pair of ear-rings for Christmas. Expensive. I felt awful when I read about his debts. But I thought he could afford them. "Makes you look exotic," he said when I put them on.' Her mind went off somewhere for a moment. To another planet.

'So you were buddies?'

'I think so. He always acted as if you were his best friend. I mean, he'd confide in you . . . tell you stuff.'

'Such as?'

'Oh, which pub he'd been to the night before. Girlfriends. What he'd done over the weekend. You know . . .'

They moved on again. Now they were in a smaller hut that contained a drinks machine, a sink and some pale fitted cupboards.

'The kitchen,' Hilary said abstractedly. 'We have a tea club. We all contribute. No, that's a lie. I don't. I like my own pot. Mummy says a teapot is better, so I brought my own in. Can't stand the dreaded tea-bags. Not the same at all. The others don't like it because I won't join the tea club, but it can't be helped.' She pushed back her floppy dark hair with fingers that were as pudgy as a child's. Flashed a nervous smile. 'Anyway, the others all pay so much a week. There's a cake machine in H block. I try not to indulge. Got to watch the old calories.'

'Oh, come on, Hilly!' said a voice from behind them.

Hilary spun round. The newcomer was a girl with long, chestnut-coloured hair. She wore a slim, green skirt and a clingy little top, gooseberry green to match her eyes. Sharp eyes. A sly-boots, Elizabeth thought for no reason at all. How old? Twenty-eight? Twenty-nine?

'Who are you trying to kid?' Sly-boots reached out to open a drawer. 'Two doughnuts and a Mars bar yesterday after lunch.' Her voice was light and offhand. 'What are we on this week? The light heavyweight diet?'

She took out a teaspoon and slammed the drawer shut. Shook her head pityingly as she whisked out of the room again.

'Bitch!' said Hilary, half under her breath. 'What's it got to do with her? Bloody vegans! We can't all be stick insects.'

Elizabeth gazed at her with some sympathy. 'Of course you can't. I've known some knockout big girls.' She pressed on with the questions while she had the advantage. 'Julian Neville . . . How did he fit in here at Draycott?'

'He didn't. Not really. If you'd seen him that first morning . . . Ever so brown, he was, like a Greek god. He'd just spent the summer over there on some island. He used to sit there looking all languid and yawning a lot. You can't sleep at work, I told him. He said it seemed the perfect place. He couldn't care less. Didn't give a damn. But . . . well, that was what made him such fun. He was so different.'

'In what way?'

'Well, he liked taking the mickey. Morgan didn't get away with half as much when Julian was around.'

'Morgan?'

'The stick insect.'

'Odd sort of name.'

'Odd sort of person. And she's Welsh.'

'So Morgan and Julian didn't get on?'

'Couldn't stand each other. Morgan fancies herself – especially since she got promotion – and Julian just laughed at her.'

'Morgan's last name?' Elizabeth asked, pulling out her notepad.

'Dundy.'

'Any relation to Gerard Dundy?'

'His wife. Until a few months back, when they separated. Can't say I'm surprised. Who'd want to live with that tight-bummed, politically correct little cow?'

Elizabeth asked, 'Did Julian make a habit of it? Taking the mickey?'

'I'm afraid he did, rather. Well, this place must have been a come-down after Oxford.'

'I'm surprised he came here.'

'Oh, Draycott's full of people who never thought they'd finish up in the civil service. Anyway, he said he was only filling in while he looked for something more exciting.' From somewhere in the next hut, a phone rang. 'Actually, I think he'd just found it.'

'Really?'

'Something had come up. He wouldn't say what. Only that he was going off first to Europe. He seemed . . . excited, that last week. Lit up.'

Elizabeth found that interesting. She said, 'Tell me something – is there anyone here at Draycott who hated Julian enough to kill him?'

Hilary looked at her as if she had suggested taking off on a flight to Mars. 'Don't be silly.' Yet there was a strange panic in her voice.

'Would any of the work he was doing here be important? Secret, I mean?'

'We all have to sign the Official Secrets Act. But, no, not really. Not at Julian's level. It was all pretty run of the mill.'

Another blind alley. 'So tell me about the other people in your office. Who else did Julian make fun of?'

'Everybody really. Even Wendy.'

'Wendy?'

'Wendy Lucas. She's the top cog in Z Block. She's also Bernard's wife – only we're not allowed to mention that fact during office hours.'

'Why not, if everyone knows?'

'Bernard doesn't like it. He likes to keep their working lives separate and then he can't be accused of nepotism. That's the theory anyway.'

'So Julian used to needle the boss's wife? Why? Because Bernard had given her a leg up, promotion-wise?'

'Good lord, no. Wendy got where she is by climbing the ladder one rung at a time. You can't do it any other way in the civil service. It all goes by how long you've worked here and no one can leapfrog. But no one. Not even the big boss's wife.'

Sounds deadly, Elizabeth thought. 'So . . . how did Julian get at her?'

'Oh, he'd play her up by handing in bits of the pantomime he was writing instead of the report she expected from him. Things like that.'

'Pantomime?'

'He was naughty. He got so bored here, filing things and sharpening pencils and opening and shutting windows. There's never enough to do really. Mick plans his holidays on his spread-sheet. So anyway, last November, Julian started writing his version of *Cinderella* on the computer. He wanted us to put it on for the Christmas party. He'd spend half the week tapping all this rubbish into it. I'm digging deep into my inner life, he'd say.'

'And what was Wendy's reaction when he handed in bits of his play?'

'Well, Julian being Julian, he got away with murder. Oh, sugar! That wasn't the expression to use.' She looked quite distressed. 'What I meant to say is that Wendy would pretend to be cross, but she wasn't. You could tell that. This one piece he gave her . . . well, I don't know what was on it, but it made her go bright red. And then he'd sit and gaze at her, all intense like . . . he should have been on stage . . . and made her even worse. He knew how to use his charm quite openly.'

'So you think Mrs Lucas fancied him?'

'Quite possibly. We all did, frankly.'

'Would anything have been going on between her and Julian?'

'Good lord, no, nothing like that. It was just a bit of fun to him. He was subversive . . . you know? Like with the pantomime. He was terrible. He'd get people to confide in him . . . charm them into letting out secrets they'd never tell anyone else. Then he'd put it into the latest scene and drop it in somebody's in-tray.'

'What kind of secrets?'

'I don't think I should tell you that.'

'Look . . . Miss Russell . . . I'm trying to track down Julian's murderer. It might have some bearing.'

A bluebottle was buzzing round the window. Hilary watched it go round and round and said abstractedly, 'Julian should be here. He spent half his time flipping things at flies with his ruler. We used to have bets as to how many he could hit.'

Elizabeth tried again. 'These secrets. What sort of things are we talking about?'

'Well—'

Elizabeth let her take all the time she wanted. If you pushed too hard, it would have the opposite effect. She waited.

'There was nothing that would tempt anybody to kill him. Honestly. It was all such harmless stuff. Like he made out that Morgan was—'

'Hilary? Why aren't you at your desk?'

Hilly jumped as an older woman came through the door behind them. She was fair and plumpish, wearing a thrusting, poppy-coloured shade of lipstick. No calendar girl, but she had once probably been very pretty. She had been hurrying and was out of breath.

'Nothing, Mrs Lucas. Nothing at all. I was just . . . showing someone around.'

'I wasn't aware of any visitors.' The woman articulated every syllable with a clarity that approached menace.

'N . . . no. Well, I thought she was Press. For the admiral's party, you see. But it turns out—'

'Yes?'

'It turns out that she's . . . well . . .'

'It's not Miss Russell's fault,' said Elizabeth, handing the Lucas woman one of her cards. 'I misled her.'

'A private detective?' A look crossed the woman's face. 'But – you can't just come in here off the street! You should have rung for an appointment.'

'I realise that. It was just that I was driving past and—'

'On the way to where?' Wendy Lucas's tone was icy.

Good point, thought Elizabeth. She turned on her most winsome smile, but it didn't get her anywhere. There was a distinctly unpleasant look in the woman's eyes. 'Another appointment,' she said blithely. 'I'm investigating the murder of Julian Neville. I believe he worked here? I don't suppose you could spare a moment or two to answer a few questions?'

'Certainly not! So may I suggest it would be in your own interests to leave voluntarily. Otherwise I shall call Security and have you thrown out.'

Elizabeth slung her hook, as requested. Winked an eye in Hilary's direction and headed for the car park. As she did so, she heard the old cow taking the girl apart.

The not-so-civil service, she thought. Everything done by appointment. With a measuring rod and tape. Not to mention copies in triplicate.

She felt a small charge of relief at getting out into a clean, warm wind that smelled of chestnut and sycamore leaves. The same relief that Julian Neville must have felt at the end of a boring, pen-pushing day?

Elizabeth stood by the car, thinking about it.

Julian Neville. As sharp as his colleagues were dim. A maverick. A complete mismatch. But just at this moment, distinctly human. Unlike some people I could mention.

CHAPTER SIX

Elizabeth was in the shop with the door wide open. Late afternoon. The place was stuffed with patchwork quilts, whole truckloads of the damned things. They spilled from the window and from the pine shelves, a knock-out of colour, if you liked that kind of thing.

Max found it a touch on the twee side. The whole place looked like one great big set for *Little Women*. He stood there eyeing it. The Shaker style rocking-chair, the Victorian fire grate, the jug of old roses.

'Something wrong?' Elizabeth asked.

'This place.'

'Yes?'

'It needs something.'

'Such as?'

'Half a dozen sticky-fingered kids. A filthy great mongrel with muddy paws.'

'Don't even think about it.'

'So how was Draycott?'

'Dire. I got chucked out.'

'Well, that's a good start.'

'Mmn. It was interesting though.' She told him about it. 'I'd like another go at Hilary Russell. If the Lucas woman hadn't turned up—'

'You'd better make an appointment,' Max said with a grin.

'I've got a better idea.'

'What's that?'

'I'm going to gatecrash their Sports Day.'

Max said, 'You always were a sucker for our quaint old English customs. I suppose you'll get out your

Miss Marple gear and your shades—'

'Miss Marple gear?'

'Yeah. That flowery frock you bought at Oxfam. And a whacking great straw hat. You could pretend to be somebody's old auntie. Perfect casting.'

He got out fast, before she could clock him one.

Gerard Dundy had moved back into his mother's end-of-terrace house opposite a row of shops in Larkhall Road, not far from the Gym and Athletic Club that he part-owned. He had just come back from the pub when Max called and it was obvious, by the way he dropped into the chair, that he'd had more than enough.

He was a man in his mid-thirties. Thin and swarthy, with wary blue eyes and brown, curly hair. He wore a green tracksuit and scuffed trainers. Strong, nervous hands kept picking at the laces. Dundy's whole attitude was defensive, his eyes were constantly watchful.

The story he'd sold to the tabloid had been the biggest whinge Max had read in ages. Packed with gripes and evasions. The police had victimised him. He'd been given a bad press. He'd had all sorts of nasty phone calls. Anonymous, of course. In short, Dundy appeared to blame everybody in the world but himself for his two failed marriages and the mess that his life was in. It was all one big, pre-planned plot, quite outside his control.

'Thanks for seeing me at short notice.' Max brought out his professional smile. 'As I explained on the phone, we've been hired by Herbert Neville to look into his son's murder.'

Useless to try and read anything into Dundy's expression, which revealed nothing. But there was something in the twist of his mouth that showed an increased nervousness.

'The police pulled you in, so I had to talk to you,' Max said.

'I had a go at the little bastard. I didn't kill him.'

'But you threatened to, at some disco at the Angel Gabriel. They all heard you.'

His voice was harsh. 'I was drunk. I've got a short fuse and he was laughing at me. I'm not in the habit of bludgeoning people to death.'

'But you were in the SAS. Let's see now . . . Germany, two spells in Ireland, one in Bosnia. The army trained you to kill.' Max flipped on through his notepad. 'And five years ago, you were done for GBH.'

'That's different.'

'Is it? You attacked a man in a fight outside a pub. I've got the details here. You put him in plaster. Broken arm, broken nose, ten stitches in an eye wound . . .'

The colour rose in Dundy's face. 'He was having an affair with my wife. They'd been carrying on for months behind my back.'

Max felt the words drop inside him, like stones into deep water. He knew what that one felt like; he had been through it with Jess. 'Yes, well. That's tough.'

'I beat him up. I didn't kill him. And I didn't kill Neville. I wasn't even in town the night he was murdered.'

'You were on a fishing trip, I believe?'

'Yes. With a mate. We left Bath at about four-thirty. Wanted to get out before the rush. Joe picked me up at the gym. Lost my nerve when I was ill.'

Max said, 'The papers said you had psychiatric treatment.'

'No. Not exactly.'

'You either did or you didn't. Which is it?'

'It was a long time back. In a different life.'

'OK. So you had psychiatric treatment. Here in Bath?'

'In Bristol actually. Caught the bus in every day.'

There's a certain kind of bloke, Max thought, when you ask a few necessary questions, he'll trip over himself trying to get out of your way. Make things worse for himself instead of better.

'Which is still in this area?'

'I suppose so.'

Max concealed his irritation 'You were being treated. Can I ask what for?'

'When my first marriage broke up, I had a kind of breakdown. Oh, not immediately, but months later when I should have been getting over it. Deborah – my first wife – had been having it off for years with different blokes, only I was the last to find out.' His voice was as lifeless as his gaze. 'Anyway, I took an overdose, but they found me in time.'

After a lapse of a minute or two, while Dundy turned his attention back to his trainers, fiddling with the frayed end of one lace and rubbing it repeatedly between thumb and index finger, Max turned the questioning back to the fishing trip.

'So where's this fishing pub you went to? How long did it take you to get there?'

'The Trout? It's down in Somerset. An hour and a half's drive. Two hours. Perhaps a bit longer, because we stopped at a Little Chef to eat.'

'You don't know what time you actually got there?'

'Didn't check my watch, but it must have been about sevenish. Just after, maybe.'

'And then?'

'We had a drink in the bar. Took a shower—'

'Did you have single rooms or share?'

'Separate rooms,' said Dundy. There was a trapped look about him – both desperate and aggressive.

'Who paid the bill?'

'Joe did. We take it in turns and it was his shout.'

'So what would you normally have been doing on a Saturday night? If Joe hadn't called?'

'I don't know. I'd probably have been slumped in front of the telly. After I'd done my five-mile jog. Army training. Old habits die hard.'

'Let's go back to The Trout. You took a shower. And then . . . ?'

'We ate in the bar. Steak and kidney pie. The best in Somerset.'

'But you'd already eaten at The Little Chef.'

'Only a snack. I missed out on lunch, because I had to take on Julie's shift at the gym. She's the rookie. She was down with some bug.'

'So . . . you had dinner in the bar?'

'Yes. And we spent the rest of the night in there over a

pint.' Dundy sounded open and honest; his hands were shaking, all the same.

'You have witnesses to prove that?'

'About a dozen. Ask the police.'

'I will. So what time did you turn in?'

'God knows.' For the first time, he sounded vague. 'Half eleven, midnight. I was in a bit of a state, to tell the truth. Crashed out on the bed with my clothes on. Didn't check the time. Felt bloody awful when Joe knocked me up at four.'

'Four in the morning?'

'We were there to fish. It's the best time.'

There was a sound somewhere in the nether regions of the house. Like a latch lifting, a door opening and closing.

'Gerry? You there?' a voice called. Female.

'Front room,' he called back. 'Business meeting. Give me ten minutes.'

'Right you are.'

All was silent again except for the tick of the clock on the mock stone fireplace. 'Ma,' he proffered by way of explanation.

'So where does your wife live now? I understand that you split up?'

'Three months back.' He said it in a strange, cramped sort of voice, as if he wanted to cut the subject short. Then he jumped up, shoved his hands in his pockets, said abruptly, 'I could use a coffee. How about you?'

'I don't mind. Thanks.'

He went through to the back of the house. Max heard low conversation; then, a couple of minutes later, Dundy came back in with a tray that held two mugs and a plate of biscuits.

'Didn't have any lunch,' he said with an over-bright smile. As if someone had plugged him in suddenly to an electric socket. Charm of a kind was now emerging. What we have here, Max thought, is a real Jekyll and Hyde.

'Morgan lives three doors down.' Dundy made eye contact again, but only briefly. 'In my house, for the time being. She's looking for a place of her own.'

'So how long has your wife . . . ex-wife . . . worked up at Draycott?'

'Two years thereabouts.'

'And she's doing well?'

'Earns more than I do. She was always glad to rub that in.' His face was sour with failure.

'So it wasn't a happy marriage?'

'She was all over me at the beginning.'

'How did you meet?'

'I went to stay with an old mate in Wales. We met at a club there.' He gave a dry laugh. 'She was going to make my life blissful again. Help me get better. We were going to turn our backs on the past. That was a laugh.'

'We? Did your wife have an unhappy past, too?'

'She's adopted. Her real mother rejected her. Mind you, she uses that as an excuse for all sorts of things.'

'You told the newspapers that she was unfaithful to you. With Julian Neville. Is that why you split?'

Dundy got up and walked over to the sideboard. Poured himself a drink. That's the last thing he needs, Max thought. It's like pouring alcohol on a banked fire.

'Yes. That's one of the reasons.' Max looked at his back and saw physical weariness. The green tracksuit seemed too big for him. But his shoulders were powerful. And tense.

'You were jealous?'

'Pretty damned natural, wouldn't you say, under the circumstances?'

Oh, yes, Max thought. I've been through all that. Jess tearing me apart and not bothering to pick up the pieces.

'We'd only been married six months when Neville started giving her lifts home. And they'd sit out there talking. I got mad once and went out there. He just laughed.'

'But you're quite sure they were lovers?'

'She admitted it quite openly. She was sleeping with him. With the office stud. And I'm possessive. Perhaps too much so, but it's in my nature. And then I get aggressive.'

'So you picked a fight with him at the Toga disco?'

'I boiled over. So would you have done, the way she was

dancing with him. Nothing left to the imagination, I can tell you. I felt a right prat when I walked in and found them at it. But I didn't kill him. Why would I land myself in that kind of trouble? I'm in a deep enough hole already. Ask anybody.'

'And what did you do after they threw you out of The Gabriel?'

'I went on drinking.'

'Where? Which pubs?'

'A couple of places down in town. The Walpole and The Princess Amelia.'

'How did you get down there?'

'I walked.'

'It's a mile and a half.'

'I was all steamed up. I was glad to work it off.'

Max parked the car in the garage behind the rugby ground. Locked the door and strode up through the narrow passage that led to Edward Street. It was four-fifteen. He liked the feel of the street at this hour, the sunlight, the paving slabs, the iron railings, the parapets topped with stone acorns.

He turned the corner. A girl was perched on the low wall above the area steps.

Jess. She got up, smiled. Her voice was husky yet collected. 'Hello, Max.'

CHAPTER SEVEN

———◆◆◆◆———

Jess, on the area steps, looking exactly the same. No. Even better. Her hair black and glossy and shorter than she used to wear it. He found himself frantically trying to drum up some normal conversation. 'You're early. I didn't expect you yet.' Not for another two hours.

'I didn't think you'd mind.'

'I don't. So . . . how are you?'

'I'm fine. And you?'

'Great. I'm great.' He resisted the temptation to reach out and touch her. Nor did he grin widely. He waved an arm towards his front door and spoke nonchalantly. 'You'd better come in.'

Thank God he'd cleared the flat up a bit. It had taken hours and the place had a certain scoured look that didn't exactly suit it. He didn't know where anything was. Went automatically to the sink, instead of the cupboard, to find wine glasses.

It seemed bizarre that she was here in his flat. Her mouth a luscious red and her long, fifteen denier legs walking themselves round and round his sitting-room while she picked things up and put them down again. He felt exhilarated, but there was also an element of trauma.

The pain he had felt when she walked out on him was still inside him. After all this time. And here he was opening red wine. But what else was there to do?

Jess checked her reflection (unnecessarily) in the mirror. 'I rang your office. The girl said she'd call you on your mobile.'

Damn it, he'd kill her. Bloody Ginger Rogers. 'Sorry. She's new.'

'She didn't sound too bright.'

'She's useless.'

'She said she didn't know when you'd be back and she had to dash off because her cat needed feeding.'

Yes, he'd certainly kill her.

'She's a bit . . .' Max struggled to find a suitable epithet. 'She's a bit new woman. Bolshy.'

'Poor Max.' Her voice was throaty yet incisive. She had shed her Manchester accent. 'You know something?'

'What?' He handed her a glass of wine. His voice sounded crazed.

Her violet eyes were all over his face. 'You've grown up.'

'Oh?' Max pushed his hair back from his sweaty forehead.

'Mmn. I like the jacket.'

He should bloody hope so. It had cost a small fortune from the Italian shop in Cumberland Yard.

'There's something so different about you.'

Suddenly he was in a panic, agonisingly on tenterhooks. There was something electric in the way she was looking at him. What did she want? Why had she bothered to come here?

'I'm not likely to be the same as when you dumped me.'

'You've got it all wrong, Max. I didn't want to leave.'

'No?'

'No. But we couldn't go on as we were.' She turned her head to stare out of the window. The profile of a beautiful boy, tilted against the haze of afternoon sunshine.

'Why not? I was happy.'

'Darling Max, that's typical, if you don't mind my saying so.' The silk skirt moved as she sat down and crossed her legs, the violet eyes blinked even wider. 'Sod what you need, I'm OK.'

'No,' said Max. 'It was never like that.'

'Perhaps not exactly. But look at it from my point of view.' She touched his hand with her long fingers. 'I needed to stretch myself. I needed London. But I can't tell you how much I missed you.'

Max gazed at that sexy but impish face and the eyes shaped

like a cat's. If he put out a hand and stroked her, like in the old days, would she start to purr? He suddenly smiled, an unsteady, nostalgic sort of smile. She smiled back as she slid lightly off the chair.

'So where are we going tonight? Any idea?'

None at all, he thought. Won't you please tell me? 'I've booked a table at The Harlequin.'

'Is it nice?'

'Excellent.' Forget how much it costs.

'Actually . . .' Her voice was husky, low, almost a whisper. 'I'm not that hungry. We could stay here, if you like.'

CHAPTER EIGHT

Balloons drifted over a sky that was blue and solid. Elizabeth wished she were up there, suspended, instead of sweating away down here in the crowd. From on high, the sports ground would look like a square, green rug with pink and white dots for the marquees. You would gaze down over all these tiny, ant-like creatures in billowing frocks and panama hats. And the long rows of huts to one side, broken only by the odd tub of scarlet geraniums.

I wish the breeze would pick up, she thought, like the weatherman promised. But it has no intention. The sun goes on burning down. Well, at least it's fine for that peculiarly British thing, a June Sports Day. So silly, so childish, but so extraordinarily pleasant. The Hundred Yard Dash, the Tug-of-War, the Silly Hats race (thank the lord that didn't get to America with the Pilgrim Fathers). Across the roped-off area, the windows of tall town houses glinted through the haze of plane trees which circled the ground: the Abbey spire shimmered in the afternoon heat, above the bright green of the newly-watered Parade Gardens. What a place. Oh, my. Elizabeth straightened her straw gardening hat. Full parade order. Mustn't let the side down. Because everything here had been organised down to the finest little detail. Painted chalk lines, raspberry striped awnings, little ornamental tables under the shade of the trees. And chaps with whistles, chaps fussing about the length of the finishing tape, rosettes, silver trophies, lemonade, tea urns.

She strolled across the grass towards the refreshment tent. White damask cloth, piles of china cups, folded napkins, a crystal bowl with roses. Someone (male or female? Hard to tell.) in a striped blue apron was serving salad rolls. Some old dear was issuing commands in a memsahib voice.

'Those cups come from J Block. Keep them separate. Yes? Next?'

'Tea,' said Elizabeth. 'Black, please. I'm looking for my niece . . . Hilary Russell.' Lord forgive the little white lie. 'Do you know where I might find her?'

'Hilary? Over there, logging the results.' Like clockwork, the memsahib slopped tea into a cup. Nodded towards a table set back under the trees. 'Help yourself to biscuits.'

The tea was stewed, the biscuit splintered into fragments as she bit it, but Hilary Russell sat beavering away at her lists in the dappled shade. She looked nannyish today in a blue frilled blouse.

Her reaction, when Elizabeth presented herself, was ambivalent. An uneasy smile followed by a great shuffling of papers. 'I'm not allowed to talk to you. Really I'm not.'

'I won't tell if you don't.'

'It's not as simple as that.' Her cheeks were stained the colour of raspberries.

Elizabeth pulled off her straw hat. Gazed at the girl with warm, green eyes. 'The truth's always simple. It's for Julian's sake. Just five more minutes?'

At last she caved in. 'What do you want to know?'

'Tell me who's who in your department. The ones I haven't met yet. It would help a lot.'

Hilly fumbled in her pocket. 'You don't mind if I have a ciggy? I know I shouldn't.'

'Be my guest.' But wasn't it interesting that she needed the prop? 'Are they all here today? Could you point them out?'

Hilly's gaze went towards a cluster of people by the refreshment tables. 'The man in the alpaca jacket and panama is Bernard Lucas.'

'Ah, yes. I see.' Wendy Lucas, standing next to him, was wearing yellow.

'The chap they're talking to . . . hair slicked back, white sweatshirt . . . is Mick Rudd. He's second-in-command.

48

Fancied himself as the office glamour boy until Julian came along.'

Greased monkey, Elizabeth thought. Hair gelled back with no parting. Very blue eyes. 'Married or single?'

'Married. His wife worked in Z block until she had the last baby. Mick's a bit flash, but very efficient. He's the one to go to if you want a problem solved. He's dead good in an emergency. When there was that car crash outside the gates last year . . . two people killed, a bad fire and walking wounded . . . Mick ran the whole thing like clockwork until the emergency services arrived. He belongs to the Red Cross in his spare time. The rest of us were running round like headless chickens.'

'Even Julian?'

'God, Julian was worse than any of us. He was so upset. Quite unlike his normal self. But we were looking out of the window when it happened. It was all so horrible. You keep seeing it all again in slow motion . . . that little patch seconds after the impact . . . like you're frozen in time. Morgan couldn't go near. Well, some can't. But give her her due, she fetched the First Aid box and made tea.'

'Is Morgan here?'

'No. She had to go to the dentist.'

Rudd had moved away from the Lucases. They crossed to join another chattering group in the shade of the trees, Wendy's yellow skirt drifting behind her.

'I'd like to meet your big boss,' said Elizabeth suddenly. 'Introduce me.'

'I can't.' Hilly looked scared to death. 'They'll throw you out again.'

'Nonsense. It's a public function.' Elizabeth put down her cup and grinned.

'I'll get the boot. I shouldn't be talking to you.'

'Then I'll introduce myself.'

'Oh, no! Please don't. You mustn't.'

'It's OK. You stay there. Pretend you never saw me.' And Elizabeth took herself off.

Terribly hot, out in the sun. Too hot. Scorched grass, tinder dry underfoot. She was cool inside, though. Elizabeth knew what she was doing.

Bernard Lucas turned as she walked up to him, his face as straight as a plank. Not cuddlesome, she thought. But he won't bite. Here goes.

'Mr Lucas? I'm Elizabeth Blair for the Shepard Detective Agency. I wonder if I might have a word?'

CHAPTER NINE

'Well, really!'

'I guess you think this is a cheek?'

'Too right, I do.'

'I just thought maybe you'd give us a second chance.'

Wendy Lucas stared in astonishment. Dramatic pause. Elizabeth thought, grab the advantage, honey, while you've got it.

'I came to apologise, actually.'

There were beads of sweat on Mrs Lucas's upper lip. Her eyes looked tired and dark-ringed. 'Oh, really?'

'I shouldn't have invaded your territory without an appointment. Look – tell me to sling my hook, if you like, but I really would like a quick word with you . . . or your husband some time? It's about young Julian Neville.'

'I've had just about enough of this—'

Mrs Lucas was about to sound off again when her husband stuck his oar in. 'For heaven's sake, Wendy – it's no big deal. By all means make an appointment . . . but during work hours, not in the middle of a social occasion.'

'That would be wonderful. I'm really most grateful.'

Good old Bernie. He had one of those faces that resembled a wooden block. Stolid, pleasant, but essentially dullsville. Elizabeth wondered how he had got to the top of his profession. Floated, probably, like a great log floats downstream. That was unfair. His lemon tie was eloquent, but then, his wife had probably chosen it for him.

'We just need to know how young Neville fitted in at Draycott. Background stuff, really. His father called us in. As you know, the police seem to have come to a dead end.'

'I really don't see how we can help. One sympathises. Quite tragic, of course, but . . .' Wendy Lucas seemed to imply that Neville Senior was deranged with grief.

And perhaps he was. The tug-of-war team had collapsed in a heap. Arms and legs all over the place, steaming and laughing.

Elizabeth said briskly, 'There might be some tiny little detail that helps things click into place. Mr Neville is quite desperate.'

The struggle going on inside Wendy Lucas was quite plain to see. But in the end she caved in. 'We'll fit you in if we can. But we'll need plenty of notice.' Then came an interview-closing smile and the look that said, That's all for today. You may now buzz off.

Elizabeth took her leave of them. They stood under the trees where she had left them, looking like extras in some old movie. *Chariots of Fire*. Waiting for the director to shout 'Cut!'

Joe Grenfell ran his own import and export business in Canon's Wharf in the centre of Bristol. He was busy when Max called on him. Sitting hunched over the morning's mail, a spruce man in his forties. Blue blazer, striped tie, brown hair flicked into a crest at the crown and slicked smartly down at the side. He seemed puzzled rather than wary. Vaguely uncomfortable, but making a brave effort to be pleasant. 'The police checked all this,' he told Max, and concentrated on the next letter in the pile as his secretary, a timid girl in a tartan top, brought in coffee and laid the tray carefully on the desk.

'White or black?' she said.

'Black, please.' Max needed it after last night. He took a sip of coffee, leaned back in the steel and leather chair and tried to get himself back together. All the windows were open, but the office was still as hot as Hades. 'I know you've been through it all before, but we've been asked to re-examine the case.'

'By whom?'

'By the victim's father. So . . . can you confirm that you were out of town on a fishing trip with Gerard Dundy on the night Julian Neville was murdered?'

'That's right. We often go fishing together. I've got an ulcer, you see. My doctor says it's stress-related. I set up my own business five years ago. It's the old familiar story. You want to do well, so you work all hours. But not any longer. A couple of years back, when it was diagnosed, I started to take more time off. I've got a new system. I work like a whirlwind for a week or two and then I break off altogether. That's when I give Gerry a ring and he joins me.'

'At a minute's notice?'

'Most often. Yes.'

'And was it like that on April 15th?'

'The day of the murder?' He said it quite casually, in the tone of small talk about the weather. 'As a matter of fact, it was. I was stressed out because I'd been forced to work most of the weekend chasing up an assignment that had gone walkies. When I finally located it on Saturday afternoon, I decided that I'd had enough. So I called Gerry – that would have been at about two-thirty or a quarter to three – and he said he could get away too.'

'Just like that?'

'Well, there was a bit of bother about the roster at the gym. He said he'd try to get someone to do his shift and ring me back and he did, about an hour later. I picked him up at the gym at about five and we drove to The Trout. It's a pub we use down in Somerset.'

'How far would that be?'

'Forty . . . fifty miles.' He winced suddenly and drew in a slow, careful breath. 'Excuse me.' He reached into a drawer, unscrewed a plastic pill box and popped something into his mouth. 'Bloody stomach. Don't ever get an ulcer. There's no sure cure.'

There's no cure for love either, Max thought. His mind veered away from the night he had spent with Jess. Too distracting by half. It moved on to a flash image of the two of them outside his flat in the early morning. The air fine, the light so pure. Small birds twittering, the houses opposite the powdery yellow of pollen on catkins.

He had walked her as far as the Pump Rooms. Empty at this hour of buskers or beggars, tourists or touts.

He hadn't envisaged so much happening so soon. That's why it all felt confused, surreal.

Her lips had curved with a delicious smile of contentment as she reached on tiptoe to kiss him. ' 'Bye, darling. I'll see you.'

She hadn't said when. Just, 'I'll call you.'

Grenfell shoved the packet of pills back in the drawer. He was easier now. The pill had done its stuff.

Max said, 'So where did you meet Dundy? How long have you been mates?'

'We met at the gym about three years ago.'

'And what do you make of his wife? Morgan?'

He shrugged. 'I only met her once. She's OK.'

'They're separated. Is that right?'

'Can't help you on that one, I'm afraid.'

'Oh, come on! You spend days fishing together and he doesn't tell you his problems?'

'We don't talk. It frightens the fish.'

'But afterwards in the pub?'

'OK. So he has marriage problems. Never seems to get it right. But that's why he turns to fishing. He says it makes him more hopeful than trying to catch women.'

Max said, 'So Dundy was with you all that evening?'

'Yes, he was. Anyone in the bar would vouch for that. We were playing poker.'

'And after the bar closed?'

'Listen, he was in no state to drive back to Bath to commit a murder. I'll tell you that for nothing. He was as pissed as a newt. Anyway, there wouldn't have been time. It was a quarter to midnight when he fell through the door of his room.'

'You know that for a fact?'

'Yes. I was going to ring the wife, but when I looked at my watch, I decided it was too late.'

'So how was he next morning?'

'Not up to much. Bit of a hangover.'

'So how many times a year would you say you go fishing together?'

'You want me to count up?'

'Roughly.'

'Last year . . . let me see . . . we went half a dozen times, at least.'

'Always to the same place?'

'Not always, no. But The Trout is a favourite.'

'Good food?'

'Excellent.'

'I'll have to try it,' Max said.

Was it his imagination or did a look of unease flicker across Grenfell's face?

CHAPTER TEN

It was a two minute walk from the spot where Julian Neville
had left what Max called Nobs' Hill to the alley on top of
Beechen Cliff where the attack took place. And quite a climb,
towards the end of a long, hot afternoon. But Elizabeth
needed to get the lie of the land; a feel of that noble hill,
whose beautiful verdure and hanging coppice, according to
Jane Austen, rendered it a striking object from almost any
opening in Bath. Catherine Morland had never been able to
walk there without thinking of the south of France. But then
the heroine of *Northanger Abbey* was a good-looking girl
with an affectionate heart and a very ignorant mind. Elizabeth
had had a profitable winter, reading her way through her
favourite author.

She walked slowly and thoughtfully up the grassy track to
the top of the hill where Henry Tilney (How trustworthy a
name. How straight and English.) had given Catherine a
lecture on the picturesque and a drawing lesson.

Catherine had been longing for the latest Gothic horror
novel to arrive from London. Aching to dive into a very
shocking read indeed, something more horrible and gory than
anything she had met with yet. A thriller whose frontispiece
would be decorated with two tombstones and a lantern.

Some things never change, Elizabeth thought. Should have
brought the book with me. There would have been time to
sit in the shade and dip into the odd chapter. Max was always
late. And sometimes taking your mind right off somewhere
liberated it. Allowed all sorts of subconscious notions to slip
in by a side door.

A southerly breeze had sprung up and the air felt as soft as a caress. She stood on a dry, tawny stretch of grass, shading her eyes against the sun. Through the branches of a great chestnut lay the whole city with its steeples and its tight amber terraces, as thick as honeycomb. A city that inspired passion. A city with an inclination for finery. You got a small charge of pleasure from every arch and pediment and door knob; every paving slab and railing. She went on gazing as if from the prow of a great ship, a fine old liner beached at the southern end of town.

'Penny for them,' said Max from behind her.

'I was thinking of Catherine Morland.'

'Who's Catherine Morland?'

'A young girl who made a fool of herself because she expected life to be like the tales of romantic horror that were her favourite reading.'

'Friend of yours?' Max asked.

'Sort of.' It would take too long to explain. Max's only acquaintance with Jane Austen was with the barge of the same name that he'd fallen out of when plastered at a mate's birthday bash. 'So did you walk up?'

'You're kidding! In this heat? I'm parked over there somewhere,' said Max, waving vaguely across the open stretch of grass. 'Lynwood Hill. Frightfully posh.'

'Did you eat yet?'

'Not hungry.'

A bad sign. It was as if, detached from his normal hefty enjoyment of food, Max freed himself to pursue appetites of quite a different kind.

Elizabeth didn't comment. She pulled the ordnance survey map from her bag and turned it so that it faced towards the allotments fifty yards further down the hillside. The garden sheds, the huge, splashy pink mallow, the steel mesh fencing and, to the right, the quiet terrace of houses each with a double row of windows.

'The body was found over there under the lamppost by the end house.' Max nodded in a distracted manner, turned to look up and down the alley and then asked, 'Where does that footpath lead? Across the way. There's a stile.'

'Up to Beechen Cliff School. It's used as a short-cut.'

'We check former pupils with form then?'

'Might be an idea. The iron railing that killed him came from a section that used to be down there by the end house on Lyncombe Terrace. Can you see? They'd had trouble with the drains and the Water Board removed the end section of the railings while digging their trench and some kind soul made off with it one night. That was about a week before the murder. But the end bit must have dropped off as they heaved it away. Three feet long with a heavy knob at one end. It was found over there in the undergrowth.'

'Fingerprints?'

'Nothing. Must have been wiped off.'

'Did they do a door to door?'

'Probably. But it won't hurt to check again. Don't groan. You do this end, I'll do the other. But first I'm going to call at the Neville house. There was something about that lady. Something she was covering up. Plus I'd like to take a look at the script Julian was supposed to be writing. If his mother doesn't have a copy, the police might. In which case, your friend, Andy, might be useful.' She hopped subjects suddenly. 'Did I hear raised voices this morning?' A mild question. She folded the map up, waited for his reply.

'I read her the riot act. Ginger. She's a bloody pain.'

'In what way?'

'In every way. She failed to pass on a message from Jess.'

Is that all? Elizabeth thought. 'She's sorted the place out, though.'

He snorted. 'I can't find anything. And I don't like her attitude.'

'Try being nice to her. So . . . how did it go, your little reunion dinner?'

'Fine. But I don't want to talk about it,' he said and started off down the path towards Lyncombe Terrace, kicking a pebble. The crack of it shattered the stillness of the afternoon.

Strung up like a mandolin, Elizabeth thought. Not at all his usual sunny self. She watched his straight back going up the first driveway. Strong, well made. It's that tiresome girl, no doubt. What's-her-name. Jess. The return of a former lover is always unsettling. And this one a perfect bitch, from all she had heard.

'And take a look around the allotments before you leave,' she called. 'Chat to the other allotment holders. See what you can find out. I'll see you back at the office. Drinks at six. Invite Ginger. I'll play referee.'

From the pavement she looked up at the Neville house. Roof tiles baking, top windows open, baggy net curtains. Albertine roses swinging prettily from the wrought-iron balcony. Henry Tilney would have felt perfectly at home here. That tall, pleasant-looking clergyman with a maverick vein of humour.

Delphiniums against every wall, all over the shop. On either side of the porch, honeysuckle with creamy tendrils poking through the trellis. Elizabeth started up the path, moving easily, her skirt flapping around her bare ankles. Ahead, on the right, a half weeded stone urn. Earth and compost scattered over the stone slabs. Someone had been gardening; someone with green fingers.

Diana, at a guess.

As if on cue, there was a movement on the slabbed path at the side of the house. Mrs Neville in a bright floral blouse.

Mouth unsmiling. Well, what did you expect?

CHAPTER ELEVEN

So here we are, Elizabeth thought, late in the afternoon of another pleasant summer's day (would they go on for ever?); and I'd love to know why you're so scared of me, underneath that steely exterior. The alarming Diana. A fine-looking woman, permanently tanned from expensive holidays, but now showing her age a little. Grey to blonde threads in her hair, two lines cut deeply between nose and lips. Something faintly reptilian about her thinnish mouth.

Elizabeth had telephoned her that morning. Surprisingly, she hadn't slammed the receiver down. They'd had a brief conversation.

'No, I'm afraid you can't see my husband. He's in London for the day. Something to do with the City firm he advises. He's away a good deal.' Then, surprisingly, 'Can I be of any assistance? What is it that you want?' Her voice suspicious, but not belligerent.

'Just a couple of questions. Nothing major. If you could just spare me ten minutes—'

And she had assented. And so here they were now, facing each other over the carved stone urn.

'Good afternoon,' Elizabeth said.

'You'd better come in.'

'Thanks. It's kind of you to spare the time.'

Diana Neville led the way through the black and white tiled hall to the long drawing-room at the back of the house. Hubert's faded chintz chair, the Turkish carpet, the nest of tables. Elizabeth took the low chair she had sat in before, the afternoon sun behind her.

'What can I do for you?' Diana sat down opposite. The

grey eyes that matched her pewter hairclip flicked a glance at Elizabeth.

'I wondered if you could vet the list of your son's friends?'

'Vet?' She was treating it as a trick question.

'Yes. Mark the half dozen or so who were closest to Julian. It'll save us a lot of time. Only he appears to have so many.'

Elizabeth fished out the list that Hubert had given her and handed it over. Went rabbiting on, in a casual sort of way. 'It's difficult enough, interviewing youngsters. Asking a load of questions when it's not always certain they'll tell me the truth. If they've got something to hide, if there are things about Julian that they don't want me to know.'

'Such as?' Diana sat stiffly, pen in hand.

'Oh . . . things that he wouldn't tell you. Scrapes he may have gotten himself into.'

'Julian did not get himself into scrapes.'

'Oh, we all do now and again, Mrs Neville. Only our mothers are often the last to know.'

Back came the expression you could have used to split firewood. Bad move. Backtrack. We need damage limitation.

'I guess what I'd really like is for you to tell me about the girls in your son's life.'

For a moment, Elizabeth thought Mrs Neville wasn't going to respond. She sat upright in Hubert's chair; finishing-school posture, one leg crossed over the other. You've blown it. Asking about her golden son's love life. The son of this bloody great, beautiful old house. The thing is, she might just have been tempted to start boasting. Doting mothers always do.

And Diana was no exception. There was a change suddenly in her expression. She relaxed, grew almost animated. There was something almost defiant about her account of her son's conquests. All those Victorias and Lucys and Emmas. It was as if some other woman had borrowed her tongue and was using it to pour out the complicated history of her son's love life.

Elizabeth completed one page of notes, tore it off and started on the next.

'What about the girl seen with him on that last night? The dark-haired girl?'

Elizabeth had tried out all the photofits in her head. Anyone who would fit the bill, especially from his colleagues up at Draycott. Morgan Dundy was a possibility. Wendy Lucas? Too old, too blonde, too heavily built. Hilary Russell? Now, if she lost a bit of weight . . . Her mind would keep flipping back to *Northanger Abbey*. What was the quote now? *A good-looking girl with an affectionate heart and a very ignorant mind, cannot fail of attracting a clever young man.* Would that still hold true, Elizabeth wondered?

Diana said, 'I have no idea who she was. I wish I did.' Again there was the cool, shiny barrier.

'That's the odd thing. No one seems to have any idea. Could it be that he picked her up in the pub, or outside?'

'He may have done.' Diana got up and walked quickly over to the windows. 'I really don't know.'

'But you have a theory?' It was obvious by the look on her face.

'Yes . . . I suppose.' Her right hand was clenched so tight that the rails must be cutting into her palm.

'Which is . . . ?'

'There was a girl . . . He was seeing her without our knowledge. Without anyone's knowledge, for several weeks in the late spring. She was here, in this house, while we were away on holiday in Madeira.'

'You know that for certain?'

'Yes. My cleaner saw her leaving, early one morning.'

'Can you describe her?'

'Tall, Mrs Hunt said. Brown skin, light brown hair worn long with a centre parting.'

'Did you tell the police?'

She actually looked uncomfortable. 'No. I didn't.'

'Why not?'

'Because it wasn't relevant.'

'How can you be sure?'

'Well, she was . . . How can one put this? A well-brought-up girl. That's what Lily said. The right kind . . . you know? The kind he might have married . . . had he lived.' There was a hint of longing bottled up in her voice. 'It didn't seem right to bring her into it. Julian wouldn't have wanted her name spread all over the tabloids.'

'Not even if she had evidence that could convict his murderer?'

Diana shook her head.

'It never occurred to you that this girl might have been the murderer?'

'Never.'

'Why? Because she didn't come from the lower orders.' Elizabeth framed it as a statement, but her scepticism was apparent.

The colour rose in Diana's cheeks. 'Look – I don't have a logical explanation. I just know she wasn't involved. Anyway, I don't know her name, so what was the point?'

There is always a moment when you want to stop asking difficult questions and act halfway human. To lose an only son is the worst thing in the world; but I'm here to do a job, Elizabeth thought, so swoop on in there.

'All the girls you've told me about have come from, shall we say, the right side of the tracks. Were there any you didn't approve of, Mrs Neville?'

'Some. He did go through a wild phase, I have to admit.'

Didn't they all? There was that dim floozie that Jim Junior once brought home. Patsy Somebody. All body and not a lot of spare room in her head. I was damned glad when that broke up.

'Can I ask you something? Might he have brought Morgan Dundy here while you were away? To sleep, I mean?'

She said harshly, 'No. My son simply wouldn't have bothered with girls like that.'

Elizabeth got up and walked to the window. Old panes of wavy glass reflected the garden and the trees beyond. 'Girls like what, Mrs Neville?'

'Cheap and scheming. He certainly wouldn't have brought anyone of that calibre into this house. And if anything had . . .

occurred . . . I can assure you that Julian wouldn't have been doing all the running.'

'You're sure of that?'

'Oh, yes. Julian was quite a catch. They all thought that. He was such an affectionate boy. The girls all fell for him.' Diana stood gazing out through the doors, her face taut. 'But he wouldn't have been interested in Morgan Dundy.'

'Did you ever meet her?'

'No. Never.'

'Then how do you know whether he would have liked her or not?'

'I just know, that's all. I know my son.'

'Do you? Can we ever fully know our children? They lead different lives from those we imagine.'

Something disturbed the pattern of the flowerbed outside the windows. A thrush – neat, brown speckles, beak pecking away – hopping among the rose bushes. 'They're getting rare,' Elizabeth said.

'I beg your pardon?'

'The thrush. You should look after the little fellow.'

'Oh . . . yes.' Her attention went almost immediately. If you weren't talking about her son, Diana wasn't listening.

'I should like your cleaning lady's name and address.'

'Mrs Hunt. Lily. 102 Blake Road.'

'You won't mind if I check her out?'

'Not at all. You'll have to bear with her. She talks rather a lot.'

'How long has she worked for you?'

'Practically for ever. Twenty . . . twenty-five years.'

'So she knows . . . knew . . . your son well?'

'Yes.'

'Good. There's one other thing. Julian was writing a pantomime script . . . He sometimes worked on it at the office.'

'First I've heard of it.'

'There wasn't a copy here, by any chance? In his room, say?'

'Not that I'm aware of.'

'Would you mind if I took a look? It might help.'

Again, that crackle of tension in the air. And the briefest hesitation. Then, 'Of course. But you'll have to be quick. I have to go out in ten minutes. There's a Red Cross meeting.'

CHAPTER TWELVE

Elizabeth sat down carefully on the bed and considered the room. Third floor (of four), left at the top of the stairs, along a passage, last door on the right. It overlooked the garden. 'This was always his room,' Diana had said. 'He bagged it when he was a little boy. Came back to it after Oxford. He never wanted a flat.'

She stroked the silky bedspread. It was a surprisingly cheerful sort of room. But why would you expect it to show some sign of its former occupant's gruesome fate? A lot of white paint. Champagne-coloured carpet, deep-pile. A small bureau – polished mahogany, inlaid, claw feet – rather pretty. An old chair on each side of the window. All very neat, almost hospital tidy. There was a bookshelf against the far wall and, ranged along it, a silver tankard and hairbrushes and rather a fine watch; an old teddy bear, glass eyes staring; a few photographs in frames. One of Julian in a boat, aged about twelve. Another of the boy with a younger and more animated Diana Neville. His hair the same colour as the wheat-field behind them. Julian a few years on, drinking champagne with a mate on Graduation Day.

Laughing, careless, not a worry in the world, on the face of it, at least. But a young man with a powerful will, which, as an only son, he had been accustomed to exercise unopposed . . .

There was no computer. Nothing to write his panto script on, but then he had the use of a machine at work, so why bother? Having looked along the bookshelves (the usual childhood stuff, mixed up with a few textbooks; nothing current, no novels), Elizabeth moved over to the wardrobe,

which was jam-packed with expensive gear. Two dinner
jackets (satin lapels), four heavy tweed sports jackets. Neat
piles of sweaters on top, half a dozen suits, two very dark,
two lighter, one greyish green, one light linen. Shirts, crispy
cotton, expensive. A whole flotilla of silk ties. Shoes lined up
in rows. You didn't buy this lot on a civil servant's salary. But
then, he wouldn't have to. Mama or Papa was there to
provide.

She closed the sliding doors. Stood gazing at the pin-board
over the chest of drawers Now this might be interesting. But
it was just a boring mix of holiday postcards. One from Java:
You'd hate it here. No pubs. Love, Beth. From Sydney: *G'day
Sport, Sheilas are something else. Thinking of staying, Paddy*.
Then there was a Bath Festival programme (alternative and
jazz); more snapshots. Julian with blonde at May Ball?
Hubert and Diana on holiday in Egypt; rugby fixture list; job
advert (Media Sales – £25,000 guaranteed).

But there's something that isn't right. What? Take mine at
home, Elizabeth thought. A complete mess. Articles pulled
out of magazines, business cards, letters to answer,
photographs, lists . . . all higgledy-piggledy. But as for this
one? It's all too neat and tidy. No, tidied . . .

Things removed, perhaps? The rest put back in rows? Don't
know. But it's a possibility.

Check the dates. Yes . . . that's odd, too. Nothing after
Christmas. And the boy died in April.

'Any help?' Diana Neville asked from the doorway. She
reminded you of one of those ballerinas on top of a musical
box. A perfectly poised, bland smile on her face, but no life
to her. Plastic lady. I feel sorry for her, Elizabeth thought, yet
I don't.

'Maybe. Hard to tell. Tell me, did he have a computer at
home?'

'Used to. It developed gremlins.'

'And?'

'And it went back to be mended. They said it wasn't worth
it. He was going to buy a new one, but—' She smiled wanly.
Pushed her hands into the pockets of her skirt and wandered

over to the bookcase. 'The bits of silver belonged to Robin. My brother. He died just before I got married.'

'Your husband said Julian looked like him.'

'The image. I saw Robin come back in Julian.' She picked up the hairbrush and put it down again. 'I gave my son all Robin's things, but he didn't really appreciate them. Young people only live in the present. That's all they seem to see. I expect we were the same.'

'Very probably.' Elizabeth picked up her bag. 'Well, thanks for your time.'

'Feel free to come back. I'm sorry we got off on the wrong foot. I was worried about Hubert. He's had one bad heart attack. Any stress . . .' A silence. 'And I get bad days, you know?'

She waved a casual hand as Elizabeth went out of the gate and back down the hill towards town; almost found a smile. 'A difficult, arrogant woman doing a U-turn,' Elizabeth said aloud. 'Funny thing, that.'

The woman with the sand-coloured hair had been in town for two hours. She trudged back up the hill carrying two heavily laden Marks and Spencer bags, one in each hand. Every now and then, she put them down, had a breather, then swapped them around. The bag containing the chicken and the fruit was heavier than the other and was cutting red weals in the palm of her hand.

At first, she didn't notice anything untoward. She turned up the steep slope leading to Alexandra Terrace, dropped the bags one more time halfway up, just where the grey, lichened steps led up to the footpath to the allotments. And something caught her eye. Not the blackbird sitting on the branch preening its feathers. Not the lizard in the grass. But something more substantial. Something human.

She saw a man lying on his back in the hedge bottom. He seemed to be snoring. Then it occurred to her that he might be groaning. To tell the truth, she didn't know what to think of it.

She left the bags on the pavement and crept nearer. He was

unshaven, his hair a matted mess, just like the beggars down
in the Abbey Yard. Cuts to his hands and head and one eye
was almost closed up. His face all purple and puffy.

He'd gone all quiet. Was he dead? Bending over, almost
crouching, she appeared to hesitate. Then reached for his
wrist. He had a pulse.

He stirred, lifted a hand towards her. 'Help me—'

She was breathing hard when she got home. Her husband
heard the sound of the door as it slammed behind her. 'Leave
it open,' he called. 'It's like an oven in here.'

She didn't hear him. She was calling the police.

'I have an appointment with Bernard Lucas. I rang this
morning. He said he could spare a few minutes.'

Down the corridor, a door slammed. A breeze must have
sprung up, but it was the only thing moving in the naval
establishment at Draycott.

'If you'd wait just a moment, I'll check that he's free.'

A mile away down the hill, tourists were boarding open-
topped buses, tapping their way into cash machines, tramping
around The Circus and The Royal Crescent. Americans
vigorously, Italians volubly, Japanese in packs of fifty. But
here at Draycott, there was a stifling stillness. It was a dusty,
monochrome sort of a place with its narrow circles of desks.
Over-warm on this summer's afternoon, inducing a kind of
paralysis of the spirit. Of the body, too, Elizabeth thought,
curling her hand round the coolness of the steel-backed chair.
She felt again a sense of sympathy for young Julian, his restless
spirit leaping like a chamois over the pen pushers who
dragged themselves listlessly from desk to photocopier and
back again, month after month, year after stultifying year.

It felt like a great padded cell. She felt an uncontrollable
urge to bang a gong and wake the place up.

'Follow me, please.' The receptionist, a short girl with frog-
like eyes, led her down the corridor and in through an open-
plan office to an inner door. Elizabeth thought it was the one
where Hilary worked, but couldn't be absolutely sure.

The girl tapped on the door and was told to enter. She

made a sort of flapping gesture with one hand, ushering Elizabeth in. The room was cooler than the outer office, with shuttered light. Furnished with a heavy oak desk, a couple of cabinets, a computer screen, a couple of good Nash prints, a rubber plant and the ubiquitous piles of paper.

Bernard Lucas glanced up as if it was bugging him to have to come up out of the file he was working on. 'Mrs Blair. Take a seat . . .' He slid the top on his pen and nodded towards the swivel chair in front of his desk.

CHAPTER THIRTEEN

'Thank you. Good of you to see me.' Elizabeth took in his stuffy-looking grey suit (on a day like today, for God's sake?), heavy, wooden expression and the slight wave in his thoroughly combed hair. Bernard Lucas was one of those men who would always have been middle-aged. As much charisma as the average wardrobe. He looked like a man who had plodded his way to the top of his profession and didn't quite know what to do with himself now that he had reached the summit. Elizabeth imagined him writing in his diary: *Climbed Everest today. Must say it was quite exciting.*

But he was courteous. 'So . . . what can I do for you?'

'Well, as I said, we're investigating the death of Julian Neville.'

He shook his head. 'I don't know what you'll uncover that the police haven't. They were most thorough. Went through this place with a fine toothcomb.'

'Nevertheless . . . I'd like your assessment of the young man's character.'

He sat there for a moment, contemplating the matter. 'The honest truth? His father might not like it. Julian Neville was careless, lazy, uninterested in his work. He had a brain, but hardly ever bothered to use it. In pursuit of work, that is. When it came to disrupting office routine, stirring up hornets' nests, generally making himself a pain, he could be most inventive.'

'So why did you take him on? He doesn't, quite frankly, seem the kind of young man who would naturally fit into this establishment.'

A shrug. 'We didn't know, when he came here, what a

73

nuisance he would prove to be. His references weren't that bad. We were short staffed. And then he was Oxbridge.'

'Third Class Oxbridge.'

Lucas touched his upper lip with a thoughtful finger. Had there been a moustache, he would have fingered it. 'True. But he was coming in as a glorified clerk. He could have done the work standing on his head. Perhaps that was part of the problem.'

'He was bored?'

'I suspect that Julian was born bored, Mrs Blair.'

'So he became disruptive. In what way, exactly?'

Lucas seemed to consider the papers in his in-tray while he reflected. 'He was just fond of setting the cat among the pigeons.'

'Could you elaborate?'

'Well, there was that damned pantomime he was supposed to be writing.'

'Ah, yes. Did you ever get to read it?'

'A couple of pages. Half a scene. He thought it a joke to hand it in with a report I'd given him to write.'

'What was it about? The panto scene, I mean, not the report.'

Bernard didn't see the joke. 'The usual rubbish that generation think of as clever. Lavatory jokes. Bad language. Sexual innuendo with a succession of Pamela Anderson types.'

'Were any of the characters based on people who worked here?'

'Some may have been.'

'The Pamela Anderson types?'

'Shouldn't think so, would you? But I can't honestly say. Didn't see enough of the rubbish. According to my wife, Mick Rudd went for him one morning. Accused Neville of making him a laughing stock. Of portraying him in his scribblings as a seedy little crook.'

Elizabeth made a note of it. 'Your wife was in the habit of reporting to you what went on in the office?'

'Not all of it . . . of course not. But you chat at home. It's inevitable that you hear things.'

'So did you ever act on her reports?'

'Occasionally. If there was something I really couldn't condone . . . something that got in the way of their work.'

'And then?'

'I'd haul them in and give them a talking to. But it would have to be something major.'

There was a knock on the door. A girl came in with a letter in her hand. The stick insect. Morgan Dundy. Green eyes, cool smile, neat gold ear-rings, trousers, but not fancy. Lucas signed the paper. 'Two copies, Morgan. One to Portland.'

She picked up the letter and gave Elizabeth a sharp look on her way out. A strangely fey face, but fierce eyebrows.

'Mrs Dundy . . .' Elizabeth said.

'Yes. You know her?'

'We've met. May I ask your opinion of her?'

'She's a good worker. Sharp, quite ambitious.'

'Is she liked?'

'Not always. A touch tactless. Rides roughshod over other people's feelings. But her work's immaculate.'

'And her private life? Is that immaculate?'

'Can't help you there, I'm afraid.'

'Your wife didn't pass on any gossip about her?'

'Not that I know of. You'd better ask her.'

'It can't make your wife very popular . . . the fact that it all went back to you. Did that bother her?'

'No. I don't think so. We're not here to be popular, Mrs Blair. We're here to run Her Majesty's Navy and keep the country running smoothly.'

Elizabeth said, 'Can we go back to this script of Julian's? What was your reaction when he handed it in with the report?'

'I read the riot act, of course. Told him that if I ever caught him being so puerile again, he'd be out on his ear.'

'Did the warning have any effect?'

'Not one bit. I'll tell you what his biggest problem was.' Lucas rubbed thumb and forefinger together. 'Money. He had too much of it. Or rather, his parents did. Even if I'd chucked him out without a reference . . . well, he wouldn't have had to bother. They'd have kept him. Damned annoying for all the other poor kids struggling with a mortgage.'

'So one of his colleagues may have held a grudge?'

'I'm not saying that. But he could be pretty irritating. He riled a lot of people. Seemed to take pleasure in it.'

Elizabeth considered the ground they had covered and changed tack. 'Can we move on to the Roman disco back in April? The fight between Neville and Gerard Dundy? Did you witness the scene?'

'Not exactly. I'm not much of a dancer. Not one for a knees-up.'

Elizabeth thought, You can say that again. Knees like logs, all the sparkiness of a table leg.

'I was in the other bar, as far as you can get from the sound system. Blasted row. You can't call it music . . . just that damned thump-thump-thump. But Wendy was there. By all accounts, Dundy just walked in and floored Neville. Gave him a bloody nose.'

'Who started the brawl?'

'Dundy, apparently. For once, Julian was blameless. Well, apart from being drunk . . . not the only one, of course . . . and smooching . . . do they still call it that? . . . with Morgan. Dundy burst in and accused Julian of purloining his wife.'

Purloining. Elizabeth very nearly laughed when he used the word. It was a perfect summing up of old Bernie. Archaic, stuffy. Standing some way off from the real world, and rocking on polished heels.

'Then he struck out with his fists. It all happened very quickly. Absolute bedlam for a minute or two, until the bouncers came in and hauled Dundy away.'

They went on to discuss Julian's career prospects (practically nil, given his attitude problem), the promotion procedure (no leapfrogging, however bright you were), the possibility of her visiting Draycott again, if there was a need.

'Don't see why not,' Lucas said. 'But I'd be obliged if you'd ring first. Rules to follow, you know? Hopeless without them.'

'Would you mind if I talked with one or two of Julian's colleagues?'

'As long as it's in their own time . . . feel free.'

She was on her way out of the place, walking briskly along the endless corridor, when her mobile rang.

'Elizabeth? It's Max. Heard the news?'

'No. What?'

'Another attack up on Beechen Cliff. Chap called Zeph Harris. Early thirties. Busker and pub entertainer. Apparently he's been living in an old shed up on the allotments.'

'Is it bad?'

'What the police call a heavy beating. Black eyes, fractured ribs, broken wrist.'

'Any idea who did it?'

'Not yet. He's in the RUH and they're not letting anyone near him at the moment.'

'OK, Max. So where are you now?'

'Hopefully on my way round to Dundy's gym to check out his mates.'

'Hopefully?'

'Car won't start.'

'But the gym's not far from the office.'

'Yeah, I know.'

'So leg it, why don't you?'

'Too hot.'

'Too damned idle, you mean.'

'I'll do it another day.'

A dark-haired girl rounded the corner, checking the change in her purse. Hilary Russell. 'How did you get on with the house calls? Lyncombe Terrace?'

'Nothing much.'

'Me neither.'

Max said, 'And by the way – I can't make the pub after work.'

Hilary selected some coins and fed them into the machine in the alcove. Helped herself to two chocolate éclairs and wrapped them in a paper napkin.

'Oh? Why's that?'

The phone went dead. Elizabeth flicked a switch and shoved the thing back in her bag. She'd call him back later, find out what he was playing at. They always had a drink halfway through the week.

Hilary Russell had seen her now and couldn't decide whether to acknowledge her or cut and run. 'Well, hi!' Elizabeth said. 'They certainly look tempting.'

'For tea. I'm taking them home,' Hilary said quickly.

'Is that the time?' Elizabeth glanced at her watch. It was barely four o'clock.

'I'm leaving early. But I started early. Flexitime.'

Elizabeth held the door open. They passed out of the stifling dimness into blinding sunshine.

'Got to dash,' the girl said. 'I'll miss my bus.'

'I'm going down to town . . . want a lift?'

Hilly appeared to hesitate, then gave in to the heat. 'OK. Thanks.'

CHAPTER FOURTEEN

A minute or two later, they were heading down the hill towards Lansdown. Hilly pushed her hair from her hot forehead and squinted through her sunglasses at the traffic. 'It gets worse every day. Even at this hour. That's where flexitime's handy.'

'Did your friend, Julian, work flexitime?'

'Yes. We all do.'

'I've just been talking to your Mr Lucas about Julian's pantomime.'

'Oh?' Hilary looked away, her cheeks shinier than ever.

'You said he'd charm people into letting out secrets that he'd use in his script. Things they'd regret afterwards. Did he ever do that to you?'

Hilary chewed her lip, stared straight ahead, shrugged a little. 'Occasionally.'

'That must have been galling?'

'Sometimes he'd keep things to himself. But other days . . . if he was in one of his moods, he'd make some awful joke about you in front of everybody.'

'So give me an example.' She saw the girl's face. 'It's OK. You're safe talking to me. Our service is confidential. Has to be.'

Hilly threw her a sideways glance. She has lovely eyes, Elizabeth thought. Dark brown and expressive . . . poetic even . . . at odds, somehow, with that dumpy little body and squat neck. And her voice is distinctive. If you look away and just listen, you can imagine quite a different-looking girl.

'Well, there was this cookery course I went on. In Normandy. And I got friendly with this French boy, but he didn't write to me like he promised. Julian let me cry on his shoulder. Said he'd had a holiday romance that went to pot . . .' Her speech turned rapid and jerky. 'But a few days later, when he was in one of his wild moods, he called out . . . right across the office . . . "Hey, Hilly – I put your Frog into the panto. Was he a good lay? Bet he taught you a thing or two?" I died. I nearly died. But he just stood there grinning.'

She sat picking at the skin around her thumb-nail. 'He'd sort of gamble with your friendship, if it amused him enough. He liked to take risks . . . with people, with money, with his job. He didn't give a damn about anything or anybody as long as he wasn't bored.'

'You once told me . . . or started to tell me . . . that he wrote something about Morgan in the panto script.'

'Oh, that. He wrote her in as a mad Welsh witch who played the harp. Harpy. Get it? It was pretty stupid really. And then he had Mick and Trev down as a pair of cheap market traders who were pinching things from Baron Hard-Up's castle and selling them on the black market. Bernard was the Baron. That seemed to amuse him no end. I don't know how he dared . . . I was a size 20 Cinderella . . . well, I ask you! And Wendy was to play Buttons. Can you imagine her wearing men's clothes and slapping her thighs?'

Elizabeth passed over that one. 'I gather Mick had a go at him?'

'Oh, Mick hated him from the beginning. Mick fancied himself as a ladies' man . . . Jack the Lad. Well, he did until Julian came on the scene and eclipsed him.'

'And Morgan? How did she react to being turned into a harpy?'

'Good casting, if you ask me. She didn't like it at first. But then he'd butter her up by telling her he'd take her off on a dirty weekend. And she believed him – I mean, she's so vain—'

'You don't think they were having an affair?'

'Only inside her own head.' There was a hard edge to Hilly's voice now. A rare but satisfying flash of vengeance. 'Morgan's another poser. She preens around with whoever she can get her hands on. And Julian was a great flirt. All the woman fell for him – even Wendy.'

'Wendy Lucas?'

'She wouldn't have admitted it, but Wendy had a crush on him, too, at one stage.' Hilly was more confident now that they had got away from the subject of her own love life. 'Julian used to play her along something dreadful. He'd sit on the edge of her desk and just gaze at her like she was the cat's whiskers. Naughty, but very funny. That was why he did it, of course. He knew he could get her going.'

The sun was slanting through the windscreen. They were down at the bottom of Lansdown Hill and nearing town. Pale apricot terraces, pretty balconies, the antiques market. A scatter of tables and chairs outside a restaurant with striped sunblinds.

'Wendy would sniff his aftershave and tell him how delicious it was. Or she'd straighten his tie or brush away imaginary specks of dust from his shoulder. When she thought our backs were turned . . . when no one was around.'

'And did it go any further than just flirting?'

'Of course not. She's old enough to be his mother. Julian would have run a mile. Like I said, he was just having fun. Life is on the wire, he once told me.'

The wire being what? Love? Danger? Anything that would give a quick (sexual?) charge, a fleeting buzz?

'He didn't care what people thought. When he came to Draycott . . . well, it was a bit like throwing a firecracker into a quiet waiting-room. People who had been stuck to their seats for a very long time started jumping all over the place.'

Elizabeth nodded, picturing the fun. For some. 'The disco interests me. Tell me about it.'

'Well, it was my idea. No, Daddy's, really. We wanted to raise funds for the Dorothy House hospice and we couldn't think of a theme and he was in the middle of his crossword and he suddenly said that spring was the month when Roman youths used to go into the fields and spend the day dancing and singing in honour of Flora. That was the clue, you see . . .

Flora. Anyway, to cut a long story short, we decided to have a Toga Night. Well, it seemed like a good idea at the time, but, quite frankly, it was all a bit of a shambles. The hotel we originally booked fouled up its dates, so we finished up at The Angel Gabriel. And there was this big, noisy stag do in the other room that kept spilling over into ours. Drunken yobs, Karen called them.'

'Karen?'

'Karen Rudd. Mick's wife. But then, she was pissed off . . . oops, sorry . . . mad at Mick. They'd been bickering all evening. Well, that was nothing new. As I said, Mick's got an eye for the ladies. He couldn't keep his eyes off Morgan that night. Her legs and her cleavage.'

George Street. On the right-hand side, Edgar Buildings. Elizabeth turned left into Milsom Street.

'Morgan turned up on her own that night. It turned out she'd had a row with Gerry about her get-up. She looked like a tart, he said, and if she didn't get changed, she could go on her own. Suits me, she said, and waltzed off on her own. She was in a right strop all that week, actually. Nobody knew what was wrong with her. Anyway, Gerry fumed away on his own at home for a while and then came storming up to the Gabriel to blow her up in public.'

'And found her dancing with Julian?'

'Yes. She had a couple of drinks and hauled him on to the dance floor. She was wrapping herself all round him. Talk about embarrassing! It's not surprising that Gerry went for Ju. Actually, I felt sorry for him. Gerry, I mean. He was in this black mood. Tortured. I mean, it was pathetic and ridiculous at the same time, seeing a grown man in that state. But pretty spectacular. They had a no-holds-barred scrap in the middle of the dance floor. Good fun, if you weren't involved. I mean, Draycott social events are usually as dull as ditchwater.'

'So who came off worst? In the scrap?'

'I didn't actually see. Somebody released all the balloons from the balcony at that point and they disappeared in the mêlée. But Trev had this photo of them dragging Gerry off in an armlock . . .'

Photos. Chase them up, Elizabeth thought. 'Who's Trev?'

'Trevor Walsh. He works for Mick.'

'Right. So did anyone else take photographs?'

'I've got a few.'

'I'd like to see yours some time, if I may.'

'OK. I'll drop them in to you.'

'So did Morgan go home with Gerry that night?'

She tried to remember, but couldn't. 'Sorry. I left soon after that. Got a cab. Mick offered me a lift, but I refused.'

'Why was that?'

'Mick's the original road-hog-from-hell. Anyway, he'd been drinking. Karen was out in the car park trying to get the keys off him. Oh, yes . . . and this other chap was having a go at them.'

'Other chap?'

'Big and meaty. Turnip-shaped head, gold ear-ring, wild hair pulled back in a pony-tail. Looked a bit like Giant Haystack. You know . . . the wrestler.'

'So who exactly was he having a go at?'

'Well, they were all three of them at it. Karen was joining in.'

'So what was it all about?'

'Well, I only heard a bit of it, because my cab turned up. And they were at the other end of the car park and I couldn't catch most of it. But I heard Karen tell Mick he could clear off if he wanted to. Self-destruct. But he wouldn't see the children again.'

Self-destruct? What was that all about?

Elizabeth said, 'One more thing. Did Julian ever borrow money from you?'

Hilary sat with her hands on her thighs. 'Sometimes.'

'Large sums?'

'No. I don't have that much.'

'But more than you could afford to lend?'

'Sometimes.'

'Any idea why he should be so broke?'

'He spent a lot. He wasn't good with money.'

Everything too easy-peasy, as Bernard Lucas had said. No

one ever said no to him. Until that last night, perhaps. So what if someone had lent him money – a lot of money – and wanted it back? And he couldn't pay? It was a possibility.

'Can you drop me here? I've got some shopping to do for Mummy.'

'You live at home with your parents?'

'For my sins. I'd like to be able to afford my own place, but they pay peanuts at the MoD. Here will do. Thanks a lot.'

Elizabeth asked one last question as Hilly climbed out of the car. 'By the way, where were you on the night that Julian was murdered?'

'I was at a friend's house. Zoe Phillips. We watched videos . . . all night.'

'And Zoe lives where?'

'25 Holland Terrace.' Said very quickly. She couldn't get away fast enough. Why was that?

Elizabeth steered the car back into the traffic, thinking of Julian Neville. The good-looking kid with the weak chin. The matinée idol, the professional troublemaker, the young man who loved an audience and took all his risks in public. Seemingly a focal point for all the gossip, the longings, the jealousies at the heart of the great vacuum that was Draycott.

As always, at this stage, there seemed too many threads to chase. How would you ever sort them all out? Such a tangle.

The usual way, she told herself. Like the old-fashioned gumboot, you just keep knocking on doors. Keep asking questions until somebody comes up trumps. Questions that go round the block and back again.

And there was one door that seemed particularly tempting in all this heat. The Trout Inn. By a river, presumably. She felt cooler just thinking about it.

I'll take Max, she thought. Tomorrow. Have a bar meal. Sort him out. Find out what's going on inside that infuriating skull of his.

CHAPTER FIFTEEN

Fishing . . . It took her back to summer vacations up in Maine. Spruce woods in the clear morning air. The dry turf path down to the lake. The horseshoe curve where you always stopped to peer up at the blue sky high above your head and to listen to all that silence. They'd had a cabin out in the wilds of Hancock County. Used to go up there every summer for a month in August. Up to the big cool.

Everything blessedly the same every year. There had been this robe she kept there. Oh, the pleasure of finding it every year, hanging, as always, on a hook on the back of the bathroom door. Hal, her brother, had called her a loony. Sloppy. But Hal had been just as bad about his darned boat.

All those memories. The goldenrod coming out just as they were packing up to go home. And the rowans and the gulls and the herring and silver water as far as the eye could see.

Elizabeth sighed, came back to the present and said to Max, 'There it is. See the chimneys?'

There was a sharp line leading from the main road down into the willow trees. A deep lane tilting downhill.

'Turn left here. By the sign.'

'I'm starving. They'd better be open.'

'Of course they're open.' She consulted her watch. 'It's five past seven. Took us an hour and twenty minutes. Dundy could have killed Julian and got back here by the early hours.'

Max nodded as if he wasn't listening and swung the Citroën into the car park. He'd been reluctant to leave town for the evening, but she'd forced him. She'd seen restlessness and boredom on his face. Bad combination, she thought.

'Deserted,' she said, bringing her attention back to the pub. 'Real piece of old England.'

'Real hole.' Max sat there looking at it, gloom all over his face.

'Odd place to come for a night out,' said Elizabeth. 'I could think of livelier joints.'

The Trout Inn was like a tottering old cottage that had shambled down to the river one dark night and slumped itself down in the ragged grass. A new wooden conservatory thing stuck on one end was misleadingly called The Commodore Room. Inside, there was dark wooden panelling, dirty yellow ceilings and windows giving a telescoped view down across the overgrown garden and a scrappy copse.

Not a place of great charm. But fishermen were a peculiar breed. Not glitzy. And you had to suppose it would perk up with a customer or two and all the little lights illuminating the bar.

Max banged the bell on the counter and then, when nothing stirred, hit it a second time with more force.

Frustration, Elizabeth thought. He hadn't managed to contact her. The dim Jess. She'd have to be dim, dumping a boy like Max.

He banged the bell again, scuffing the grubby bar rail with his foot.

'Can I help you?' The barmaid wore a mauve top and startlingly pencilled eyebrows.

'If it's not too much trouble,' Max said. 'A Fosters and a gin and tonic. Plenty of ice and lemon.'

'And the menu,' Elizabeth chipped in.

'Have you thought what the kitchens will be like?' Max whispered.

'You're starving.'

'Not that starving. There was a decent place a couple of miles back. We'll stop on the way back.'

They stood sipping their drinks. 'So what was wrong with you last night?' she asked. A mild question. 'I had to go home and cook myself supper.'

'Sorry. I was supposed to be meeting Jess.'

'Supposed to be?'

'She didn't turn up.'

'Why not?'

'I don't know, do I? Haven't caught up with her yet.' He was already halfway through his pint, just pouring it down him. Anxiety probably; he couldn't settle.

The barmaid slopped around stacking a tray with glasses. She pushed a cupboard open with a thud.

'We wondered if you could give us some information?' Elizabeth pulled an agency card out of her bag, slid it along the counter.

'Detectives?' She looked more curious than startled. 'What's it about?'

'We're making enquiries about one of your regular customers. A Mr Dundy. Gerry.'

She looked blank. It wasn't difficult.

'Gerry Dundy. And his friend, Joe Grenfell. They come here to fish, I believe. I've got a photo somewhere.' Elizabeth did some fishing of her own. Among the rubbish in her overstuffed bag. 'Here.'

The girl looked at the blurred mugshot snipped from the Bath *Chronicle*.

A double-take. She hooked a wad of hair behind one double-pierced ear. 'Oh. That Gerry. 'Course I know him. Nice bloke. Likes his country and western. Always on the quiz machine. Yes, I've seen him.'

Max said, 'You could hardly miss him in this crowd.'

'Sarky, isn't he?'

'Crossed in love,' Elizabeth said. 'Ignore him.'

'Glad to.'

'So . . . how often does Gerry stay here?'

A shrug. 'Hard to say.'

'But if he comes regularly . . .'

'I don't, though, do I?' She picked up a tea towel. It didn't look very inviting.

'You're not full-time?'

'Right. There's two of us. And he's always messing us about.'

'Gerry?' Elizabeth's ears pricked up.

'No. The old man. The boss. Chopping and changing our shifts.'

'When you get a rush on?' Max studied the contents of a murky jar on the counter.

'Shut it, Max—'

He shook the jar around a bit. 'What precisely are these?'

'Pickled eggs. What did you think?'

'Hard to say. Ploughman's whatsits?'

Elizabeth kicked him under the bar and said quickly, 'Was Gerry staying here on the night of April 15th, do you know? With his friend, Joe Grenfell?'

'Wouldn't know.' The girl glared at Max. 'I was off sick.'

'You remember the date that clearly?'

'Listen – I broke my arm. I was away for weeks. All of April.'

'Then could we speak to the other barmaid?'

'She's not here.'

'Your boss, then?'

'Gone into Taunton.'

'Right. The lady of the house?'

A flicker of emotion on the solid face, almost a sly grin. 'If you like. Hang on a minute.'

She slouched off through a curtained alcove at the back. Elizabeth looked at Max critically. 'Lumpen,' she said. 'Probably inbred. But you're not helping matters.'

Somewhere at the back, a phone rang. Life, a wide-awake sound in a dead place.

'Not in the mood,' said Max.

'I can see that. Mood's got nothing to do with it, Max. It's work. It pays the bills.'

'Bloody boring work. Didn't need two of us.'

'Real little ray of sunshine, aren't we? I don't happen to care for drinking on my own. Anyway, I wanted to talk to you.'

'Oh, God—'

The curtain parted. The barmaid was back, followed by a thickset man in a blue tee-shirt.

'Well, hi!' said Elizabeth. 'You're back from Taunton.'
He wiped his oniony fingers on his apron.
'Taunton?'
'I was expecting your better half.'
'You got him,' said the barmaid.
'I'm sorry?'
'This is Bertie. The lady of the house.' She smiled sweetly
at Max as if to say, Now who's the clever clogs?

CHAPTER SIXTEEN

'How was I supposed to know?' Elizabeth said.

'That the pub was run by a couple of gays? You couldn't.' Max had recovered his grin. 'Sexist thing to ask for, though . . . Showing your age, Betsey. The lady of the house!'

'OK. Have a good laugh and get it over with.'

'What was that word you used? Lumpen?'

'So she made me look stupid. I can live with that.'

They sat opposite each other at The Three Crowns, a more salubrious establishment with rough whitewashed walls, polished wood floors, copper warming pans and rosy pink curtains.

Elizabeth said, 'What did you think of Bertie? All the stuff he gave us about the big darts match?'

'Convenient that it was on April 15th. That Gerry was their star player.'

'A bit too convenient, if you ask me. All that guff he gave us . . . who won what, down to the last arrow. Rehearsed, I thought. Like they knew we were coming.'

She helped herself to bread from the basket. Fresh-smelling, crusty, perfect with tomato pasta. Max tucked into his bubble and squeak, his face cheerful again. 'Did you check the Bargepole crowd? Anyone know the dark-haired girl he was seen with?'

'Haven't had time have I? Caroline's gone gadding off to London for a couple of days, so I've been stuck in the shop. You must have noticed?' Well, perhaps not, she thought. In your present state.

'What's she up to in London?'

'Something to do with a solicitor and a legacy. That's all I could get out of her. Anyway, I'll start on the Bargepole crew tomorrow.'

A fresh, green summer evening outside. Shadows lengthening, bats dipping in and out of the tall trees at the far end of the beer garden.

Max said, 'I checked all the Draycott alibis. They seemed to hold water.'

'No more shop,' Elizabeth told him. 'Listen – I'd like you to be nicer to Ginger.'

'She's been moaning, I suppose?'

'Not at all. But she's a good girl. She could use a friendly word.'

'I could use a bit of respect from her.'

'OK, so she's blunt. But she means well.'

'She bloody doesn't!'

'You shouldn't rub her up the wrong way.' She shoved a fork into the pasta. 'So you didn't hear from Jess?'

A moody look. 'Nope.'

'Do you think she's being evasive?'

'How the hell would I know?'

'Max – are you getting in above your head again?'

'That's my business.'

'OK. OK.'

'Maybe I want to be in above my head. Maybe I like it that way.'

'Maybe you're just plain dumb,' Elizabeth said. 'Letting her walk all over you a second time.'

'It's not like that.'

'No?'

'No. Look – we had a good talk the other night. She explained why she left me.'

'As I heard it, she didn't just leave you. She waltzed off with your best mate.'

'She's changed since then. Matured. So have I. So butt out.'

She had to say, 'OK, sunshine. Have it your own way.' There was no alternative. For the time being. Max was in love again . . . or at least, in lust. But it wasn't making him happy, only restless and unsatiated. It didn't please Elizabeth to see him living his life in false memories, refusing to see any defects in the returned goddess, diving down some blind alley in pursuit of insubstantial dreams.

Lord, help us survive our passions, she thought. Or at least, come out of them relatively unscathed.

Max had telephoned Morgan Dundy from the office and said he'd like to call on Thursday evening, if that was convenient. Morgan came to the door fanning herself with a small notebook. She apologised for the place being in a tip, only she was in the middle of packing her things.

'You're moving?'

'I'm buying my own house up by the Assembly Rooms. The mortgage hasn't come through, but I've found a rented place in the meantime. I'm fed up of Gerry's mother glaring at me every time she walks past.'

'You don't get on?'

'That's an understatement. She never approved of me. She wanted me out of here weeks back, but I told her I wasn't about to make myself homeless to keep her happy.' Morgan shifted a half-filled box of china from the rug to the pine chest and some books from the sofa so that he could sit down. 'It's absolute chaos. I'm sorry.'

'No problem.' Max set down the tape recorder. 'I hope you don't mind? As I explained on the phone, we're interviewing anyone that Julian Neville worked with. All the usual stuff. Background. Relationships. I'll try not to keep you long. First of all, how long have you worked at Draycott?'

'Two years, roughly.'

'And before that?'

'I lived in Wales.'

'That's where you met your husband?'

'Ex-husband. He'd just left the army. He came up to Wales on holiday.'

'And what kind of work were you doing in Wales?'

'Inland Revenue. Dead boring. I should have gone to university, but my mother was ill. I went to pieces. Couldn't face the exams.'

'So you went into the civil service straight from school?'

'After a year travelling around the world . . . Greece and Singapore and India.'

A light little voice to go with the light little frame. Morgan was the kind of female who looked frail, but was bullet-proof. Combative green gaze, something feline about her. Something scratchy and faintly unpleasant, as if she might have claws.

'So . . . you followed Gerry Dundy back to Bath?'

'I came here to be with him, if that's what you mean.' A dry laugh. 'I found him attractive, for some strange reason. To be fair, he was good to me at a time when I needed shelter, just after my mother died. I was lonely.'

'I'm sorry.'

A shrug. 'You get used to it.'

'So are we talking about your real mother or your adoptive mother?'

A quickly flung glance. 'How did you know about that?'

'Your husband told me.'

Morgan reached for a cigarette and lit it. 'He'd no right.'

'I'm sorry. I don't think he meant—'

'He'd no right. It's my business and nobody else's.'

'I'm sure.' A tense silence. Touched a raw spot, Max thought. That's interesting, but better go careful. Using his most caring voice, he said, 'You didn't answer the question. Was it your real mother who—'

'No. She died when I was a baby. She committed suicide.'

'I see. I'm sorry.'

Morgan shrugged. 'It was a long time ago. It was my adoptive mother who died just before I moved to Bath. I was very close to her. She was everything to me.'

Max felt awkward. Wrong-footed. Nevertheless, he pressed on with the questioning. 'So . . . your relationship with your husband was happy at the beginning?'

'For a while. Yes.'

'Could I ask what went wrong? Why it failed?'

'I just got bored. I felt trapped. He's . . . well, he's not a very happy person. Not warm.' She wrinkled her brow, frowning as if to express all the emotions packed inside it.

'You mean physically?'

Another shrug.

'Your sex life wasn't brilliant?'

'Ask his first wife.' Something foxy about that little smile.

'You're saying that the marriage failed because he was useless in bed?'

'No.' But she was implying it, quite definitely. 'I just thought it would get better, but it didn't. And when I complained, he got moody. Violent.'

'He hit you?'

'And the rest. That's why there are new locks on the door. Have you ever seen one of his rages? They're unpredictable, destructive. He once flung a chair at that wall. You can see the dent. He has these evil moods. One night, after a row, he tore up all my clothes and set fire to them.'

'And Julian Neville. When did he come into the picture?'

'Julian?' She looked quickly at Max, then away.

'Yes. We heard you were dancing rather intimately with him at the Toga disco.'

'I wasn't the only one. Wendy Lucas was playing up to him as well.'

'The boss's wife?'

'Yes. She hauled him on to the floor and made herself look quite ridiculous.'

Max stowed that one away for future use. 'It's your relationship with Julian I'm concerned with at the moment. Was your husband right to be jealous? Did you have an affair with Julian?'

'Yes. I slept with him.'

'Where?'

'Sometimes at his house.'

'What about his parents?'

'It was when they were away on holiday.'

'You said sometimes. Where else did you sleep with him?'

An odd little flicker. 'He had the use of a friend's flat in town.'

'Where exactly?'

'Fosse Road. Number 63.'

'And the friend's name?'

'Sorry. I don't remember. But he runs a furniture shop on the ground floor.'

'Did your husband know what was going on?'

'Not at the time.'

'But he found out?'

'I don't know how. We were very careful.' The green eyes were very bright.

'You found it exciting?'

'Of course. Julian was a dish. They all fancied him.' That little look again. 'I never encouraged him. He dropped a note in my in-tray. Would I meet him for a drink one night? He made all the advances.'

'So how long did the affair go on?'

'It didn't really go on, as you put it. I mean, it was now and then. As the mood took us.'

'It wasn't serious?'

'Julian was never serious about anything in his life.'

'Did you mind?'

'Why should I? It was just a bit of fun. He was a wonderful lover. Fantastic in bed. But not a stayer. I knew that from the beginning.'

'So how many times did you sleep with Julian? Roughly?'

'Hard to say. It was just . . . sporadic. A dozen times, maybe.'

'And the night he was murdered? Where were you?'

'I was in London visiting a friend. All weekend. Your partner, Mrs Blair, rang me and I gave her the address.'

Which, presumably, Elizabeth had already checked. So there was no mileage in that one.

The city rooftops were sharply outlined against a serene blue sky. Sky and stone meeting in an elegant jumble of amber-tinted chimneys and parapets, attics and gables, stone pineapples and pyramid-shaped pavilions. From the doorways of the many little restaurants came a hint of cooking, a whiff of garlic. Elizabeth had been late night shopping to buy a birthday present for Kate, her daughter. She had found what she wanted – some Provençal table napkins – but they had cost a bomb. Kate had better like them, she thought as she walked down a narrow alley and through an imposing hollow square of eighteenth-century lodging houses into the Abbey Yard. Better not dump them in the wash with her blue jeans like she did with the last lot.

Useless on the domestic front, that girl. Never figured out how to empty a garbage bucket. Or perhaps she preferred somebody else to do it.

No fool, our Kate.

Past a flower-filled balcony, a bow-fronted coffee house, the Victorian pillar-box and the beggar and his dog asleep on the steps of the Guildhall.

The street musicians all gone home. The mews deserted.

Elizabeth liked this time of day. No more hustling; just thinking time.

Thinking about the look in Max's eyes. Something dark there. Something disturbing and perhaps destructive. I'd rather see him laughing than wagging his tail after some silly little siren who once took him apart. Can't seem to get through to him that all he wants is a nice, ordinary girl with a warm heart. Someone to love. The trouble with young people these days is that they want it all with knobs on. Physical perfection, perfect sex (is there such a thing?), champagne lifestyle, the excitement of instant gratification . . .

I'm getting old and crusty, Elizabeth thought. But our generation took what they could get and made the best of it. No great harm done either, Jim used to say.

She unlocked the door to the shop. Pleasant at this time of the evening. No customers breathing down your neck. No Caroline. That wasn't fair. Caroline wasn't a nuisance, just a touch irritating at times, so that you ended up wanting to crack your head (or hers) against the wall in frustration.

This morning, for instance, when Elizabeth had asked about the legacy, instead of revealing who had died, under what circumstances, expected or unexpected, Caroline had simply said, in one of her longer speeches, 'Lame duck. Obliged to go for Mother's sake. OK if I desert you until Tuesday?'

Well, it wasn't OK, as it happened. Couldn't have been a worse time. But on the whole, the girl was—

A board creaked above her head. She stopped to listen. Max? Couldn't be. He never came back in at night. Overtime? He didn't believe in it.

There was a pause. Then another creaking sound . . . this time on the other side, towards the landing.

Elizabeth stood stock still, listening. Then, grabbing the pepper pot that she kept behind the till, shot towards the door.

Too quickly, as it happened. Tripping over a corner of the Triple Rose quilt that Caroline had left draped over the rocking-chair, she overbalanced and went crashing into the bookstand.

By the time she had picked herself up and reached the staircase, the intruder had clattered down the stairs and got clean away.

But there was plenty of evidence of his visit. The office was a shambles. It had been well and truly ransacked.

CHAPTER SEVENTEEN

'Anything missing?'

'Hard to tell in this mess.'

Files slung all over the place, drawers pulled out, contents dumped, papers scattered. Elizabeth picked her way carefully over to the desk.

'The petty cash tin's gone,' Ginger said.

'That's all right. It was empty. Max raided it yesterday.'

Ginger bent down and started to collect up papers with methodical, nifty fingers. 'Suppose I shouldn't really. Fingerprints and all that. Are you going to call the police?'

'Not sure. What do you think, Max?'

'I'll mention it to Andy.'

'Who's Andy?' Ginger asked.

'Max has a buddy in the local constabulary. A drinking companion.'

'Oh . . . I see.'

'What do you see?' Max took a handful of ballpoints and dropped them back into the pot.

'You're mates. You go to the pub together.'

'Anything wrong with that?'

'Nothing at all. God, you're suspicious! Here – paper clips. Put them in the ashtray for now. Why is there an ashtray? Nobody smokes.'

'Clients,' Max said, 'have been known to.'

'What you need is a No Smoking sign,' Ginger said. 'Much healthier.'

'I decide what we have on the desk.'

'Children . . . children.' Elizabeth righted a chair. 'So . . . what were they looking for, I wonder?'

'The Neville case notes?' Ginger suggested.

'A possibility. But unless they went into the computer...'
Max said, 'At least that wasn't nicked. Cost enough replacing it last time we were done.'

Across the way, Elizabeth saw George Godwin from The Music Box watering his hanging baskets. The morning was simmering gently. Already a scatter of early tourists in the mews below. Normality, thought Elizabeth. Comforting, the breeze from the open windows, coffee brewing in the shop downstairs, pigeons flapping on the roof edge three feet away.

'So what are our plans for the day? After we've cleared this lot?'

'You tell me. I can see you're dying to.' Max flopped into his chair.

'Dundy's fitness club? You could go pump some iron.'

Max said, 'You're more in need of it.'

'Well, thank you kindly, but I'm happier exercising my brain cells. Got to keep up with you English intellectuals.'

She went on clearing up the mess. Ginger, a faint grin on her face, did likewise. A creaking of metal; George pulling down his striped sunblind. Elizabeth picked up the bits of a broken plant pot, dumped them in the waste-paper basket, put the kettle on for coffee and decided on her own first call for the day.

The first name Diana Neville had marked on her list. Toby Perrin. Morgan Dundy had mentioned him, too, though not by name. *He had the use of a friend's flat in town.* The flat above a furniture shop in Fosse Road. An over-priced furniture shop, judging by the price tag on the pine dresser that took centre stage in the window.

But it wasn't the dresser she was interested in. 'Toby Perrin?' she asked, closing the door behind her.

'Yes.' A young man with clear, pale blue eyes stepped out of the back room to greet her. Something indolent about him. Fair-streaked hair in a surfer's bob. His voice, heavy and expensive, said, 'What can I do for you?'

'My name is Elizabeth Blair.' She handed him her card.

Silence. Then, 'What's it about?'

'I believe you were a friend of a young man I'm making enquiries about . . . Julian Neville.'

His gaze didn't flinch. 'That's right. We were at school together.'

'Where?'

'Marlborough.'

'Boarding?'

'You've got it.' He had picked up the tone in her voice. Stood there staring back at her. 'You disapprove?'

'To be honest, it does seem a touch dim to go to all the trouble of having children and then send them away for someone else to raise. However . . .' She kept her cheerful tone. 'How long have you had the furniture shop?'

'A couple of years. And it's creative wood design.'

An upmarket carpenter. Probably best not to say so. 'I believe you were one of the crowd at The Bargepole on the night Julian was murdered?'

'For a while . . . yes. May one ask who's employing you?'

'Certainly. Hubert Neville, the young man's father. How long is "a while"? Accuracy would help.'

He stared past her out of the window, avoiding her gaze. Elizabeth waited. In the end, he said, 'I was with him until about eleven.'

'And what sort of a mood was Julian in that night?'

'He was OK. Quite high, actually.'

'Drinking a lot?'

'Probably. We were all knocking it back. It was Rex's birthday.'

There wasn't a Rex on the list of Julian's friends. 'Rex who?'

'Rex McFall. He's a hairdresser. He part owns a salon up by the Assembly Rooms. A lot of our crowd use him.' His eyes were fixed on the list in her hand. 'You're interviewing everyone at that party?'

'I'm afraid so.'

'Rather you than me.'

'Tell me about it.' She smiled ruefully. 'So . . . how close were you and Julian Neville?'

'Not very.'

'So you didn't see each other regularly?'

'Good God, no! Who told you that?'

'His mother, actually.'

'OK. So we were mates when we were teenagers. That's a while back.'

'His father said you often gave Julian a lift home.'

'Not really.'

'So it isn't true?'

'Julian may have told him that.'

'Why would he do that?'

'I'm sorry. I haven't a clue. We didn't see each other that often. Not of late.'

'But you were at the same party the night Julian was murdered.'

'Listen – everybody was at that party. Rex is a nice guy.'

He's not going to admit to anything, Elizabeth thought. She gave him a hard look. 'So what's your home address, Mr Perrin?'

'Why do you need to know that?'

'I might want to contact you again.'

'What's wrong with coming to the shop?'

'It might be urgent. Out of office hours.' She waited, pen poised.

A pause. 'Actually, I live here . . . over the shop.'

'Now that's interesting.'

'Is it?' His voice was cool. 'I don't see why.'

'Tell me something . . . did you ever lend your flat to Julian?'

'Lend it? In what way?'

'In the usual way. Did you ever let him use it for his own convenience?'

'I don't follow.'

'Oh, come now. You must know what I'm driving at.'

'No.'

'Then I'll spell it out for you. Did Julian ever bring women to your flat? Use it as a knocking shop? Is that clear enough?'

'No. He didn't.' His voice was clear and incisive, but there was a pulse ticking away in Perrin's jaw.

'You're quite sure?'

'Positive . . . Look – I'm due to meet a client. Quite frankly, you're holding me up.'

'I won't keep you much longer. I'd just like some details about the girls at Rex's party.'

'All of them?' He looked incredulous.

'No. Just any that Julian may have been interested in.'

'That would take all day. And I don't really have the time. Look – all I can tell you is, he was talking to Amanda towards the end of the evening.'

'Amanda—?'

'Amanda Tolley. Yes. She's a designer. Designs wedding dresses. Runs her own business in Burlington Gardens. Amanda was celebrating too, that evening. She'd just landed a big export order. Julian cracked open some champagne for her and sprayed the whole room.'

'What time would that have been?'

'Not sure. Ten thirtyish. Just before I left to go on to another party.'

'Did you speak to Julian before you left?'

'No. I went to the bog. When I came back, he'd gone.'

'On his own or with somebody?'

'How do I know? I wasn't there.'

'But someone must have seen him leave?'

'Rex said he buzzed off without a word.'

'Was that unusual?'

'Yes, it was, as a matter of fact.'

'Might he have been meeting somebody?'

'It's possible.'

'Which one of you was it that saw him outside with a girl?'

'Amanda. She went out to see a friend off.'

'Was there ever anything between Julian and Amanda?'

'Only schoolboy stuff.' He tossed back his hair. 'He crossed her off his list years back.'

'Did she mind?'

'Shouldn't think so. She's living with some film editor. Is that it?'

'For now.'

There was some satisfaction in keeping the rich college kid dangling. Something about him irked her. Some kind of pervading arrogance . . . impudence . . . in the way he looked at you. You can't catch me out, his eyes seemed to say. There was something smug about his parting look. It lingered a while in her mind.

CHAPTER EIGHTEEN

Martha Washington was quiet, but there was life in Max's office upstairs. Voices. One male, giving orders; one female – Ginger's? – seemingly arguing back.

Elizabeth stopped in the curve of the staircase to listen. Not a full-scale row? Please, no. She'd had plans for that little girl. No, not plans exactly . . . more of a hunch. There was something about her. She had character and personality. She was just the kind of girl Max could do with. Down-to-earth, sensible, a dry sense of humour; and not at all bad-looking behind those darned granny glasses.

I thought they might get on. Well, eventually. It seems you were wrong. So much for instinct. That red hair, of course. And Max such an expert on riling you on purpose.

The office windows were wide open to the mews below. Max stood leaning against the piano, in his shirtsleeves. 'You knew where I was. You could have walked it in two minutes.'

'I couldn't leave the office.'

'You could have shut up shop for ten minutes.'

'And what if a customer had turned up?'

'Sod the customer. There are things more important.'

Ginger had picked up her rucksack and was prodding her spectacle case down through the hole in the top. 'Such as super-models with big boobs and an attitude problem? Why are men such suckers?'

Elizabeth stood in the doorway and coughed.

Ginger swung round, her grey eyes startled. 'Oh, hi! I didn't hear you.'

'Evidently. What's going on?'

Max said, 'Jess was here. And Miss Clever Clogs here didn't call me.'

'I did! Three times. It's not my fault if you left your phone in your car boot.'

'He's always doing that.' Elizabeth eased off one shoe. Her feet were killing her.

'Max, dear, pour us all something cold, there's a good boy. We're all frazzled.'

Ginger said, 'I think I'll push off for lunch, if you don't mind.'

'I don't mind in the least.' Max slammed the drawer shut.

'Max—' said Elizabeth. 'Three glasses of orange juice. And plenty of ice.'

Max glared over the desk at Ginger. 'She doesn't want one. She's leaving.'

'Now that's not very civil of you.'

'That's OK,' said Ginger. 'I'm used to it. He's like his girlfriend. Ill-tempered.'

'Ill-tempered?' Max was spluttering.

She thought about it. 'No. Querulous.'

'You must have said something to upset her.'

'No.' Her expression was guileless and innocent. 'It was difficult to get a word in, actually. She's got no manners. Swanning in here and demanding to know where you were.'

'So why didn't you make her a coffee? Ask her to wait? I suppose that didn't occur to you?'

'It didn't actually.'

'Why not?'

'Because, quite frankly, she was a pain in the butt. And I had work to do. Somebody,' she pointed out, 'has to keep the place going.'

'Didn't she leave a message?'

'Sorry. But I wouldn't lose any sleep over it.'

'What do you mean by that?'

'Well, she's—' Ginger stopped.

'What?'

She swung her rucksack over one shoulder. 'I'd better not say it. You won't like it.'

'Go on.'

'Oh, well, if you insist. She's a bit . . . well, Page Three, don't you think? A bit over the top for Bath. A bit . . . dated.'

'I'll get myself a drink,' said Elizabeth, heading for the small back room. 'If I can't interest anyone else. If neither of you will join me.'

'She looks all right to me,' Max said furiously.

'Yes, well.' Ginger shook her head sadly. 'There's no accounting for taste. I'm off. See you, Elizabeth.'

The allotments lay warm and somnolent against a backdrop of green hills and the incomparable spires and terraces of the city. Hazy gold clouds, very thin and gauzy. The tail end of a breeze sighing and riffling over the dog daisies.

She was in luck. Zeph Harris was standing in the doorway of his customised garden shed (it had taken some finding), a glass of something long and brown and cool in his hand. He stood leaning against the door jamb as he watched her scrambling down the cinder path.

'Hi. Nice afternoon.' He was a tall, polite man in his thirties, wearing a faded collarless shirt tucked into washed-out jeans. Red hair, some of it – the long top bits – out of a bottle. There was the remains of bruising around his left eye.

'Isn't it? I'm looking for Zeph Harris.'

'Then you've found him.' He smiled pleasantly.

Elizabeth smiled back, a touch inanely. Said what a nice little home you have here. Quiet. A real laid-back sort of a place.

'I like it. I can sit up here of an evening and watch the trees and the trains and the clouds.'

Elizabeth could imagine it. She thought, he looks as if he belongs here. Don't think it, don't even think that he looks like Worzel Gummidge. It takes all sorts to make a world. He's probably as sane as you or me.

'I'm Elizabeth Blair. I'm a private detective.' She explained why she was there. 'I just wondered whether there might be some connection between the Neville case and the attack someone made on you the other day.'

'Wouldn't imagine so. Can't see why there should be.'

'But if I could ask the odd question or two . . . You never know. It might help.'

'You'd better come in.'

'Why, thank you.'

The shed smelled of candle grease and joss sticks. There was a guitar in the far corner and a fiddle propped up next to it.

'Take a pew.' He hooked out a single plastic chair.

Elizabeth sat on it. 'So . . . Mr Harris . . . just a bit of background information. What do you do for a living?'

'I'm a poet.' He nodded vigorously, repeating the phrase.

'Really?' There wasn't a deal else you could say about that.

'I've had some published.'

'You did?'

'A couple of years back. Doesn't pay, though.' He sighed. 'I rely on street theatre in order to eat. And I do a Friday night spot at the Pied Horse.'

That made more sense. He was a busker.

'So tell me about your act.'

'I do this comic history of the city . . . in ballad form. Finish off the act with a melody or two. I'm like one of the old Elizabethan actors.'

Sounded like a bundle of fun. Elizabeth's green eyes gazed at him, steady, enquiring. 'I suppose you read about the Neville murder?'

'Didn't everyone?'

'Very probably.' She leaned forward, her hands lightly clasped around her knee. 'I guess it would have been the talk of the allotments?'

He didn't seem to have heard her. 'I'm peckish,' he said suddenly, out of nowhere. 'How about you?'

'Not really.' She couldn't imagine what he would come up with. 'You cook in here?'

'When I have to.'

'But where?'

He pointed to the camping stove on a packing case behind the dilapidated linen basket that had a whiff to it.

'I'm really not hungry, thanks all the same.'

'A drink then?'

It was the lesser of the two evils. 'OK. I'll have whatever you're having.' She hoped she wouldn't regret the statement.

He found another glass and filled it with something beige-coloured with steam coming out of it. She glanced at it as he handed it to her. Took a surreptitious sniff.

'It's decaff,' he explained.

'Oh . . . right.' The hut was oppressively hot. Cars formed tight little lines down on the ring road. The little breeze rustled the roses outside.

Harris looked up from the camping stove. 'Actually, I knew him.'

'Knew who?'

'Julian Neville.'

She found that surprising. 'How?'

'He gave me a lift up the hill one night.'

Elizabeth tried not to look disbelieving. 'How come?'

'I'd been celebrating something or other. I was in a bad state. Having one of my evenings. He found me at the bottom of the hill.'

Good Samaritan stuff.

Harris had found some pitta bread in the shopping trolley that held an assortment of foodstuffs and proceeded to stuff it with beans from a saucepan on the camping stove. 'I may have been staggering a bit. He stopped to ask if I was OK.'

She waited.

'Anyway, he helped me up the hill.'

'And—?'

'Well, that was all there was to it.'

'What time was this?'

'Late at night. After the pubs shut.'

'You're absolutely sure it was Neville? I mean, in the dark?'

'Sure. We bumped into each other a week or two later. I was sober this time. I thanked him and he said don't mention it. We had a bit of a laugh.'

'It must have been a shock when you saw his picture in the papers?'

'Not half.'

'Did you contact the police?'

'What for? I didn't know anything. I knew the guy superficially. That was all.'

Odd story, Elizabeth thought. 'Were you up here the night he was killed?'

'No. No, I'd had a skinful that night. Couldn't get back up the hill, so I kipped down in a friend's squat down in town.'

Elizabeth moved on. 'So what can you tell me about the night you were attacked?'

'Nothing. I don't remember a thing. I was concussed. It's all gone.'

A handy story. Convenient, if you have things to hide.

'That's a shame,' she said. 'Tell me about what led up to it. All you can remember.'

'The last thing I remember . . . honestly . . . is walking up the hill from town. Turning into the alley.'

'What time was this?'

'Eleven. Eleven-thirty at night.'

'Don't tell me. You'd been celebrating?'

'No. Not this time. I'd been to the buskers' meeting. I was stone cold sober.'

'The buskers' meeting?'

'Yeah. We're fed up of amateurs invading our pitch. We formed a committee to do something about it.'

'Such as?'

'Petitions. Letters to the Council. All legal and above board. Anyway, I turned into the alley and somebody must have jumped me. I'm afraid that's all I can tell you.'

'Did they take anything?'

'My wallet. That's where they were unlucky. It was empty. I was spent up.'

'Do you have any enemies, Mr Harris? Anyone with a grudge?'

'Not that I can think of.'

And that was all she could get out of him. Elizabeth thanked him for talking to her and began to take her leave. As she stepped out into the evening air, she said, 'Here's my card. Keep it handy. And if you think of anything else—'

'Doubt if I will.'

'And I can find you here if I need anything?'

'That's the only way you can contact me, I'm afraid.' He smiled that dry, foxy little smile. 'Sorry about that. My fax machine's out of order.'

CHAPTER NINETEEN

Amanda Tolley's was a typical small Regency terraced house. Three storeys, but thin. A cat sitting sunning itself in one window, a beetroot coloured ceramic bowl and a pink kelim cushion in the other.

She opened the door almost before the bell had stopped ringing. Stood there smiling in a cool, blue print dress that showed off bare, deeply tanned arms. Shining brown hair caught up in a braided plait. Freckled nose, little-girl look about her.

'Mrs Reynolds! Do come in. You're early, but it doesn't matter. My last client cancelled.'

A stunning bowl of roses and delphiniums behind her in the hall. The scent drifting out on to the sunny doorstep. She was gazing, with a short-sighted air, along the broad pavement.

'Your daughter's not with you?'

'I'm afraid my daughter's back home in New York.'

'Really?'

'She'd go anywhere if she thought I disapproved. That's kids for you.'

A pause. Then a rapid calculation. 'You're not Mrs Reynolds?'

'I'm afraid not.' Elizabeth introduced herself.

The girl was floundering. 'I'm sorry. I don't understand. A detective agency?'

Elizabeth explained the reason for her visit and mentioned her previous call. 'I called on a friend of yours. Toby Perrin.'

'Really?' The alarm in her blue eyes was abating.

'If you could just spare five minutes. I really would be grateful.'

'You'd better come and sit down.'

They passed through the hall into a room done out in milkshake colours. A huge, sludgy pink sofa, apricot linen cushion covers, creamy yellow walls. Like the girl who lived there: young but sophisticated. Tranquil but cleverly structured. Glossy magazines on the coffee table, exquisitely framed watercolours, a small but perfectly formed Portland stone fireplace.

'If I understand rightly, you were talking to Julian towards the end of the party on the night he was murdered?'

'Yes. Yes, I was.' She sat fidgeting with the edge of the cushion cover.

'Could you tell me what the conversation was about?'

'It wasn't a conversation . . . not really.' Her cheeks were flushed, her eyes suddenly bright.

'What was it, then?'

'A shouting match.'

'You were arguing?'

This might be interesting.

'No. It's just that you had to shout to make yourself heard above the din. All those people and the music thumping.'

'But you did communicate?'

'Yes. But you missed bits.'

Elizabeth nodded. And waited.

'Ju . . . well, he was having a lot of fun that night. He was on a high. He kept teasing me about my New York buyer who'd given me a big order. He said I'd get way too big for my boots. The papers . . . they made him out to be an absolute shit. But he wasn't. Well, not all the time. He could be very sweet.'

Watery eyes suddenly. There was a pause during which Amanda found herself a tissue. 'Sorry.'

'You were fond of him?'

They were all fond of him; half the darned females in the city.

'He was my pin-up when I was a lot younger.'

'But not recently?'

'God, no. It's just scary... knowing someone who got murdered.'

Music tinkling on Radio Two at the back of the house. Sun on the ticking clock and the sketchbook stuffed down the magazine rack. Amanda gave a shiver, sat staring at her screwed-up twist of tissue.

'Was Julian in a relationship that you know of? Anyone special?'

'No. No one special. He... he just enjoyed himself.'

Playing the field. 'So tell me about the girl you saw Julian with. As I hear it, you went outside to see a friend off...'

She got up and walked round the room. 'Yes. There wasn't much air that night. Before I went back in, I stood there for a while, to cool down. And I saw them down by the river. Julian and this girl.'

'No one you knew?'

'No. She had her back to me. But it was no one from our crowd.'

'You're quite sure?'

'Positive. I'd have known. This girl was tall... quite striking.'

What could be so striking about a back? Elizabeth wanted to know.

'It's hard to explain.'

'Try.'

'She was... well, I'd lost one contact lens, so I wasn't wearing them, but... there was something foreign-looking about her. Italian. Or Greek.'

'What was she wearing?'

'A silvery jacket. Quite jazzy. That was what caught my eye. And jeans, I think.'

'Anything else you remember?'

'Her hair. It was thick and shining. It caught the light. They were under the lamp.'

'You didn't speak to them?'

'No, I wasn't that close. Anyway...' An odd, constrained

look on her face. 'They were having a quick snog. He was oblivious.'

'So why didn't he bring her to the party?'

'I don't know.'

'And how did you get home that night?'

'A lift.'

'What time would that be?'

'I don't know. About a quarter to midnight.'

'And there was no sign of Julian?'

'No.'

'So how do you imagine he planned to get home?'

'It wasn't far. He'd probably have walked. If only—'

'Yes?'

'Well, Toby usually gave Ju a lift home if he'd been drinking.'

'But he didn't that night?'

'No.' Once again that awkward little look.

'And why was that?'

Silence.

'Toby told me he went on to another party. Was that the reason?'

The girl seemed to hesitate. 'I don't know if he did or not.'

'But there's something else that's troubling you?'

She shook her head and looked away.

'Miss Tolley. Amanda. If you want Julian's killer found . . .'

Her face suddenly looked distraught. 'I don't like saying this. But they had a bit of an argument, Toby and Ju.'

'About what?'

'Not sure.' She was struggling with her conscience. 'Something about some money Ju owed him. Something about rent for the flat.'

'But Julian lived at home with his parents.'

'Yes.'

'So why would he have owed rent?'

'I'm sorry, but all I heard was a snatch of conversation. There was a lot of noise in there. I'm sorry. You'll have to ask Toby.'

CHAPTER TWENTY

Mick Rudd was about as welcoming as cold porridge when Max introduced himself and explained the reason for his call. He slicked back his dark hair. 'I hope this won't take long. We're expecting guests. Friends coming over for dinner.'

There was no smell of cooking, no table laid. Unless, of course, it was going to be a split-second affair. Marks and Spencer shoved into the microwave. Mick's wife, in a tired denim skirt that matched her tired eyes, certainly wasn't dressed for entertaining. She was an unnoticeable little woman. Brown hair hanging in a curtain when she dropped her head.

'It shouldn't take long. I need to know what you thought of Julian Neville. How you got on with him?'

He nodded, but there was still no expression on the face that was going to seed a little. The face that might have belonged to a second-hand car dealer; something foxy about him. Disingenuous, dodging.

'That's easy. I didn't. The man was a prat, a complete poser. Couldn't walk past a mirror without tossing a hand through his hair and admiring himself. Liked himself, didn't he?'

'So he got up your nose?'

'Exactly. He seemed to think himself better than the rest of us. Which was a laugh, because we carried him most of the time. Dead idle bugger.'

A messy, toy-strewn living-room that smelled of burnt toast. A television talking to itself silently in the far corner. Stacks of CDs. Outside the netted window, a thin slice of lawn, roses that needed dead-heading and a lupin patch clogged with convolvulus.

Mick wasn't much of a gardener. Nor much of a conversationalist either. Waiting, shrewd and watchful, for the next question to come, but giving nothing away in small-talk.

'I've heard the pay's lousy at Draycott. Is that true?'

'It's OK.' Had he been expecting this question? He showed no sign of surprise, appeared to have a formula answer. 'I'm not exactly rolling in it. But we get by.'

'There were rumours that Julian was always broke. Borrowing money.'

He shook his head. 'Not from me he didn't.'

'OK. Could we talk about the Toga do? You and your wife attended?'

Again Max had the distinct feeling that Rudd was being shifty. 'Yes. But we'd left before Dundy burst in. Karen had a headache . . . she gets these migraines. Nothing works on them . . . can't do anything except get her home to bed fast. It was as hot as hell in there and she couldn't stand it any longer, so I took her home.'

'What time would this be?'

'Ten-thirtyish? About then. I just know that we'd left before Dundy turned up. We didn't see any of that.'

'You couldn't exactly have left.' Max sounded affable, but puzzled. 'You offered Miss Russell a lift and she saw Dundy attack Julian.'

'Then we were outside in the foyer when it happened.'

'In which case, you'd have seen Dundy as he came in?'

'Not necessarily. The place was packed out. And there's more than one entrance.'

'So which one did you leave by?'

'The back door that leads to the car park.'

'Is that where you were when you spoke to Miss Russell?'

'By the small cloakroom at the back. That's right.'

Max waited in silence for a moment, then said, 'So . . . then you drove your wife home?'

'No.' Rudd's voice was calm, almost detached. 'As you no doubt know already, Karen wouldn't let me.'

Max nodded with apparent understanding. 'You weren't

getting on too well that evening, I heard?'

'Well, you heard wrong. Karen wasn't too happy, but you're not when you're in pain.'

'It wasn't anything to do with Morgan Dundy?'

'Morgan? What's she got to do with it?'

'Someone said you couldn't keep your eyes off her that evening.'

'Bloody rubbish! I wouldn't have touched her with a bargepole, after she accused me of sexual harassment.'

'When was this?'

'When she first came to Draycott. All I did was try and be pleasant to her. Show her the ropes.'

'Is that right?'

'Ask anybody. All I did was offer to buy her lunch at the Gabriel. A working lunch, I might add, to talk about general office procedures. And she had the cheek to report me to the Union rep. Women these days . . . talk about aggressive!'

Max thought of Ginger (he was still mad at her) and was inclined to agree with Rudd. You gave females an inch and they took a mile. Perhaps he should have put her down right at the beginning. Showed her who ran the concern.

'She didn't report bloody Neville! He could get away with anything.'

Max decided to broach another subject. 'He was writing a script, I hear? You didn't like what was in it?'

'Someone told him about the sexual harassment business. He wrote an exaggerated version.' Rudd's face was suddenly suffused with anger. 'I lost my rag with him. As did a lot of other people when he decided to include them in the plot.'

'So who else did he write about?'

'Pretty nearly everybody in the office.'

'So what did he write about them?'

'I can't remember half of it. Wouldn't repeat it anyway. He just made fun of people. That was his idea of a joke.'

Karen, who had gone to deal with a screaming child in the other room, was back watching by the door. She looked stressed out. Her face pale.

'I see.' Max said. 'So . . . you didn't have any hankerings after Morgan?'

'Of course not.'

'OK.' Max's blue eyes were bland. He chose his words carefully. 'You weren't ogling Morgan at the Toga Night and you weren't quarrelling with your wife. She wanted to go home, but you weren't fit to drive. What happened next?'

'I called a cab, but we had to wait about twenty minutes. They were busy.'

'So where did you wait?'

'In the foyer at first. But then out in the car park.'

'Quieter out there, I expect?'

'Yes. Yes, it was.'

'Many people around?'

'Not really.'

'Except the drunks from the stag night.'

'Except them, of course.'

'You didn't have any trouble with them?'

'No.'

'Nobody picked a quarrel with you?'

'No.'

'Strange, that, because someone told us there were raised voices.'

His face was no longer deadpan. In fact, it had become almost animated. 'Oh . . . that! Yes. I'd forgotten.'

Max waited. Karen looked like a frightened rabbit, over there by the door.

'The bloke who pranged the other bloke's car. Came out too fast. Hit the bumper.'

'You witnessed an accident?'

'Nothing major. But he was about to drive off. I yelled at him to stop.'

'And did he?'

'No chance. He just put his foot down.'

'Can you describe the man?'

'Difficult. It was dark. Forties, overweight. Business type. Thought he knew it all. Gave me a mouthful back when he should have been apologising.'

It was a brilliant piece of improvisation, but Max didn't believe a word of it. 'Funny,' he said. 'Our witness didn't mention a car.'

'Your witness?'

'The person who heard the row.'

'Hilly Russell? Well, she's as blind as a bat. And the car park wasn't well lit.' He hid his nervousness under an elaborate attempt at nonchalance.

Max said, 'No cabs went to your address that night either.'

'It was a mini-cab. Lots of them don't register.'

'And I suppose you can't remember the name of the firm?'

'Sorry. Slipped my memory.'

Well, what a surprise. 'So is there anything else you'd like to add about the evening?'

'I don't think so.'

'Or your wife? Would you like to add anything?' Max smiled in her direction.

'Karen was in too much pain to register anything. She was right out of it, weren't you, darling?'

Karen nodded, avoiding Max's gaze.

'One last question. Where were you on the night Julian Neville was murdered?'

'I was at a Red Cross training weekend up in Chippenham. Ask Trev. He'll tell you.'

'Trev?'

'Trevor Walsh. The lad who works for me.'

Max took Trev's address. Out in the cul-de-sac, a child was wheeling around on a ramshackle bicycle. Not a wealthy area. In which case, Mick's new camera and expensive hi-fi system were interesting. Out of place among the rest of the shabby clutter.

Four young kids and a badly paid job, thought Max. I wonder how he manages to pay for his little luxuries?

CHAPTER TWENTY-ONE

'I'm sorry, Elizabeth, but he's been and gone.' It was ten minutes to one the following afternoon and Ginger was studying something intently on the computer screen.

'He'll be at Dixie's.' It was a cheap and cheerful diner down below Trim Street. She paused, then said, 'They do a good lunch. Join us, why don't you.'

'Thanks.' Ginger smiled benignly from the revolving chair. 'But I don't think he'd be delighted.'

'How are things between you two?'

Ginger drew a finger across her throat. 'Don't ask.'

She reminded Elizabeth of one of those angels in Piero della Francesca. Open, clear brow; that hair; mouth delicate and graceful but firm enough to tell you things very straight.

'Any news on the Page Three girl?'

'He kept calling her hotel.'

'And?'

'No joy.'

No, he wouldn't get much joy from Jess. Or was that unfair? She had never met the girl. 'Sure you won't join us? We could ignore what Max thinks.'

'We could. But he'll get on my nerves and I'll get on his. Anyway, I brought sandwiches.'

Elizabeth walked down through the Trim Street arch to Dixie's Diner, past lamp posts hung with geraniums and trailing petunias. The alleys at the back here were silent. No sun underneath the stone walls; just a deep lunchtime shade. There was a way through the little garden by the pie shop. She bought a paper and walked through low rose beds, past a bird fountain, a cluster of pecking sparrows, then across the small square of grass by the church that had been turned into the Festival box office.

She pushed open the restaurant door and walked over to where Max sat in the window. 'Hi. Thought I'd find you here.'

Dixie's Diner had a real American feel with good blues music thrown in for good measure. The walls were festooned with New York cab doors, baseball banners and portraits of Bessie Smith and Blind Lemon Jefferson. There was a little bar in the corner and a cheery young staff serving burgers (veggie if you were squeamish) and relishes that you would murder for and the best clam chowder this side of the Atlantic.

Max looked at her warily.

'You ate already. If you'd waited, I'd have joined you.'

He didn't look ratty any more. In fact, there was something quite chippy about his light linen jacket and plum-coloured tie.

'Thought you were up to your Yankee ears.'

'I was, but there's always time for a working lunch.'

'That's what I was trying to get away from. Work.' He was already pushing his chair back.

'Can't you stay while I eat? Have a beer or something?'

'Sorry. Something I've got to do. I'll catch up with you later.'

Just what was so pressing that he had to rush off in such an all-fired hurry, Elizabeth couldn't imagine. She was still pretty much ruffled by his attitude as she rang the doorbell of No. 65 Fosse Road. But if he wanted to act like you were some sort of disease he didn't want to catch, well, she wasn't going to waste time worrying about it. For now, at least.

It was just after three when the old man opened the door. Rather a handsome old man in a white summer jacket of the kind that clergymen wear. Long, stork-like legs. White hair.

'You'll be from the Environment?' He didn't wait for a reply, so Elizabeth didn't provide one. 'It's about time. I've been waiting in all day. 11.30 means 11.30, you know, not six minutes past three. You'd better come in.'

Elizabeth followed him through a dusty hallway into a stuffy sitting-room. Faded Edwardian, like its owner. White dust sheets over the spare armchair in the window and a line of newspapers cobbled together to cover the strip of carpet the sun fell on. He shuffled into the room behind her. 'Take a pew. Now—' A resonant voice. 'I don't know who complained, but I shall not be cutting it back. It's doing no harm to anyone. In fact, it's probably giving a good deal of pleasure.'

'It is?'

'That buddleia has been hanging over those railings for years and years. And what's more, I object to the threatening tone of your card. Your second card. Cut it back, you said, or we'll do it for you. Well, I'm not having it! I'll go to prison rather than have that beautiful thing amputated, so you may as well go ahead and arrest me now.'

Elizabeth assured him that she had no intention of carting him off.

'I'd like to know who reported it. It was him, wasn't it? That young puppy next door.'

Time to own up. Elizabeth couldn't go on deceiving a senior citizen. 'I'm afraid I don't know, Mr . . .'

'Griffith. Edward Griffith.'

'Mr Griffith. I'm not from the Environment. I'm a private detective.'

'Good lord!' Momentarily, he was stunned into silence.

'I can't help about your buddleia, but I am interested in your neighbour, the young puppy next door. If you mean the young man who keeps the furniture shop. Toby Perrin.'

'I knew it! He's up to no good. What's the young so-and-so been doing?'

Elizabeth said in a steady, friendly voice, 'I'm not sure he's done anything. Yet. I'm investigating a serious crime and I'm very much interested in the comings and goings next door.'

'Well, now . . .' He seemed almost pleased at the information.

'I'd be interested in anything you can tell me about Mr Perrin's lifestyle.'

'That's not difficult. He sits in his cellar and hammers all day.'

'How long has he lived there?'

'Five years or so. This house was wonderfully peaceful until he set up shop. You have no idea how much noise he makes. That's why I rang the Environment. I plan to counter-attack. I'm going to complain about the row he makes. Bang, bang, bang . . . twelve hours at a time. It makes the whole house vibrate. And he's not registered for business purposes. I checked.'

'It seems quiet enough at the moment.'

'That's because he's gone off to some trade fair.'

'So did you tackle him about the noise?'

'Frequently. Now when I go in, he pretends not to hear the bell. And when I do manage to corner him, all I get is a parcel of abuse. Last time, I almost hit him with my stick. I've only been in a temper two or three times in my life and that was one of them.'

Elizabeth nodded in an interested fashion. 'Tell me something. Does he let anyone else use the flat? Say when he's away? That's what I'm most interested in.'

'You mean, the prowler?'

'The prowler?'

'That's what this fellow does. The friend who borrows the flat. Prowls around a lot while he's listening to the radio. It's in the kitchen that I hear it most. They built an extension on to the shop. The back bit sort of extends over my kitchen.'

'Can you be sure it's not Mr Perrin? The prowler, I mean.'

'Oh, quite sure. He never plays the radio. He just hammers.'

The curtains billowed gently. 'So . . . you think he lends the flat to a friend?'

'I know he does.'

Elizabeth felt her pulse quicken. 'And can you describe the friend?'

'Can't help you there, I'm afraid. The buddleia restricts my view of the shop front. And his back door is tucked away at . . . well, the back. And the prowler always wore a baseball cap. Don't they all these days? Dreadful fashion. Should be sent right back to the States.'

Elizabeth smiled an agreeing smile, wrinkled her brow in concentration. 'But you can swear to it there was someone different in there? Even though you never saw him?'

'I don't need to see. You get to know a person from the sounds they make. Perrin thumps up and down the stairs like an elephant. Slams doors. His friend was very light-footed.'

'Was? Past tense?'

'Yes. He hasn't been there lately.'

A prickle at the back of the neck. 'Not since when?'

'A few months ago. March . . . the end of March. Just before I went on holiday to my son in Norfolk.'

Excitement mounting, Elizabeth scarcely dared ask the next question. 'And did he ever have visitors? The prowler?'

'Yes. One or two.'

'Did they ever stay over?'

'I wouldn't say so. I'd say they stayed a couple of hours, then went home. You'd hear footsteps go down the stairs.'

'A car start up?'

'No. No car. I'd have heard it.'

Elizabeth nodded. So whoever visited, parked the car down the hill and walked up. Edward Griffith pushed his hands into the pockets of his jacket, ancient by the look of the stitching, but venerable and worn with dignity.

'Can you describe any of the prowler's visitors?'

'Well, mostly, I just heard footsteps on the stairs. But he had a girl in there one night. They had a big row. I don't know if that's any use to you?'

Is it just? But Elizabeth's face betrayed no emotion; no sign of the excitement that was growing inside her.

'Possibly. Go on.'

'Well, I was baking a cake and I overcooked it. I was in the kitchen, attempting to scrape off the blackened bits, when I heard this almighty row going on. Backwards and forwards. Shouting at each other. Two voices. A man and a woman.'

'Not Perrin?'

'No. The prowler. Definitely. It was the only time I heard his voice.'

'Can you describe it?'

'Well-spoken. That's all I can say.'

'So what was the row about?'

'Difficult. I only caught snatches. Something about a diary. Letters. She was screaming and he was trying to shut her up. There was a fair amount of effing and blinding, if you know what I mean. In the end, she went down the stairs like a bat out of hell.'

'You saw them?'

'Her. Not him. He didn't follow her down. I imagine that's what riled her. That's what made her heave the stone through the shop window.'

Elizabeth almost couldn't bring herself to ask the next question. She sat on the edge of the sagging chair, one hand clasped tight on its arm.

'You said you saw her.'

'Several times, coming or going. Outside in the street.'

'Can you describe her to me?' Please, please don't say she wore a baseball cap.

'Dark-haired girl. Long, dark hair. Very thin. Like a stick of rock, I remember thinking—'

The hotel lobby was quiet.

'Would you tell Miss Boyd I'm here?' Max asked the receptionist. 'Jess Boyd.'

'Your name, sir?'

'Max Shepard. I'm an old friend. She'll know.'

'Room number, sir?'

'Haven't a clue. Sorry.'

She consulted something under the desk and dialled a number. 'You're to go up,' the receptionist said at the end of a short conversation. 'Room No. 103. Third floor.'

'Thanks.' Max strode towards the lift, looking relieved and marvellously pleased with himself.

He rapped briskly on the door marked No. 103, adjusted his tie, examined the bunch of red roses he was carrying.

The door opened. A smartly-dressed man in striped shirtsleeves stood looking at him.

'Oh . . . sorry. They must have made a mistake. I was looking for Jess Boyd.'

'You just missed her.'

Max stood there for a moment in silence, clutching the roses, noting the other chap's expensive watch and blond streaks. 'And you are?'

'Tony Wilson. Her agent. Want to leave a message?'

'Just . . . just tell her I called. Max Shepard.'

'Okey-coke.'

'We go a long time back, Jess and me.'

Was there any need to have staked his claim in such a marked fashion? Flex his muscles? Max couldn't make up his mind. He was all of a jangle, as usual, where Jess was concerned.

CHAPTER TWENTY-TWO

'Whopping, aren't they? They bag all the prizes at the Show. I enter them in Arthur's name.'

'Arthur?'

'My husband. He had a stroke . . . five years ago, come September.'

'I'm sorry. Is he—'

'Oh, no, dear. Still with us. But he's in a wheelchair.'

'Well. That's a blessing.'

Elizabeth wasn't sure if that was the right response. The woman on the doorstep had made some small deference to the heat. She had undone the top button on her pink cardigan. Her face was old and battered and she had the disconcerting habit of licking the corner of her mouth with the tip of a wet tongue. But she was proving talkative and helpful, which was not to be sniffed at when you were on check-the-neighbours duty. A good curtain twitcher could save you a deal of time and shoe leather.

'That pink one – Elizabeth of Glamis – that's Arth's favourite,' the old woman told Elizabeth.

'Really? I wonder if I might trouble you for your name? Just for our records.'

'Mrs Pike. Edith.'

'Thank you, Mrs Pike. And this is No. 37 Larkhall Road?'

'It is.' The tongue flickered out once more, like a lizard's, while she dug out something from the nether regions of her memory. 'Years ago, when we were on holiday in Cromer . . . at Mrs Hartley's on the seafront . . . Arth spotted that little beauty. And he wouldn't rest until we'd ordered one for our little patch.'

'Well, that's wonderful. I wonder if I might ask how you get on with your neighbours? The Dundys?'

'That's easy. We don't.'

'Oh, dear.'

'Between you and me, we got off to a bad start. I asked him not to park that vehicle of his right outside our house. That's Arth's only entertainment, the view from the window. He's lost his speech. And he's paralysed, so it's all he's got to do all day . . . sit there, looking out. And if that great Japanese jeep thing is parked there . . . well, Arthur can't see a thing. Anyway, it did no good. He still parks the thing in front of our windows. Arth gets that frustrated. Sometimes he wishes he was dead, but I tell him he mustn't think like that. While there's life, there's hope.'

'That's very true.'

'I had another go at him the other day. Mr Dundy, not Arth. He was most abusive. Mind you, I probably caught him at the wrong time. He'd just been rowing with his wife.' Her marshmallow tone changed. 'Yelling fit to wake the dead, both of them, on her doorstep. You'd never believe what we have to put up with.'

'Really?' said Elizabeth. 'What were they rowing about?'

'Money. He wanted to discuss the terms of the divorce and she told him he'd have to deal with her solicitor. Which didn't seem to suit him. And that's an understatement. Of course, I should have left it until he'd calmed down, but fools rush in. I said to him, maybe you don't get on, but, frankly, your home life isn't my problem. Arth is.'

'And what was Mr Dundy's response?'

'Gave me a mouthful, as usual. And I wasn't having him talk to me like that. To hell with him, I thought. I'll have that great ugly thing removed or I'll get the police to do it. So I called them. I explained the situation and they went round there to talk to him. And eventually he moved it.' The tongue came out, then went back in again. 'I hope we understand each other better now, I told him. Meaning that he'd understand better what I'd do if he parked it in front of our property again.'

Elizabeth nodded as if in interest.

'And . . ' Edith Pike's voice hurried on. 'I told him that his gentleman friend had better not park there either.'

'Gentleman friend?'

'The chap that visits him on a Friday night after his mother's gone out. I said to Arth, there's something fishy about that.'

'To have a friend visiting? Surely not?'

'That's just it. He never has friends in. Wouldn't know he had any. Keeps himself to himself. Bit of a loner.'

Of course, it might mean nothing at all. But there again . . . 'So how long does this friend stay?'

'Not long. Half an hour or so.'

'And how long has this been going on?'

'A few months now.'

'And always when his mother's out?'

'That's right. She goes to see her sister on Fridays.'

'So can you describe this friend of his?'

'Fortyish. Smart. Drives a blue thing as big as a bus.'

A business associate? Elizabeth wondered. An ex-army mate? But it won't hurt to check.

Trevor Walsh was painting his hall when Elizabeth called on him. 'Oh, dear,' she said. 'Did I come at the wrong moment?'

He wiped his hands on pristine overalls. 'Not really. Would you say that ceiling is yellow or cream?'

'Yellow.'

'That's what I thought. It'll have to be done again. Cheryl will go mad.'

Trevor was a pleasant young man, if a touch on the gormless side. Anorak man, Elizabeth thought. He corroborated Mick Rudd's story about the Red Cross weekend. There had been a talk with slides on accidental injuries on the night of Julian Neville's murder. It had finished at nine-thirty and then they had all adjourned to the pub round the corner, where Mick had treated Trev to a couple of pints and a bar meal as recompense for driving him up there and they hadn't turned in until well after midnight. So that's that, Elizabeth thought.

Cheryl, Trev's fiancée, who was a nurse at the Royal United, had got him into the Red Cross. Part-time, of course. He liked the uniform, was good with bandages, did a lot of garden fêtes, summer events. It was a bit hot this weather, but you had to put up with that. And it was amazing the people you met . . . really famous people. Well, not The Spice Girls . . . but Cilla Black. He'd got Cilla to sign his autograph book . . .

Trevor had an endearing compulsion to tell you about everything except what you wanted to know. He skidded around from one topic to another with hardly a pause. He wasn't a do-gooder, but you had to give something back to society. Cheryl thought so too. They saw eye to eye on most things. 'We never squabble, Cheryl and me. Not even when her sister comes to stay. Paige. Do you know, Paige brings her own coffee? Ours isn't good enough. But me and Cheryl, we laugh about it. We're right on the same wavelength.'

Radio Two, with knobs on.

'We go caving together.' Trev was unstoppable. 'On the Mendips. I was always getting stuck, when I was a beginner . . . wet behind the ears.'

Not very dry now, Elizabeth thought. There was a touch of the rabbit about old Trev. Something to do with his goofy smile and the way his teeth needed a good brace.

'Did you know Julian Neville?' She got it in quickly, before he could start again.

'Julian? Not really. Not my type.'

You're telling me.

'A bit peculiar, I always thought. But you shouldn't judge people. That's what Cheryl says. And she's right. I mean, that day there was the accident on the crossroads, he went up in my estimation . . . out there helping pull people out, regardless of his own safety. Afterwards it hit him, mind. Sitting there at his desk, he was, wearing a deathly kind of smile. Almost in tears. But that's the thing. You never know about people. I mean, Morgan Dundy . . . women's lib, hard as nails . . . she couldn't go anywhere near. I found her skulking in the kitchen drinking coffee. Couldn't take it.'

'Morgan's not your favourite person?'

'You can say that again. Still, it takes time to get used to the blood and gore. And you learn when you take the job on that it's not all vicarage tea parties.'

'I'm sure.'

Trev leaned forward confidingly. 'Mind you, a vicarage fête has its own hazards. Old dears with sunstroke. Kids that fall through windows. And you're always being bamboozled into buying draw tickets . . . or jigsaw puzzles from the White Elephant . . .'

Elizabeth got up out of her chair, told him that she really must be on her way. 'One last thing. In your opinion, was Morgan having an affair with Julian Neville?'

'I wouldn't know about that.'

'But they were dancing together at the disco.'

'She was dancing with him,' said Trev. 'She asked him. Women fell for him like billy-ho. And he'd fix them up in a trice, I shouldn't wonder.'

'Hilary said you might have some photos of the Toga Evening?'

'Yes. Hold on a sec. They're here somewhere.' He found them at last in the bottom of the dresser. 'I'll need them back. Only Cheryl's sister—'

'That's all right. I'll only need them for a day or two.'

Trev walked with her to the front door, waffling on about some fête at a stately home in Wiltshire. Belonged to the Marquis of Something-or-Other . . . small aviary, bed slept in by Wellington, tea-rooms in the courtyard.

'Fascinating,' Elizabeth said, edging backwards.

'That was where I found the boxed set of Elvis records. Bit of a bargain really. I had this old school chum who collected Elvis . . .'

School chum? Did anyone still use terms like that?

'I have to go. Thanks for talking to me.'

'. . . but I lost his phone number, so I thought I'd take them round to Mick Rudd. He's into Fifties stuff.'

Elizabeth paused on the threshold.

'He was off sick that week, so I drove round there after work with them to see if he was interested.'

'And was he?'

'He might have been. Karen certainly wasn't. Too much damned junk around the place already, she said. But luckily, Mick's brother was there. Warren. He took them off my hands. Went mad about them, actually.'

Something prompted her to ask. She would never know what. 'Tell me about Mick's brother. Are they alike to look at?'

'Not a bit. Warren's big and fair. I'm not being funny, but he looks like something out of a fairground. Beer belly, gold bracelet and ear-ring.'

'He'd make a wrestler?'

'Exactly. How did you know?'

'Just something somebody said.' And blind instinct. 'Tell me something. Did Warren come to the Toga Night, by any chance?'

'Funny you should say that. I did wonder what he was doing there. We don't bring guests. Stick to hubbies and wives, usually.'

'So he was where, exactly, when you saw him that night?'

'In the hotel foyer.'

'Talking to Mick and Karen?'

'No. Talking to Mr Lucas when I saw him. Mick was nowhere in sight.'

CHAPTER TWENTY-THREE

———◆◆◆◆———

Elizabeth stitched away at the Shoo-Fly while she listened to Bach. The Goldberg Variations. Coming out of herself, through the music and the needle dipping in and out of the cotton print. Making seams where there had been none, quilting in a feathery line. Outside, the geraniums were drying out, their petals paper-thin in the brassy sunshine and the brook, down at the bottom of the field, was almost dying in its bed.

Snip, snip, went the scissors. She had been working on the yellow and rose scrap-quilt for a year now. Making a thousand little decisions. Would the sailor stripe fit in there by the yellow herring-bone? Probably not. The rose madder pink then, bleeding its pattern with the dusky rose square left over from a coverlet she had picked up at one of St Swithin's rummage sales. There was something very soothing about putting two aimless scraps together to find that they made one another sing. And about removing a print that dominated and putting in its place a jazzy, sunsplashed little number that was sharp, but not strident. No blueprint. That was the fun of it. Just a piece of scrapwork. Like life, really.

The tape clicked and ran out. She got up to turn it over, changed her mind, selected another one – Mozart this time – and began to play it. Stood gazing for a moment at the barley and wheat out beyond Church Farm. At two blackbirds scratching around on the bleached and prickly grass outside the patio doors. Never a cloud in the dry, blue sky. It couldn't go on for ever . . . could it?

I swear we shall burn up, one of these fine mornings.

There came a hefty shuffling of feet out in the porch. Dottie

Marchant, her elderly neighbour. Damn it! Elizabeth thought. Not now. I'll bet a dollar watch she's collecting for something.

'Anyone at home?'

Wasn't it obvious, with the music blaring out? 'Yes, there is. Come on in.'

'I hope I haven't called at an inconvenient moment?'

'No . . . no.' A good, stiff-necked lie, but you tried to make it sound convincing.

'My cake turned out well. For the vicar's coffee morning.' Dottie walked creakingly over to the windows. She looked like a plump pigeon in a blue polka-dot blouse, peering at you with beady eyes as if stolidly trying to get you to feed her.

'That's good.'

'Date and walnut. The fruit didn't sink. It's another scorcher. Paddling in the brook weather.'

Paddling? At Dottie's age? But Elizabeth had trained herself not to react to English eccentricities.

'We used to tuck our frocks into our knickers and build dams. Great fun!'

Panic over. Dottie was simply back in the past again. She wasn't going to trot down the field and throw herself into the brook. Pity, really.

The old girl was smiling her good-old-days smile. 'Pa's head always got shiny this weather. There wasn't a breath of air last night. I finished up watching that film. The girl on Martha's Vineyard. Smoochy ending. In the book, he hit her with an axe.'

'He did?'

'The blind boy, of course.'

'Sorry?'

'Cupid, dear. Unrequited love. The cause of most of the world's crimes. There was rubbish on after the film, so I switched on the radio. Cheap tunes for cheap people, Pa would have said. He wouldn't have one in the house. We had to go up to Perce Chedgy's to hear the dance bands.'

Snip, snip. Elizabeth cut the thread.

'Perce's brother, Stanley, used to do the Charleston like

nobody's business. Or was it Daniel Chedgy? I'm blessed if I can remember. At any rate, his wife wasn't all she might have been. A harlot, Mother always called her.'

Was there any point to the old girl's ramblings? Sometimes she looked quite mad. Elizabeth threaded her needle with sand-coloured silk and started on a new feather wreath.

Dottie put up her hand to swat at something. 'You want a fly paper.'

'I've got a spray.'

'They're no use at all.'

In one of her moods, Elizabeth thought. Arguing with every blessed thing you said. A breeze trickled in through the door, making the papers rustle.

Dottie cleared her throat and fingered the flimsy mauve scarf that was wrapped round her neck; the request, when it came, was just what Elizabeth had been expecting. 'Could I ask you for a donation for the Ruandan Amputees Appeal? It's our project this month at the Bright Hour. And I always think that as long as one has a penny, it should be doing something useful.'

Like keeping the wolf from the door or appeasing the bank manager, Elizabeth thought. But she coughed up. It was the quickest way to get rid of the old battle-axe.

The hum of a fly. The ticking of the clock. Elizabeth lifted the hair from the nape of her neck, sat there thinking about Julian Neville pestering his colleagues up at Draycott. Pestering them all like a gadfly. Bites here, nips there. Try and shoo him away and it only made him buzz round the more.

Shoo-fly – don't bother me!
I don't need your company.

The more you flipped and flapped with the swatter, the more annoying he got.

But somebody had finally landed him. Someone who had got tired of his little games at the MoD? Or someone who had been partying with him at The Bargepole, the night he was killed? Someone on that long list of people who were supposed to be his friends? Elizabeth hadn't liked them much. A tightly-knit group of rich kids who had made it clear that no one had seen anything. But that only made you more certain that they had something to hide. More determined to keep on digging.

'Julian? An absolute sweetie,' one of his former girlfriends had said. Isabel? Or was it Sophie? Hard to tell them apart. Their oval faces empty of any experience of real life. Desirable young bodies, sudden surges of magpie chatter that told you absolutely nothing. 'No, we didn't go out for long. Actually, he used to go out with my sister and I sort of inherited him.'

'It wasn't serious?'

'No. He was much older than me. And much too clever.'

'In what way?'

'At keeping you on the back-boiler. He always had a new pot to boil.'

'How many pots? Among your crowd?'

'Let's just say that he wasn't anorexic.'

'He liked his food?'

'He was quite a gourmet, our Ju.'

'Could that be why someone killed him?'

'I don't know. I'm sorry, I have to go now . . .'

It had been the same story with his Oxford friends, the ones they had tracked down. Ju was a bright star in the social calendar. A free spirit. They all remembered him vividly. But as for lasting relationships . . . Forget it. All you drew was a blank.

She tape-measured the border.

So you came back to the people he worked with up at Draycott. To more digging below the topsoil. And there was always something lying down there half excavated; always something deep down in people that you were unaware of. Like the Roman city, Aquae Sulis, lying only fifteen feet below the streets of modern Bath.

I wonder, she thought, letting the quilt drop on her lap, why this thinking business makes you so damned tired?

Perhaps by closing her eyes, she could shut up her thoughts . . .

. . . she was sliding down a water shute with Dottie behind her. Tilting sideways into the biggest, bluest waterfall you ever saw. It wasn't the splash at the bottom that woke her, but Max's voice. 'Elizabeth?'

'What? Yes.'

He was standing there with a bunch of drooping roses in his hand. Looking whacked. 'I'll put the kettle on,' he said. 'Or would you rather have a beer?'

CHAPTER TWENTY-FOUR

Max dumped the flowers in her lap, dug his hands in his pockets and stood staring out of the window at the sun-burnished fields.

'For me?' Elizabeth asked.

'Nobody else here.'

'So what did I do to deserve this?'

'Just put them in a bloody jug.'

'Such chivalry!' She supposed it was a kind of apology for his oafish behaviour at lunchtime. Yet his mood was quite odd; she didn't know what to make of it.

They sat in the relative cool of the kitchen with a plate of nibbles. Max on the stool by the open door, morosely chewing at a fingernail.

'Coffee or iced tea?' Elizabeth asked.

'I don't care.'

Elizabeth knew she had to snap him out of it. 'OK. What's wrong? Come on. Out with it.'

And surprisingly, he told her. Slowly at first, but then accelerating into the full, sorry story.

'So you think Jess is sharing a room with this guy?'

'I don't know.'

'But you suspect she is?'

'Yes. No. I don't know what to think.'

'You know what I'm going to say?'

'Yes. But I don't want to hear it.'

'Well, you're going to. She's got you jumping through hoops, my boy. Is that what you want?'

'No. But—'

'But what, Max? You're young and – I wouldn't normally

admit this – bright. What are you going to do about it?'

'Ask her, I suppose.' He sounded utterly miserable. 'If I can catch up with her.'

'If? You mean, when! OK. Look at it this way. You're a detective. A professional. You could check up on her in five minutes.'

'Wouldn't be right.'

'Why not?'

'Because it's not work. It's personal.'

'All the more reason—'

'No.'

'OK. But think about it.'

But maybe he didn't want to. Maybe he was scared of what he would find out. The blind boy, Elizabeth thought. No kind of friend to have.

Having aired the subject, she decided to let it drop. There was a point when advice could backfire on you. Better to drag Max back into the outside world, distract him, force him to exchange his own problems for somebody else's. 'About the Dundys,' she said. 'I've been organising my thoughts.'

'Makes a change.'

Sarcasm. Well, it was one step away from self-pity. Elizabeth propped her elbows on the draining board. 'Let's assume, for the moment, that it was Morgan who was with Julian that night outside The Bargepole.'

'OK.'

'Gerry had been watching them for weeks. We know that. He'd had a go at Neville at the disco a week earlier. His blood was raging. So . . . he saw them having a snog out by the river and then he followed them up to the allotments from town. Maybe they were having if off up there.'

Max's hooded gaze went out through the window, avoiding hers. 'Why would they do that when they had a borrowed flat to go to?'

'I don't know. It was a warm night. Perhaps it made a change alfresco.' She bit into a square of Cheddar cheese. 'Trouble is, he'd have to walk her all the way back downtown again afterwards.'

Max barked a laugh and shook his head. 'God, you're old-fashioned. Girls take themselves home these days.'

'At that time of night? On her own?'

'Called a cab, didn't she? From the phone box at the bottom of Beechen Grove.'

'Then there should be a record of it. I checked the cabbies and nobody of Morgan's description was picked up that night. Anyway, surely Dundy would have attacked both of them if his wife was there? And she'd have gone to the police.'

'OK. Then let's say Julian left her in town and Dundy followed him up there and killed him. He's set up the fishing trip as an elaborate alibi. He drove straight back down to The Trout and got his mates to lie for him.'

'It's possible. Or else he paid one of his ex-Para mates to do the job for him. Did you think of that?' Elizabeth bit into a cracker. 'Then there's Dundy's mysterious Friday night gentleman friend.' She stared thoughtfully out at the field. 'I'd like to know what that's all about.'

Max tried to concentrate, but you could see that his heart wasn't in it.

'Let's try another theory,' Elizabeth said. 'Let's say that Morgan killed him.'

'She's weird enough. I hate women like that.'

'Like what?'

'You know. Wild feminist. Vegan. Nostrils flaring . . . She'd chop your balls off, slice by slice.'

Elizabeth winced. Looked across in an almost pitying way at her strapping partner.

'Why would she kill Neville,' Max asked, 'if she had the hots for him?'

'Well . . . let's see now. Morgan is bored with Dundy and sets her mind on getting Julian between the sheets. A few weeks' sexual abandon in Toby's flat, borrowed especially for their grubby little assignations. But for Julian, the affair would have a limited shelf life. Plenty of other women chasing him and he's not known for his staying power. So . . . he gives her the brush-off. And Morgan's not the passive type, as you said.' Something pinched about her, something spiteful.

'She's unstable and she'll retaliate. She takes her immediate vindictiveness out on Toby's shop window.'

'Sorry. I've lost you.'

She filled him in on what the old man had told her. 'And later, when Julian just laughs at her... Julian the joker... and when he starts seeing this other girl – the one he met outside The Bargepole – Morgan decides to kill him. She tracks him back up the hill after he leaves the pub. There's a drama just waiting to happen, when you think of it. She was in a strop all week, Hilly said.'

Max had his doubts. 'Is Morgan strong enough to have battered him to death?'

'Hell hath no fury, Max.' There was something about Morgan. Elizabeth remembered the little exaggerated movements of the girl's hands. Yes, you could imagine Morgan waiting, her energy rigorously contained, until she found the right time and the right place. Then she'd lash out.

'But she said she was in London.'

'Yes, well. We shall have to work on that.' Max was fiddling, now, with a square of pizza, pushing it round and round the plate.

'Are you going to eat that stuff or not?'

'Not. Not hungry.' He shoved the plate away, said vaguely, 'Did you get Hilly's photos?'

'Not yet. I will do. I went through Trev's. He's good at cutting heads off. And getting his thumb in the way.'

'Nothing that helps, then?'

'Only one thing. He said that a couple of prints went missing when they were doing the rounds.'

'Do we know what was on them?'

'That's the annoying part. He couldn't remember. But there are now thirty-four instead of thirty-six. They were all there when Mick Rudd brought them back.'

'So who had them after that?'

'Hilly. And then Wendy.'

'You don't suspect the boss's wife?'

'Not the likeliest candidate, I must admit.' But theories, like buses, tended to come along in threes. And sure as hell

Wendy hadn't liked them asking questions.

Wendy Lucas. A fussy, select little woman. Or made herself out to be. Well into middle age. Too old, surely, to have had any serious interest in Julian? But you never know, Elizabeth thought. Julian would have been flattered . . . tickled. And if he thought the boss's wife could give him a leg up, career-wise . . .

Wendy Lucas was another one who might just have wanted to shoo away the gad-fly. If she'd been indiscreet and he'd made himself a nuisance. For the moment, however, Wendy remained a rank outsider.

'Anything from Andy?' she asked. 'About the office break-in?'

'He took down the facts, but it happens a lot. Probably kids, he said. And nothing's missing, so . . .'

So it didn't warrant a call. 'I almost forgot,' Elizabeth said, her face lighting up in anticipation. 'There's something I've got to show you. Something that nice old man gave me.'

She disappeared for a few moments and when she came back, there was a sheaf of papers in her hand.

'Well?' Elizabeth said, as Max flipped through them.

'Well, what? They look like time sheets.'

'That's exactly what they are. Copies of the time sheets that Edward Griffith filled out for the Environment people. Times and dates of the noise nuisance from the flat next door. Should be useful, don't you think? With any luck, we can work out exactly when Julian used that flat. Now – am I a genius or what?'

CHAPTER TWENTY-FIVE

Elizabeth sat munching a sandwich – tuna and mayo – in the park. School holidays had started. The city (well, the residential area) was growing emptier by the day, as families took off for the coast. And Henrietta Park was growing dryer; the lilac trees in the Blind Garden looked as if they might faint flat-out; only the great, wide-spreading chestnuts stayed alluringly green. You wanted to crawl under the shade of their branches and close the leaves around you. But there was work to be done. As Elizabeth ate, she cast an eye over the print-out of the Neville notes. Those time sheets had been fascinating. If her analysis was correct, Julian (if, indeed, the borrower had been Julian) had used the flat pretty regularly at weekends – and occasionally during the week – until about three weeks before the murder. That was the pattern established by the quiet patches, when the radio dried up. It was a pity that Edward Griffith couldn't positively identify the young man. That his eyesight was too ropey. That the baseball cap had covered Julian's very distinctive flop of blond hair.

The baseball cap, to be honest, troubled her somewhat. Julian didn't seem the type to bother with disguises. Too arrogant, too devil-may-care. As was Morgan Dundy, on the surface of things. She hadn't bothered to cover her hair with a baseball cap, even during her window-smashing bonanza.

She'd forgotten, probably. Would you care what you had on your head when the man you were madly in love with had dumped you? Would you hell? As Elizabeth shook the crumbs from her skirt, she decided that her reasoning was sound. Morgan storms off home and Julian has no more use for the flat. Their affair is past history. He still has to deal with her at work, of course – tricky, that – but the facts fit in there very nicely. Hilly had testified that Morgan had been throwing around a lot of two-edged remarks at work. And two weeks later, she's trying to get him back again by playing the sex kitten at the disco.

All to no avail.

Morgan was in this business up to her ears. Diana would try to knock the theory on the head, of course. Had tried. 'Utter nonsense,' she had snapped on the telephone last night. 'Julian renting a flat? Why would he need to, when he could bring his friends back here?' Brushing the crumbs off her lap, Elizabeth remembered the quick panic in Mrs Neville's voice. 'Julian never stayed away from home,' she insisted.

Which was plainly absurd. Ridiculous. All kids spent the night away now and again. Elizabeth recalled what Hubert had said when he called in at the office a couple of days back to see how things were going. 'Of course the boy stayed out from time to time. Yes, usually at weekends, when he went clubbing.' Hubert didn't doubt for one minute that Julian sometimes shacked up with a member of the fair sex. Good God, even in his day, all that went on. Just as much as now, if not more, he shouldn't wonder. Elizabeth got to her feet and started to stroll back. Past the tall, old champagne-coloured houses of Henrietta Street, right at the fountain in Laura Place. She crossed the Pulteney Bridge (Adam) that had taken five years to build; the only bridge in Britain to be built over from end to end. Tall Venetian windows balancing domed pavilions at either end. And as she crossed the road by the Guildhall, her mind was still cross-hatching and filling in tones and shadows.

That cleaning lady of Diana's . . . Lily Hunt . . . an elderly woman in a melancholy blouse . . . amazing how she had parroted every single detail of her employer's story. No dickering. No hesitation. Wasn't that just a tiny bit flaky? Oh a very nice class of girl Lily had seen coming out of the front door with Master Julian. (Master Julian? Ye gods!) How did I know that, Lily had asked, when she didn't open her mouth? Well, you can tell, dear. You know. Nice clothes. Classy. And a lovely figure. Oh, don't get me wrong, she didn't make it obvious. But there was plenty up on top. Men like that, don't they? That was the difference between my sister and me. She had a chest and I didn't. Makes all the difference in the world. She married a bank manager and I got my Reg.

Yes, witnesses who were ultra-sure of their facts made Elizabeth suspicious. She had this feeling that money may have changed hands, that Diana had bribed Mrs Hunt to say what she wanted her to say. But why? That was the puzzling thing.

'Name?'

'Max Shepard.'

'On the books?'

'Nope.'

'No chance then, mate.'

'Is that right?' Max said.

The bruiser lounging on a swivel chair behind the reception desk was watching Sky while he guarded the entrance to the gym. His nose had been broken at some time or other. He wore designer shades, black jeans and a black silk shirt that had somehow eased itself over fat biceps. Shogun driver, Max thought. Souped up on steroids and God knows what else. Comes from some parallel universe. Hates students and posh people. 'Actually, I don't want a work-out.'

'No?' The bruiser took off his sunglasses and glanced at Max without altering his fixed expression of boredom. Then, 'If you're selling, forget it.'

'I'm not. I wanted to enquire about becoming a member.' A lie, but it was the only way he could think of to get a look around the place. Suss out Gerry's colleagues.

'No chance,' the bruiser said once more without feeling.

'Why's that, then?'

'Waiting list.' His head turned and, with it, a pair of peculiarly colourless eyes. Max noted the tattoo on the bloke's forearm. Blue parachute with a motto underneath. One of

Gerry's ex-army mates? Fit and tough, anyway; trained to injure or worse. In a fight, he wouldn't be quick to slam the emergency brakes on. Or slow to pick up the odd length of iron railing.

'Well, how about putting me on it?'

'No point.'

'Why's that?'

'Because it's as long as my arm.'

'You should be in PR,' Max heard himself saying.

'What's that supposed to mean?'

'Nothing. Listen – what's your name?'

'Lee. Jason Lee.'

'Any relation to Bruce?'

'No.' Irony obviously wasn't in his repertoire.

'Sorry. Stupid joke. Look, Mr Lee, any chance I could, like, look round the place? See what you have to offer? If some time in the future you actually let me join your waiting list?'

'You deaf or something?' asked Lee. His voice was turning nasty. 'I said there are no vacancies.'

'That's a big word,' Max said. Then got out while the going was good.

But then he found a side alley that led round to a back entrance, where he happened to bump into Louie Gennaro. Now Louie (baptised Luigi) was a different kettle of fish entirely. A stocky, bow-legged, half-Italian back-room boy (eighteen or nineteen perhaps) who liked a chat and was on his coffee break. No trouble, mate, he said, glancing at himself and adjusting his hair in the mirror in the little kitchen at the back of the changing rooms. You seen the boss already? I've seen the boss, said Max. Well, a few days ago, he thought a touch guiltily, but we won't quibble about dates.

He asked about the set-up at the gym and found out that Lee was Gerry's partner in the business and that, yes, they'd been in the army together. They employed two more casual staff (both women) besides Louie, whose job it was to check all the equipment and keep the coffee bar going and do all the odd jobs and chat up the decent birds. Well, you got to have some perks, ent'ya? Louie asked with a grin. The pay's so-so, but it won't take you off round the world, if you know what I mean. However, Gerry was a fair employer. Louie wasn't so keen on Lee. Not an easy bloke to deal with, not very sociable. To be honest, a funny-tempered sort of a git. His girlfriend sometimes came in with marks on her. Jason sometimes boasted about it. But (here Louie shrugged) everybody's different. He had no real gripes. The night the kid was murdered? Yes, Lee had been around, because Louie had stayed late to tidy up some stuff and Lee was watching the golf when he left. What time? Eightish. Eight-thirty. And, yes, the police had interviewed him, but he'd told them he'd gone out clubbing with his girlfriend that night (he'd gone straight from the gym into town); had spent the whole night with her and it must have been true, mustn't it, because they didn't keep him long?

Louie said, 'Anything else you want to know?' But there wasn't.

Max thanked him and took off.

Caroline came drifting into the back room with a sheet of wrapping paper and a roll of Sellotape. Her smile flickered on and then off again. 'Telephone, Mrs Blair. Squadron-Leader Somebody or other.'

Elizabeth tried to tell herself it wasn't. 'Not Jones? I'm not here.'

'I already told him you were. Sorry.'

In the shop, the customer was patiently waiting for the Flying Geese wallhanging to be wrapped. Out in the mews, the striped awnings had an air of faded gentility.

Which was more than you could say for Jones the Onion. His voice sounded snappy, anxious and exacting. 'I've got one of the little beggars!'

'I'm sorry?'

'One of those blasted kids. Caught him vandalising my property. Caught him fair and square and he'll stop there locked in my shed until you get here. Under lock and key.'

'But surely it's the police you want?'

'You never spoke a truer word. But will they come, Mrs Shepard?'

'Blair.'

'Are they interested? That's what you have to ask yourself. I called them, but they practically told me to hobble off.'

And who could blame them?

'So it's up to you. How soon can you get here?'

CHAPTER TWENTY-SIX

◆◆◆

'You'd better go,' Elizabeth told Max. 'It might be a job for muscle.'

Max sighed. 'I've only just got back in. How long's he had the poor little sod locked up?'

'No idea. He's several blocks short of a quilt. You realise that?'

'Mad as a hatter. But you took the case on. And I've got an appointment at the Council offices.'

'Well, visit the allotments on your way, there's a dear boy.'

It was miles out of his way, but for once, he gave in to her sweet talk. Anything for an easy life and better outdoors than in on a day like today. The office was unbelievably stuffy, the sense of tension and imprisonment inside himself – he hadn't yet been able to get hold of Jess – was like a dull ache that he couldn't shift no matter how hard he tried.

He drove up Nobs' Hill and parked the car in the shade of an overhung alley. He was out and walking up the path to the allotments before the sun could get to him. Beech leaves hung listless in the windless air above his head and the bright paint of tethered barges gleamed motionless down on the distant ribbon of the canal. There was no one about. Empty gardens, high walls like barriers of stone on either side. Then the steep slope downwards, slippery with dust and gravel and dried twigs. It went down in fits and starts, between little wooden huts and beanstalks and vegetable plots and thin wattle fences.

Squadron-Leader Jones, tapping a brass-topped walking stick, was watching for him with a gleam of triumph in his eye.

'Took your time, didn't you? Still, you're here. Mrs Shepard's lad, I presume?'

Max put him right. He could see the hut, the size of a signal box, behind him. 'Is he in there?'

'Unless he tunnelled out when my back was turned. He's quieter than he was last night. Given up cussing and swearing.'

Max eyed the stout lock on the outside of the door. The dangerous moment would be just after the key was turned. If he charges, Max thought, I'll use a rugby tackle.

'You've had him in there all night?'

'It was just before ten o'clock,' Jones said. 'I'd been pruning my roses . . . raking a bit of hay. And I heard something going on at the back of the hut. They were only trying to set it alight. An armful of dry hay and a box of matches. Everything tinder dry. It would have gone up like a torch. Only I saw red and I charged at them and clobbered one of them with my stick. The others ran, but this one . . . well, I dragged him inside and slammed the bolt.'

'So he may be hurt?'

'Serve him right if he is.'

'How big is he? How old?'

'Fourteen. Fifteen.'

'Then someone will have reported him missing?'

'Not necessarily. Parents these days . . . don't know where they are. Don't give a damn, most of them.'

'He might be concussed. How hard did you hit him?'

'Didn't get him over the head. Just whacked him across the back.'

'Even so.' Max looked at the Squadron-Leader, his eyes askance. Fascist old bastard, Max thought. Stubborn and agitated and obsessed. Thinks he can do anything and get away with it. I should ring Andy. Or a doctor. Instead, he said, 'You stay there. I'll go in.'

'Want my stick?'

'No, thanks. Just give me the key and keep back out of the way.'

Max approached the hut and inserted the key in the

padlock. Still no sound from inside. Cautiously, he turned the key . . . ran back the bolt.

Behind him, the Squadron-Leader was crouching like a baseball player waiting to whack the ball, sucking in his breath, the stick braced at right angles to his body.

'Rush him,' he said in a stage whisper.

'Shut up. Just shut up.'

Max's mouth was dry, but his brain felt clear and controlled. He banged the door open, swung in behind it and, as he stood squinting into the unaccustomed murkiness, he jerked himself into the hut.

The boy was sound asleep on the floor at the back. Curled into a ball with an old sack dragged over him. 'OK. Come on. Wake up,' said Max, poking at him with one foot.

'Wha'? Leave me . . . Wha's happening?'

The dozy little sod scrambled to his feet. Stood there swaying a little like a corpse coming back to life. He wore baggy shorts and the inevitable baseball cap; there was a smudge of dirt over one piggy little eye.

'Thought you said he was big,' Max said to the Squadron-Leader.

'Never mind that. Let me get to the little blighter.'

'Keep him off me!' yelled the boy.

His name was Bradley Pitt, he was thirteen and a half and he lived down by the embankment. A bit pathetic really, Max thought. A shivering little inadequate, his voice hoarse with shouting, his fingers gripping the side of the hut, that blue weal down the back of his leg.

'You'd better get that looked at.'

'He done it. He's a nutter.'

I know, Max wanted to say, but that's his problem. He actually felt sorry for the kid, but he wasn't letting him off the hook just yet. You never could tell what a few questions might yield.

'So what was the idea of setting fire to the hut?'

'Nuffink. It was just a bit of fun.'

The Squadron-Leader, behind him, was about to have a fit.

'Bloody silly idea of fun. Your idea, was it?'

'No.'

'Then whose? And it had better be the truth—'

The boy threw a frightened glance in the Squadron-Leader's direction and coughed up names and addresses. There were four of them and he was the youngest. They hadn't set fire to anything before; they just messed around, sometimes up here, sometimes down by the canal.

'Thieving little bastards,' said the Squadron-Leader.

'I never stole nothing. Well, only a couple of gnomes once for me Nan.'

'Ever see anyone else nicking anything?'

'No.'

'Sure?'

''Course I'm sure.' But his gaze had dropped to the wooden floor. He was very still all of a sudden.

'I think you're lying.'

'No, I aint. I never saw nothing. Honest.'

Max let his voice sound more chill. 'So who did? See something?' He had this feeling.

The boy shifted uneasily. 'Nobody. None of us. It was too dark to see.'

'Too dark, was it? Well, that's a shame. Don't you think so, Squadron-Leader?'

'I didn't see nothing, I tell you!'

'But?'

'But . . . I might have heard something.'

'So what might you have heard?'

'Nothing much. Just voices . . . up by *his* hut.'

'His hut? Whose hut?'

'That Zeph. The weirdo.' The boy pulled his baseball cap tighter over his shorn head.

'Harris? He's lying. Harris is too damned wet to run a thieving racket.'

'I didn't say he ran anything. I said I heard them talking. We was up there because Rod wants to be in a group. He thought we might get hold of some guitars. Stuff like that.'

'You said you didn't thieve.'

'We didn't, because he was there, wasn't he? So we had a quick fag over behind the pallets, waiting to see if he'd go out.'

'And—'

'And we heard them telling him. If he kept his mouth shut, he'd be OK. If not—'

'If not?'

'They'd duff him up.'

Which they did, Max thought. Which somebody did.

'But you didn't see who they were?'

'I told you. Too dark. Now can I go?'

'No, you bloody well can't!' the Squadron-Leader said.

'I'd like some names,' Max said. 'Did you hear any names?'

No names, no more details, no matter how much he was questioned. The boy jumped a little as the Squadron-Leader tapped his stick, wondering which way to run. 'Can I go home now? Please?'

'Yes. You can go home.'

The boy stared past him at the old man.

'It's all right. He won't stop you. Get going.'

Max got back to the office at ten minutes past two. Starving, sweat-soaked and not in the best of moods. Elizabeth wasn't in the shop and Caroline was, seemingly, serving three customers at once. No hope of a sandwich from that quarter, then. It would have to be Marks and Sparks, once he'd made a few phone calls.

He pushed open the office door and immediately recognised the perfume. French. Very expensive. Jess . . .

CHAPTER TWENTY-SEVEN

She sat there in his swivel chair, her mouth set ominously tight. He'd forgotten that look. Ants in her pants, his sister, Fran, used to call it.

'Jess!' He felt an indescribable mixture of delight and apprehension.

'I've been here for hours,' she said in her icicle voice.

'She rang to see if you were in,' Ginger explained. 'I said you'd be back at one. Which is what you told me.'

It was ten past two. Max apologised profusely. 'Why the hell didn't you ring me?' he said to Ginger.

'Because your cell-phone was here on your desk.'

Max saw that Jess's eyes were like blue molten glass; and opaque with some unreadable emotion. Judging how she would react in this kind of situation was sometimes hazardous. He drew deep on his experience and decided on a breezy, I'm-here-now smile.

'We'll have coffee,' he said rather grandly to Ginger.

'Fine. Make mine black.' She went back to sorting the mail.

'What I meant was, would you make it?'

'Sorry. Elizabeth wants these done by three. *She* could make it,' she said with a nod in Jess's direction. Nothing else to do, her look implied.

He thought, for one moment, that there was going to be trouble. But Jess contained herself – just. 'I keep getting these phone messages. I thought you were keen to see me.'

'I was. I am. I never wanted to see anyone more in my life.'

A stifled moan from behind the other desk. Ginger. He'd get her later.

'I've got a shoot in half an hour,' Jess said stiffly. 'I don't have time for coffee.'

'Can't you skip it? Couldn't we grab a late lunch?'

'Sorry. Impossible. Anyway, I don't eat lunch.'

'Got to watch your figure?' sympathised Ginger. 'I have the same trouble. Cellulite. It's hell.'

Somebody's heels went rappity-tap along the mews. Sparrows were cheeping irritably in the downspout outside the open window. A gull wheeled loose above the rooftops, heading for the grey-green haze in the distance that was Beechen Cliff.

'She's a bit temperamental,' Ginger said after Jess had stalked out. 'Does she always talk to you like that?'

'Like what?'

'Like you're the slave and she's Cleopatra? By the way, a parcel came for you. Would you like a doughnut? There's one in the second drawer.'

'No. I wouldn't. And how dare you talk to her like that! If you'd been nice to her. Looked after her . . .'

'If she'd been nice to me – OK. I'm sorry if I upset her. But she was hard work. Bloody opinionated. And she treated me like dirt. I thought you'd have gone for somebody more bubbly. And younger than you are.'

'She is younger.'

'You're kidding?'

'No,' said Max.

'You could have fooled me. Must be all that war-paint.'

'Jess always looks immaculate. That's her style.'

'Soulless, if you ask me.' Ginger moved past him towards the cabinet and picked up a stack of cardboard files. For the first time, Max noticed that there were paper stacks all over the floor.

'What are you doing?' he asked.

'Sorting all the old rubbish in the cupboard. Some of it's been nibbled. Mice, Elizabeth thought. I've thrown out the worst of it.'

'You didn't? For God's sake—'

'It's in the yard in black bags. In case you want to check through.'

'Those are my records.'

'Nobody could keep records that badly.'

'That's it!' Max said. 'You're fired.'

'OK.' She was peering round the office as if looking for something. 'Now where did I put that parcel?' She acted as if she didn't give a fig. Max was narked. No sign of despair, not even resignation. Just a shrug of the shoulders and that 'OK.'

Ginger said, 'By the way, there are two cheques under the paperweight.'

'Cheques?'

'For the Bailey account and someone called Lionel Close.'

'Bailey and Close?' He was stunned. 'They coughed up?'

'Yup.'

'In full?'

'Yup.'

'How on earth did you get them to do that?'

'I pointed out that we had a barrister friend in the courts.'

'But we haven't.'

'I know that. You know that. They don't.'

Max found himself speechless. He'd been trying to get money out of Lionel Close for almost three years and had practically given up hope. He shook his head, but, in the circumstances, could hardly offer fulsome praise. Ginger shoved the last file in the cabinet, grabbed a few things and stuck them in her rucksack. 'I'll be off, then. Ah – there it is.' She reached on top of the filing cabinet and lifted down a brown-wrapped package. 'By the way, did you mean to collect your suit from the cleaners?'

Past tense. Max looked at his watch. Ten to three. Damn it, they were closed on Thursday afternoons.

'Actually, I collected it for you,' she said sweetly. 'It's hanging behind the kitchen door.'

He didn't know whether to be grateful or irritated by the expression on her face. The one that said she'd pulled the rug from under his size ten feet and was thoroughly enjoying the sensation.

'I'm not going to change my mind,' he muttered.

'Fine. Didn't expect you to. I'll be off, then. 'Bye.'

She always managed to get the last word. Sod it. After her figure had disappeared down the staircase, Max picked up the cheques. He shook his head again and flopped into the chair which Jess had recently vacated.

Her squalls were violent, but short-lived.

Shut up, Max. Don't go back to all that. Don't even think about the bad times.

He'd go round to the hotel this evening. Apologise again and sort out that business about the bloke in her room. There'd be some sort of explanation. Bound to be.

He picked up the parcel. Square and – he shook it – light. Printed label. Postmarked Bristol. He stared at it for a bit longer, then opened it, struggling a bit with the securely-fixed Sellotape.

'Ppffrgh!' What a smell!

Good God, what was it? Some kind of animal remains? He picked gingerly at the poly bag that contained . . .

A rotting rabbit's head.

CHAPTER TWENTY-EIGHT

Elizabeth, meantime, was keeping a date on a park bench with Karen Rudd. 'You wanted to see me?' The girl sat there feeding the pigeons with crumbs of biscuit her toddler had half eaten.

'I did.' Elizabeth sat down beside her. 'Cooler out here than in the office, I thought. A nice shady corner.'

'I've got nothing to say to you.' Karen wasn't as shy as she made out. There was some other emotion lying behind the quick, sideways glance. Something stronger than reserve. Hostility even. 'If Mick knew I was here—'

'No reason why he should. It's quite confidential.'

The child, a boy of two or so, was hopping around on the scrubby grass, talking to himself in a nonsense language. He must have told a good joke, because he started to laugh.

'Nice little fellow. How old is he?'

'Billy? Fifteen months.'

Elizabeth missed nothing of what was going on in the girl's mind. At least the little one couldn't tell anybody where she had been that afternoon, couldn't tell any tales.

'It must be hard work?'

'Yes.' Karen searched for, and found, a tissue and proceeded to blow her nose.

'Had four myself, only more spread out than yours. There are days when you want to cut and run.'

Karen shrugged lightly, twisted her wedding ring, shoved the tissue back in her pocket.

'You need to keep time for yourself, now and then.'

'You must be joking!'

'No. I mean it. Let your husband take over. Grab the odd afternoon.'

Karen almost laughed.

'He's not the type?'

No reply.

'Of course, some men aren't. You have to work on them a little. Why, when Jim and I were—'

The girl shifted suddenly, impatiently. 'I don't have time to waste. Can we get on with it?'

Elizabeth said she didn't see why not. 'Something's puzzling me. The guy your husband was supposed to have had a quarrel with in the car park. The business type. Why on earth would he wear an ear-ring and have the build of an all-in wrestler?'

For a moment, Karen looked down at her feet, quite frozen. Her face had gone white.

'My dear, I know your husband was lying about that encounter. What I can't work out is why.'

'I told him it was stupid. But he always knows best.' Karen shifted her gaze from her scuffed sandals to her son. He was standing, stumpy legs apart, hypnotising a pigeon.

Karen was as still as a rock, silent.

'My guess is that the business man was his brother. Warren. Am I right?'

'If he'd had any sense, he'd have told you. Only he hasn't. Not as far as Warren's concerned. Never did have. Never will.' A short pause. 'Yes, it was Warren he was arguing with in the car park, the night of the disco, but he didn't want you to know that.'

'Why not?'

'I'm coming to that, if you wait a minute. Mick didn't ring for a taxi to come and pick us up. He rang Warren, who said he'd be there in ten minutes. What he didn't say was that he'd just got in from the pub. When he turned up at The Gabriel, he was so obviously over the limit that I refused to go in the car with him. And Warren got funny about it, so they had a bit of a barney.'

'I still can't see why your husband didn't tell Max about this in the first place.'

'He thought you might tell the police. Warren had a slight accident after he left us. Bashed the side of a parked car in Bathwick. Only he didn't report it.'

'I see.' It seemed to make sense. Elizabeth paused to think about it. 'I'll need to contact Warren, if that's OK by you?'

Karen shrugged. 'Do what you like. But don't tell him I told you.'

'So where does he live . . . your husband's brother?'

'Compton Gurney.'

'Sounds familiar somehow,' Elizabeth said. She couldn't understand why.

'He advertises in the papers. He runs his own business from the old brewery at the back of his house. Regency Reclamation.'

'The place where you can buy old knobs and fireplaces and such? I've often meant to go up there, but never got around to it.'

'So now you will,' Karen said abruptly. 'Be careful what you say to him. He's pig ignorant. He could make a lot of trouble for me.'

'You don't sound too keen on your brother-in-law?'

'I hate his guts.'

'Well, that's honest. Do you mind my asking why you told me all this?'

Her eyes flicked away suddenly. 'Because Warren told us not to. He wants the rest of us all zipped up and in his pocket. Wants to click his fingers and have us all jump. Well, I don't care if the police catch up with him. Might teach him a lesson. Mick's brighter than him, older, got more education. But Warren still orders him around like he's a half-wit.'

Old scores to settle, Elizabeth thought. 'My partner tells me you have a good camera. Did you take it to the Toga Night?'

'Sorry. We meant to, but we forgot it.'

'And how did you get home that night, if you didn't go with Warren?'

'I rang my mother. She came and fetched us.' Karen picked up the child's hat and shoved it into her bag. 'I've got to go.'

'Thanks for your help. If you think of anything else—'

'There's nothing else.' Very quick, very certain.

'OK. Bye-bye, Billy.'

The child gave her a funny look.

Swift, suspicious.

For the first time, he looked exactly like his mother.

'I met your Jess this morning,' Elizabeth said, when she got back to the office. 'She didn't seem too happy.'

Max looked daggers at her.

'So where were you?' Her tone became jocular. 'Keeping a girl waiting like that.'

'I was working. And if that bloody Ginger hadn't riled her—'

'Did she?'

'Yes, she did. And she went too far this time. I fired her.'

'You did what?'

'She had it coming. She was impertinent.'

'You mean she wasn't a yes-girl? You'll regret it.'

I don't think so, Max thought. She was only another little temp with a sharp-edged tongue. He shoved the spilling waste-paper basket under the hole in the desk.

'I liked her. She had character.' Elizabeth's voice sounded dry and disapproving. 'What the hell's that smell?'

He told her.

'You are joking?'

'You didn't order anything from the butcher's?'

'Nothing that old.' She was still wrinkling her nose. 'What did you do with it?'

'Chucked it in the bin. So who's got it in for us, do you think?'

'Take your pick.' Elizabeth hadn't a clue. Threats of one kind or another, abusive phone calls, came with the territory. The deviousness (and sheer nastiness) of unfaithful husbands or seedy fraudsters caught on camera sometimes had to be seen to be believed.

But it was no good worrying about it. 'Listen – I'm off to see someone. I wondered if you'd have time to check out

Zeph Harris's background. Anything you can find out about him before he arrived in Bath. Jobs. Friends. Has he got a police record? That kind of thing. You might start at that pub he frequents. The Pied Horse.'

'I've got other stuff to do, you know. Photos to deliver to Jarvis and Co.'

'Who are—?'

'Solicitors. The surveillance job.'

'So you can call in at The Pied Horse on your way back. You'll like that. A pie and a pint.'

Max would have felt angry at her bloody annoying Yankee bossiness, if it hadn't been so hot. After all, it was his business (well, he'd started it) and he was the one with all the experience in the job. For which he got scant credit. He made a face at Elizabeth's back as she went out through the door. Sat there with his sweat-soaked shirt stuck to the chair. Poured himself a Diet Coke and was looking for the pack of surveillance photographs and his car keys when the phone rang. He leaned over to pick it up. 'Shepard Agency.'

'Hello? Is that you, Max?'

Jess. She sounded sweet, gentle, generous. 'I just wanted to say I'm sorry. You know how I get when I'm tired. And I was so looking forward to seeing you and that girl of yours just seemed to make it all ten times worse. But I shouldn't have lost my temper—'

'Yes, you should. She overstepped the mark. But it's all right. I fired her.'

'You didn't? Oh, Max – now I feel dreadful.'

He loved it when she used that soft little voice. It felt like somebody stroking his heart. 'Don't worry about it.' He fiddled with his keys on the desk, picked them up, put them down again. 'She had it coming.'

There was this very short, very loaded silence. Then she said, 'So . . . are you going to buy me a drink? If you still want to?' Knowing perfectly well that he did.

'Great. When?'

'Tomorrow night?'

He felt his heart leap. 'Fine. Where?'

'Where is there?'

For a moment, he was going to suggest The Pied Horse. But worn rush matting and dropped chips weren't Jess. Then he thought of another pub he'd been meaning to check out. Kill two birds with one stone. 'There's a place called The Angel Gabriel up above Lansdown. I'll pick you up at the hotel.'

'No need. I'll probably come straight from work, so I'll get a cab and meet you there. What time?'

'Eightish?' His mood was changing. The frustration was seeping away. It was going to be all right – he knew it was, this time.

'Eight o'clock, then. See you.'

CHAPTER TWENTY-NINE

Gerry Dundy obviously didn't take after his mother either in looks or temperament. Glenda Dundy was solid (and stolid), with a bosom (that was the only word for it) like a barrage balloon and an olive complexion that had faded to sallow.

She showed no hostility towards Elizabeth. Was glad someone was trying to get to the bottom of the case, because it would clear her son's name. People gave you funny looks, she confided over tea and biscuits; chatting away as if glad to air Gerry's problems with someone who would listen.

'My son isn't a murderer, Mrs Blair. He hasn't got it in him. Oh, I know how it looks. He's possessive. He boils over. Sometimes he does stupid things. But not that stupid.'

She grew fierce, clutched at the little dog she held in her lap, when Elizabeth asked about her son's first wife. 'I shouldn't say it, but I shall hate that little trollop for the rest of my born days. He idolised her, you understand. That was the highest point of my boy's life . . . having Deborah and the baby on the way. He was happier than I've ever seen him.'

'So what went wrong?'

'She went off with some man she'd been involved with before she met Gerard. And she took the baby with her. We haven't seen either of them since. Oh, he's tried, believe you me. He's been all over the country following leads . . . but nothing.' Her eyes filled. 'Crushed, he was. Depressed. Right down. Wouldn't say a word for days on end. Sat there, hour after hour, on my sofa, crying his eyes out.'

Elizabeth felt some sympathy. She knew what it was to worry like hell about your grown-up kids.

'She said they weren't suited. It wasn't exciting enough. I

171

don't know what they expect these days, I'm sure. Thunder and lightning and a symphony orchestra in the background. They'd conceived a child, hadn't they? There's nothing wrong with my Gerard. He's had girls galore and none of them ever complained before.'

Nevertheless, there was something about the set of her mouth that suggested doubts. And evasions. Mothers sometimes deceive themselves, Elizabeth thought, out of what they call love.

'Love and a bit of attention, that's all he ever needed. Girls these days . . . they're too selfish. At least, that's my opinion.'

'What about Morgan? Is she selfish?'

'That one! Fell for her on the rebound, didn't he? They were never suited, but you couldn't tell him.'

Elizabeth nodded. Loneliness sometimes made strange bedfellows.

'If he'd only waited. He was just picking up. Getting over what Deborah had done to him and up he picks with another little . . . grasshopper. I despaired. Honestly, I did.'

'You didn't approve of her, then?'

'That's the understatement of the year. She was useless in the house. Never cooked him a decent meal. He came round to me a lot of days. Or else he had to fend for himself.'

'While she was doing what exactly?'

'I'll give you three guesses.'

'You mean she was seeing another man?'

'Of course she was.'

'Julian Neville?'

'He used to bring her home in his car, didn't he?'

'That's hardly a crime. Is that all the proof you had?'

'We didn't need proof. She was quite brazen about it. Used to taunt Gerard. She enjoyed that.'

'Tell me—' Elizabeth perched on the edge of the easy chair, her hands grasped round one knee. 'Someone visits your son on a Friday night when you're out. A man in his forties. Smartly dressed. Drives a big blue vehicle. Do you have any idea who that might be?'

'It's news to me,' the answer flashed back. 'Who told you that?'

Elizabeth recounted the story that Edith Pike had told her.

Glenda relaxed again. 'That old nosey-parker. She's a pain. She makes things up. We've had nothing but trouble with her ever since we came here.'

The shrill of a doorbell made them both jump. Glenda Dundy heaved herself up looking a touch relieved at the interruption (or was that Elizabeth's imagination?) and went to answer it. Elizabeth heard voices. Female. Then the dog yapping and a kind of scuffle approaching.

'I saw her park her car,' Morgan's voice said as she came through the door. Today she wore bright red lipstick and her frizzy hair was looped up in a green ribbon. 'What's the old bitch been telling you? His doting mother . . . Now there's an unhealthy relationship, if you like.'

'Why, you little—'

Morgan dodged Glenda's grasping hand and slid round behind the sofa, out of reach. 'She never liked me, you know. Never accepted any woman who attracted her precious son away.'

'That's not true!' Glenda retorted.

'No?' Morgan was talking, moving round the room, a little spark glimmering in her green eyes. Her voice was sweetly sharp. 'You made Deborah's life hell and you thought you could do the same with me. You want everything done your way. Did you tell that to the lady detective? The slightest little excuse and you criticised. You never once made me feel welcome here. Nobody would ever be good enough for your precious Gerard.'

'Lies. All lies.'

'But let me tell you something. He's no great catch either, with his lunatic rages.'

Glenda shook her head in disbelief. 'You can talk. I'm broad-minded, but—'

'Broad-assed—'

'Filth! You're a filthy little tart. That's what.'

'Better a tart than a cow.'

173

'Why, you little—'

The dog started yapping suddenly between them. Morgan aimed a furious kick at him. 'I bloody hate him, too!'

Glenda grabbed the dog, scooped him up. 'Mitzi doesn't like you either. Never has. That's because dogs know a liar when they see one.'

Something lacking in the caring, sharing department, thought Elizabeth. Old rows, old taunts, old divisions bickering on. I'd better stop this before someone gets hurt. She placed herself between them. 'Look—'

But Glenda wouldn't be silenced. 'Mitzi knows you tell lies about all the men you bring home. And where you get the money for all the fine clothes you put on your back.'

'Excuse me one moment,' Elizabeth said loudly. She addressed herself to Morgan. 'Just out of interest . . . did Julian Neville ever buy you clothes? Jewellery?'

'Who told you that?'

'No one. But Hilary Russell happened to mention that he bought her some ear-rings and I wondered—'

'Hilly? You don't believe her, do you?'

There was something about Morgan's smile. 'What do you mean?'

'I mean that Hilly's not half so sweet and innocent as she seems. Mummy and Daddy don't know the half of what goes on in her life. Dear me, no. You ask her some time.'

CHAPTER THIRTY

———◆◆◆———

Now and then, Diana Neville thinks, life departs from the script. And you're left flailing around in a blind panic, waiting for the prompt that doesn't come.

She sits on the kitchen chair, writing things like Parmesan, Olives, Basil on a small, white pad of paper. She is on automatic pilot. The surface part of her brain seems to be coasting along all by itself, which is just as well, because the rest of it is in tumult.

She is drawing up a list of the things she wants in town. Correction . . . needs, not wants. Damn it, damn it . . . Hubert has invited the Rawlinsons to dinner. Do us good, old girl. Take your mind off it. He doesn't even like the Rawlinsons much: they are acquaintances rather than friends. Geoffrey Rawlinson will drone on and on about falling share prices and Anne has no conversation beyond her bloody needlepoint. But the truth is that Hubert can't bear another night with just the two of us facing each other across the dining-table.

Propped up opposite each other for the rest of our barren lives. So . . . he has invited the Rawlinsons; who will doubtless be dreading the occasion almost as much as I am. It's getting harder by the day. Ignoring the panic in people's eyes when they no longer know what to say to you. Keeping your face blank, your voice clear and firm as you answer the inevitable question. *Oh, we're coping. You know. Going along from day to day. The only way to get through it.* But underneath, there's this raw, ulcerous mess that burns and throbs, day and night.

Relax, she tells herself. Close your eyes, do your breathing

Lizbie Brown

exercises. But the pain only burns more strongly. There is no way to ease it. No medicine, no balm. Nothing anyone can do. Which is nonsense, of course. There is always something . . . even if the relief is purely temporary.

Abruptly she rises and pads barefoot (long, bony toes) into the dining-room, which is all tulipwood and beeswax. Circular windows overlook the garden; the graceful arc of the sideboard is stacked with Royal Doulton. She stands for a moment staring blankly at the photograph of Julian in a silver frame. The blond hair, his smile shining out at her. My boy. The only one who mattered. The light of my life. So like Robin . . . and now they're both gone. Well, you know what he would say. His voice comes through clearly. Along her spine and the marrow of her bones. Chin up, Ma. Don't let the bastards grind you down.

So I won't. Diana presses a hand to her throat, which is suddenly tight with unshed tears. And I won't let them tarnish your name either. It won't happen. I'll fight tooth and nail. I'll do anything.

Which is why she has already worked out a careful plan of action. Nothing rash or impulsive – she touches her son's face with a carefully manicured finger – that's where you went wrong, my darling. I did warn you. But youth does its own thing. It never listens.

You didn't listen either, she tells herself, or you would have picked up the signals earlier. Her face, reflected in the mirror above the sideboard, is pale and drawn with pain. She sets the frame back in its place. Bends her head and kisses him lightly. I look a real old hag. It's a good thing you can't see me. Dreadful, you'd say. A bit of a let-down, Ma. Sort yourself out. Well, I will, I promise you. I'll sort them out, too . . . don't you worry.

Morgan flails her arms in the corner by the window. A young woman in scarlet lipstick and a don't-give-a-damn mood. Red lipstick, glossy hair, green eyes would have been beautiful if they had any feeling in them.

Morgan should be at work, but she has rung in with some

176

excuse. Why bother? She has other funding now, which is why she's playing her music at a thumpingly loud volume. Why she's dancing wildly, shaking her head around, flopping her chestnut mane all over the place. She is also smoking a cigarette that smells funny. Makes you feel good, though. Like you're someone else entirely.

She wraps her arms round her skinny body and pulls off her silk shirt, dropping it on the floor. Doesn't matter if it creases. Plenty more where that came from. Galliano. Ghost. She can afford it all these days. The music thumps on, making the floorboards vibrate, but that's OK. She hopes the old cow – Glenda – will come past the house and hear. Let her glower. Get her knickers in a right old twist. It's a laugh.

Might sell my story to the tabloids, Morgan thinks. Might just ring them. That would be fun, too. She shakes her head until it hurts, then drops, exhausted, into the chair. She stubs out the cigarette and lights another, moodily, then throws the spent match into the sink.

The phone shrills. Let it. Morgan drags hard on her cigarette and blows the smoke in a ring above her head. She has no intention of picking up the receiver. She examines a thin wristful of silver bangles and smiles and waits. At last it stops. She leans over, dials 1471, listens a moment, her smile widening, then drops the receiver. She has no intention of ringing back either. She just likes to know, likes the feeling of power it gives her. Power is better than sex. Sex is nothing. All that rolling and moaning that you see on films. Play-acting. When she's in bed with a man, she feels nothing.

I just like to be in charge. To have them beg. To see them humiliated . . . that's the supreme pleasure. I dictate and they have to obey. Which reminds me . . . Morgan rolls sideways out of the chair, wobbles over to the bureau and draws pen and paper from the drawer. She pulls the top off the felt-tip and starts to write, in sinuous loops:

Remember the last time we saw each other? Remember the figure we arrived at? Well, I've been thinking. It's not enough . . . It's an expensive old world these days. Let's double it, shall we? You'll find it from somewhere . . .

* * *

Elizabeth was fiddling about on the computer, giving a false impression of knowing what she was doing when Max ran up the stairs at ten minutes to two.

'Hi! Where've you been?' she asked.

'The Pied Horse.'

Harris's pub. 'Anything interesting?'

'Not a lot,' said Max. 'He was born in Norwich. Comfortable family, it seems. Father ran a market garden.'

'Now there's a thing.' More bloody horticulture. It ought to have slotted in somewhere, but she was utterly lost.

'But they don't seem to keep in touch. There's a sister who writes at Christmas.'

'Jobs? Before he took to busking?'

'He started life as a postman. Worked in the kitchens of a London hotel for a while. That's when he took to show business. Used to do spots in a pub in Tooting before taking to the road.'

'Any form?'

'Hauled up in front of the magistrates for begging with menaces three years ago. But they let him off with a fine. Apparently he was stoned out of his head, celebrating his birthday.'

Elizabeth tapped a key. 'Nothing much there then?'

'I wouldn't say that.' Max dropped into his chair. 'I saved the best for last. Guess what?'

'I haven't a clue.'

'He used to work for Regency Reclamation.'

'You're not kidding?'

'Part-time . . . for almost a year.'

Elizabeth sat back and considered what Max had said. 'Past tense?'

'He got the push. Upset the boss.'

Elizabeth sat and gazed at the screen-saver. Warren would be upset again when the police went to see him about a certain unreported accident in Bathwick. He needn't think he was going to get away with that one. She'd felt obliged . . . correction, she had positively enjoyed tossing that choice little titbit in Andy's direction. 'Go on.'

'Well, there was this fireplace. Meant to be Victorian. Well over-priced. Zeph let the customer know that it was repro.'

'Brave man. So Warren was on the fiddle?'

'Yup. And there's something else. It may have no significance, but Warren opened a nursery section about a year ago and supplied gardening stuff to a surprising number of people who worked up at Draycott. I headed up there after I left the pub.'

'What did Mick say when he found you were nosing about Warren's business?'

'Not a lot. Just that it's a natural extension to his garden statues and such. And of course, they all bought stuff because Warren had him stick an advert on the notice-board. Ten per cent off for Draycott personnel.'

'So who bought what, exactly? Do we know?'

Max pulled out his notepad and flipped it open. 'Let's see. Hanging baskets . . . ready planted with geraniums and lobelia . . . easiest thing in the world to pinch . . . for Hilly. Bought them for Mummy's birthday . . . a snip at a fiver each. Bernard bought a wooden bench. Special offer in April. Trev bought tomato plants in Gro-Bags. Oh, and a mock-Victorian carriage lamp, complete with post. And Morgan bought some window boxes.'

'All stuff he could have pinched from the allotments . . .' Elizabeth sat wrapped in thought. 'I called on Toby Perrin again this morning.'

'And?'

'He knows a lot more than he's admitting to. And he changed his tune somewhat about the flat. Admitted that Julian had occasionally borrowed it.' Elizabeth saw in her mind's eye Perrin's shifty expression. Trying much too hard to appear nonchalant, he'd achieved the exact opposite.

'OK, so I let him use it once or twice.'

'So why lie about it?'

'I just didn't want to get involved. Anyway, it was a private matter. Irrelevant.'

'Not if he took women back there. You know, I find it hard to believe you don't want to help find his murderer.'

'I didn't say that.'

Elizabeth had said, 'But maybe you know already.'

'I don't have to take any more of this.' An arrogant glance. How she would like to have wiped it off his face.

'Your friend, Amanda, said you were arguing with Julian at The Bargepole. Something about money he owed you for rent of the flat.'

'It was a joke,' Perrin said. 'Ju was always borrowing money from me at school. We had this running joke about him one day paying me back.'

Back in the present, Elizabeth pushed something towards Max. 'You might have a look through these.'

'What are they?'

'Trevor Walsh's photographs of the Toga Night.'

'Anything interesting?'

'Not that I can see. But take a peep anyway.'

Max examined the photos one by one, registering streamers, balloons, a litter of glasses and wine bottles. Here was Wendy with a laurel wreath plonked on her head. Bernard (in blue jacket and pale trousers) waltzing in stately fashion with Hilly, whose toga was of a startling (and unexpected) scarlet brocade. Karen looking as if she were going to throw up. Julian, draped in a cornflower blue bath-towel that matched his eyes, holding up a glass of wine to the camera. A girl carrying a cardboard shield.

Elizabeth said, 'That's Cheryl. Trev's girlfriend.'

Several of them showed Hilly striking silly poses. Sticking a cocktail umbrella into her very considerable décolletage. Standing on one leg like a giggling stork in the middle of the dance floor. Stretching her arms forwards (blind as a bat without her glasses) as she led the conga line. It was a relief to get on to the last two. A shot of the draw prizes in the foyer and one of Julian, over by the bar, about to buy himself a drink.

Elizabeth was right. Nothing much to give them a lead. As he went to slide them back into the envelope, he noticed numbers faintly pencilled on the reverse side. Did a quick count. 'That's funny,' he said.

'What's funny?' Elizabeth shot the computer a look of extreme irritation.

'The two missing are Nos. 30 and 31.'

'Probably didn't come out.'

'Then he wouldn't have made the last one No. 34.'

He was right, of course. Elizabeth said, 'What about the negatives?'

Max searched the little flap inside the envelope. 'Can't see any.'

'Then I'll have to get back to Trev. Did you recheck Morgan's alibi for the night of the murder?'

'I rang her friend yesterday. She wouldn't budge. Morgan was with her all weekend and they went clubbing in Leicester Square on the Saturday night.' He dropped the pack of photographs on the window sill. Then thought, there's something wrong with this place. Something different.

'What's missing around here?' he said with a frown.

'Ginger's pot plants. She came and collected them.'

The window looked bare without them. Max swung his chair around. 'I suppose she had a moan?'

'Not at all. As a matter of fact, she seemed quite chippy. She's working for some water company. More money and she's got her own office.'

Bollocks, Max thought. They were welcome to her. She was only another little temp whose sharp-edged tongue had got her into trouble. Elizabeth was only trying to make him feel guilty. In the wrong.

But he wasn't.

CHAPTER THIRTY-ONE

Elizabeth prowled slowly round Regency Reclamation and decided that too many people nowadays made a living out of selling old rubbish at a fat profit to those who aspired, for one reason or another, to link themselves to a grand past. The English mania, she thought. Rummaging around auction rooms and car boot sales, hoping against hope that you would happen across a blue Spode dinner service, a worn Queen Anne dining chair, a Regency planter or a Victorian sofa with its horse-hair hanging out. Plundering the attics of those who had had a good clear out or had fallen upon hard times.

Warren Rudd's business was housed in a tall, nineteenth-century brewery that overflowed with Portland stone fireplaces, Edwardian cast-iron baths (chipped), window sashes, bulbous Thirties radiators, pine banisters, chandeliers, doorknobs, steamship trunks and baskets that the stately dog had slept in (complete with stately blanket).

You name it, Warren had it.

Elizabeth bent down to admire a handsome brass fender with curly bits at the corners and, behind it, a portly cast-iron fire dog. Nearly died at the price tags. And doubtless, it had been bought for a song from a house that was about to be demolished.

She creaked to her feet again. Wandered, still examining price tags, over to the arched window. A grey-blue sky pressed down on to a yard filled with stone angels, Roman goddesses, wrought-iron railings, boot scrapers, terracotta tiles, chimney pots, stone urns planted with miniature roses. I wonder where they came from? You could slip a few hundred nicked plants in there, Elizabeth thought, without anyone noticing.

What we should do, she thought, is make a return trip with the list of items stolen from the allotments. But for the moment . . . she stretched a slim, brown wrist to check her watch. It was two minutes to three and she had an appointment with Warren Rudd.

His office, which had an outer reception area that housed the sales assistant, was coolly shaded with vertically slatted blinds.

'He won't be a sec,' said the birdlike little girl who showed her in. 'Take a seat.' She stood there hovering. Her cropped blonde hair was the colour of Wensleydale cheese, her eyebrows dark and her fingernails a delicate shade of lavender. 'He's sprucing himself up. Just got back from buying his lottery tickets.'

'Really?' Elizabeth said, stirred by this confidence.

'I get mine on a Saturday. You ever win anything?'

'Afraid not,' Elizabeth said.

'Not even a tenner?'

'Sorry.'

'That's bad luck.'

'Not really,' said Elizabeth. 'I never buy any.'

The girl's expression was one of disbelief. Elizabeth wanted to tell her not to worry, it didn't hurt much, but then, from behind her, she heard footsteps approaching.

Rudd was out of breath. 'Sorry. Winded. Had to come up from the bottom yard. Out of condition.' He was a weighty man with straw-coloured hair drawn back into a pony-tail. His blue eyes – screwed up into a salesman's smile – were lost in a heavy face that was the colour of glowing brick. A boozer's face. A heart attack face, most probably, in a year or two.

'Now – what can I do for you, Mrs Blair?'

Get rid of that cigar, she thought, or I shall throw up. Elizabeth explained her mission. 'I'm hoping you can help with a murder enquiry.'

'Murder?'

'Your brother worked with the victim. Julian Neville.'

'I still don't see—'

'Basically, I'm checking statements made by Draycott staff. So . . . I wondered if you could tell me where you were on the night your brother and his wife attended a disco held at a pub called The Angel Gabriel.'

There was a cautious silence. 'Did Mick send you round here?'

'No. I just heard that you may have been at The Gabriel that night. Someone thought they saw you.'

He paused, propping the cigar in an ashtray. His piggy eyes eventually met hers. 'Mick called to ask me to come and fetch him. So I went over there.'

'What time was this?'

'Not sure. Elevenish? Some time around then.'

'And you drove them home? Your brother and his wife?'

Another pause. 'I didn't, as a matter of fact. We had a bit of a barney.'

'An argument? What about?'

'I'd had a few. My dear sister-in-law thought I may have been over the odds. I wasn't, but she gets a bit touchy. Insisted on having a cab instead.'

'So you drove off in a huff?'

'Yeah. I did as a matter of fact.'

'And a parked car leapt out at you?'

'Who told you that?'

'It's my job. Finding things out.'

He seemed momentarily taken aback, but then regained his bluster. 'These things happen. Nobody was hurt.'

This time, Elizabeth thought. 'So how long were you actually at The Gabriel that night?'

'Not long. Five . . . maybe ten minutes.'

'Where did you meet your brother and his wife? Inside or out?'

There was indecision in his eyes.

'You don't remember?'

'Of course I remember.'

'Then you can't decide what to say?'

'I met them inside. In the foyer. They were waiting for me.'

'Did you talk to anyone else while you were there?'

'Not that I can recall.'

'Think carefully, Mr Rudd.'

A shifty look. 'I don't think so . . . no.'

Elizabeth knew he was lying. She had just made a connection in her head that proved it. She waited a second or two, then timed what she hoped might be her trump card very carefully. 'Now that's interesting, because I have a photograph that says otherwise.'

'A photograph?' He looked startled.

She looked at him in a calculating way, remembering the shot of Bernard Lucas, his arms full of draw prizes. 'Of course, I can't absolutely be sure . . .' He'd had his back to the camera and she had thought at first that he was a bouncer. 'But there aren't many men around of your size with such a distinct hair-style. I'd swear it was you, smoking a cigar and talking to your brother's boss.'

A double take. 'Oh . . . yeah. I bumped into him in the foyer when I was looking for Mick. We had a word or two. That's right.'

'So you know Mr Lucas? I find that quite surprising.'

'He bought some stuff from me a while back. Garden tubs. And a bench.'

'Right. So . . . did you speak to anyone else that you forgot to tell me about?'

'No. I didn't. Look,' he said, fetching his smile out again. 'I may be a bit thick, but I don't see what all this has to do with the murder.'

'To be honest with you, neither do I at the moment. But someone attacked Neville at that disco and I have to check.'

He seemed relieved. His whole face brightened. She watched him finger the cigar. Ostentatious watch on a very hairy wrist. Big, red hands. Thick fingers stained with something browny-green. Machine oil? Paint?

Elizabeth said, 'This is quite a business you have here. Quite some property.' *Other people's property?*

'We do all right. The turnover's pretty good.'

'You've got some great stuff. A mite expensive for my pocket—'

'People seem happy to pay it.'

And you're happy to stick their fat cheques into your bank account. Elizabeth said in a most Yankee-ignorant voice, 'Where in tarnation does all the stuff come from?'

'All over. I was up clearing a house in the Brompton Road last weekend. Carted it down the M4. Buy cheap, sell high, that's what my old father used to say.'

He was good at bragging. And he obviously wanted to make a good impression. The sun went on streaming through the window. 'Isn't that taking advantage?' she asked mildly.

'It's business. These days you earn a penny wherever you can.'

'Well, you do seem rather good at it, I must say.' She waited for his response.

'What makes you say that?'

'Oh . . . let's see now. The meteoric rise. You had nothing five years ago, but now there's a seven-bedroomed house with six acres of grounds and a swimming pool.' Elizabeth had the file she had compiled on him in her lap. She continued to stare Warren Rudd in the eye. He was giving off the first whiff of anxiety.

'I bought the house for next to nothing,' he said. 'Practically derelict. Got a builder friend in. Spent a year getting rid of dry rot and the damp. But how I see it, it's an investment.'

Some investment. 'Lucky old you.'

'All you need is an eye for such things.' He was trying to be big and breezy, but his body language was saying other things. He kept glancing down at his agenda sheet. His crib notes. Fiddling with the gold-plated ear-ring.

'And the right contacts, I imagine?'

'It helps.'

The blonde girl came back in and whispered in his ear. He murmured instructions to her that Elizabeth couldn't hear and she toddled off out again on spiky heels.

'Tell me something. What would you do if you found out that an item in your stock was stolen property?'

He looked surprised. Then hurt. 'It wouldn't be.'

'How can you be so sure of that?'

'It wouldn't, I can assure you. Everything's strictly checked. This is a respectable business.'

Elizabeth kept her tone light. 'So you're an honest citizen?'

'I try to be. Yes.'

'So honest that you didn't report bashing somebody's car?'

'It was you that reported me to the police. So who told you?'

'I'm afraid I can't disclose that to you.'

'It was that bloody Karen, wasn't it?'

'Karen who?'

'My brother's wife.'

'Is that what you think?' Before he could give a reply, she fired another question. 'They tell me you've opened up a garden nursery. Is that true?'

'Only a small one. A sideline really. There was this nursery that went out of business last year. Camley Court. I bought up some of their stock along with a load of old flagstones. It was a one-off. I wouldn't do it again, quite honestly, because I caught a nasty cold. Half the plants had been affected by frost, only I didn't know that at the time.'

A lie as big as Texas. He seemed pleased that he had managed to talk himself out of a tight corner. The blonde girl was hurrying across the yard outside the window . . . brandishing an arm towards the gates. What was that all about?

'I suppose that would fit in with what Mr Roberts, the manager of The Angel Gabriel, told me when I dropped in on him.' She whipped over a page of her notes. 'You sold him some pelargoniums . . . let's see now . . . in May of this year. And some potted palms that died a death within the week.'

'You have been checking up, haven't you?'

'It's what I'm paid for.'

'Yes . . . well. I can't always be responsible for what I buy in. Denny Roberts wanted a few plants and I did him a favour.' Rudd was in charge of himself again and talking hard. 'He's a personal friend. We play golf together.'

'Are most of your customers personal friends?'

'I'm on good terms with a lot of them. Yeah. It's good business practice. And I'm a sociable bloke.'

I bet you are. When it suits you. 'Do you know a man called Zeph Harris?'

'That layabout!' Rudd left the ear-ring alone and leaned back in his chair. 'He used to work here, but I fired him.'

'Why was that?'

'He was bone idle.'

'I heard another story.'

'Yes . . . well. You'll get a lot of stories from that one. Most of them fairy tales.'

'So . . . did you know that Mr Harris was beaten up a week ago on Friday?'

'Can't say I'm surprised. Drunk, was he? Or high on drugs? Probably asked for it.'

'You don't say? So where were you that night? Any idea?'

'Let me see now. I was down in Cornwall, clearing a house.'

Convenient. 'Nowhere near the allotments by Beechen Cliff then?'

'No.'

'And on April 15th? That's the night the Neville boy was murdered, if you were going to ask.'

'That's easy.' Too easy, Elizabeth thought. Much too pat. 'I was here, all evening, doing the stocktaking. Drives you bloody mad.'

'All evening?'

'Until midnight. No, I tell a lie. Half past midnight. Ask Linda. The girl who showed you in. She was here helping me.'

'On a Saturday night?' Elizabeth looked sceptical.

'I paid her double time. She's saving to go to Bermuda.' He put his two hands on the desk top and rose. 'Now . . . I'm afraid I've got another appointment in five minutes. So if you'll excuse me . . .'

He was plumb eager to see her go. Too eager, Elizabeth considered, but mistrust him as she did, she couldn't pin anything down, and she left and drove thoughtfully back into town. Which was a pity, because a few minutes after she left, all hell broke loose in Rudd's office. Linda flying up and down the stairs from the safe to the cupboard behind the till. Rudd touched on the raw by some discovery; bellowing at the girl, his temper growing more unsafe by the minute. The nature of the panic unknown to the customers who happened to wander into the eye of the storm.

But it seemed to be something to do with a box that was missing. And the key to the safe.

CHAPTER THIRTY-TWO

'I think I wiped the stupid thing—'

Elizabeth pecked at the keyboard with one finger. Technically, she was a halfwit, Max thought. He'd bought her a new manual – the one for dummies – and had gone through it with her, but she was still clueless.

'I told you not to try it on your own—'

'If you hadn't come in and made my finger jump—' Elizabeth stabbed at another key. Irritation was the mother of invention. 'Computers are a pain in the butt. A whole hour wasted and not a damned thing to show for it! Ginger used to print things out for me,' she said. 'That kid could find all sorts of stuff that was hidden in there. Stuff I didn't know existed until she came up with it. I remember asking her how she did it and she'd laugh and say pure genius and, do you know, I reckon she was right. But what happened? You got rid of her.'

'What is it that you want?' asked Max.

'Hilly Russell's address.'

'That's no problem.' Max reached across her, gave the keyboard a few taps and a name and address came on the screen. 'There you go.'

A long pause. A very long pause. 'I guess you're not so dumb as you look,' said Elizabeth.

'Not as dumb as you.'

'Oh . . . horse manure!' she said and stomped off down the stairs.

Two minutes later, she was back again. 'I rang Trevor Walsh. There were thirty-four photographs when they came back from Boots. He lent them to Mick Rudd and Wendy

Lucas. And he can't understand why the negatives are missing.'

The Angel Gabriel was a comfortable sort of place, with honey-coloured walls, bowls of flowers and a Dutch still-life over the fireplace. Max glanced up at the pub clock and saw that it was ten minutes to eight. He ran a hand over his newly groomed hair.

'Can I get you something?' the barmaid said. 'Another pint? Or the menu?'

Max's eyes turned again towards the open door. He shook his head. 'Maybe later. I'm waiting for someone.'

The barmaid said in quite a different voice from the professional one she'd used before, 'I'm not pushing you. It's just that while I'm out here, they can't be giving me a hundred other jobs to do.'

Max gave her a smile. 'You've had enough?'

'You're telling me. I've been on all day. Preparing vegetables, laying tables, washing dishes.'

'What time do you finish?'

'Ten o'clock.'

'That's a long shift.'

'I know. But it pays the mortgage. Benny – that's my partner – lost his job, so I'm keeping the ship afloat.' She leant over to pick up a glass, grinned widely. 'Don't worry. I'll survive. There are perks.'

'Like what?'

'Lentil Bake.'

It didn't sound like a perk, not to Max.

'I got the left-overs last night. Carried them home on the front of my bike.'

Max wondered, quite out of the blue, if Ginger had a mortgage. Or a partner. Bet she gives him a hard time, poor sod.

'How long have you been working here?' he asked the girl.

'About six months. Before that, I worked at The Princess Amelia up in Walcot Street. Do you know it?'

Max did know it; it was one of the pubs Dundy had

mentioned visiting after the Toga disco. 'I was in there last week,' he said. Asking questions and drawing a blank. Nobody seemed to know Dundy; he was instantly forgettable, it seemed.

'I'd better not ask which bar,' the girl said.

'Why's that?' said Max.

She leaned back to hook a glass above the bar. 'One of them's a gay bar. Didn't you know?'

'No. I didn't.'

'There are two bars. If you turn right as you go in, you're in the straight bar. Turn left and go down the steps if you want the gay one. You didn't find it or you'd have known. I always worked in the gay one. Less rowdy. Nicer type of customer.'

'Well, blow me,' said Max, with genuine surprise. So what if Dundy was a closet gay? What might that lead to? A concrete reason, he thought, for the failure of two marriages. He could imagine what Morgan might have said about it – sad bastard; you should have told me; well, I'm off to find myself a real man . . . But it didn't lead to any radical new conclusions.

In his inside pocket, he still had the bunch of mugshots from his visit to The Pied Horse. He pulled them out and showed them to the barmaid. 'I don't suppose any of these were regulars at the gay bar?'

'I seem to know him,' she said, pointing to the surveillance snap he had taken of Toby Perrin outside his shop. But not Dundy or Grenfell. Or Julian. Well, apart from having seen his face splashed all over the tabloids. And she hadn't been on duty on the night of the Toga disco. 'A couple of us were down with the flu, so the boss had to take on temporary staff, what with both function rooms booked and the restaurant full to overflowing.'

'Max. Darling! Have you been waiting long?' A voice cut through from behind them. A smooth, lazy voice. Jess. She was pushing her way through the tables towards him. She wore a scarlet linen mini dress that set off her bronzed arms, her luminous eyes. 'Sorry I'm late. Blame our art director. Useless git. He wanted to keep us there all night.'

'Yes?'

'Yes. I could murder a gin and tonic. Ice and lemon. Loads of ice. I am absolutely exhausted!'

The barmaid, signalling that she had heard, moved towards the bar. She looked suddenly big and solid and clumsy around the legs.

'God, what a day! Stuck in this hotel dining-room for hours on end and no air conditioning, would you believe?'

'Tough assignment, eh?'

'You can mock. Ned – that's the art director – decided we were going to nibble at paw-paw and goat's cheese. Only the paw-paws dribbled juice down over us and the cheese started to melt under the lights and smelled absolutely foul. I said to Kim – that's one of the other models – I won't ever look at a goat again.'

The barmaid placed a gin and tonic on the table. 'Thanks,' Max said. 'So . . . how long more have you got in Bath?'

'Three days. Four maybe. God knows.'

'Then it's back to the smoke?'

'I suppose.'

What did that mean? 'So where are you living . . . in London, I mean?'

'Camden.'

'A flat? A house?'

'A house. I bought it about a year ago.'

'On your own or sharing?'

'On my own. Why?'

'No reason. At least . . . Well . . .' He took a deep breath. 'All I wondered was . . . Well, when I called at your hotel the other day, there was this bloke in your room.'

'Not true, actually.'

'Jess – I was there. I saw him.'

'I know. He said. But he wasn't in my room.'

'The girl behind the desk said—'

'She said I was in 103. Yes? Well, I was, originally. But 103 was noisy . . . traffic right under the window. So Tony offered to swap with me. In this business you need your beauty sleep. OK?'

'OK.'

'I do believe you thought . . . Max – I do believe you were jealous.'

'No.'

'Yes, actually.' Her fingers brushed his face. 'Sweet. OK, so now it's my turn. Are you . . . attached to anyone?'

'No.'

'Good. So that's all settled. Now we can get down to the important stuff. Are we eating here? Only I'm absolutely famished. Haven't had a crumb all day, except for the bloody paw-paw. I spy a menu board. Back in a tick.'

'Your girlfriend . . .' the barmaid said as she cleared the table next to him. 'She's in show business, yeah?'

'She's a model.'

'You can tell.'

'Yeah?'

'Cheekbones. Wish I was that skinny.'

'You're all right.'

'No, I'm not.' She gave the table a final wipe. 'You know the trouble?'

'What's that?'

'The Lentil Bake. I like it too much.'

They exchanged a grin. The girl went off as Jess came back. 'What was that all about?' she asked.

'Oh, nothing. She's a nice kid. Just having a joke.'

'I noticed.'

'Now who's jealous?'

'Of that? You must be joking? Yes, you are. I'd forgotten your absolutely wicked sense of humour. There's nothing on the board that I fancy. Tell you what, there's a place someone mentioned . . . it's called Les Delices. Should we try that, do you think? It sounded quite luscious.'

CHAPTER THIRTY-THREE

The first thing that struck Elizabeth about Hubert Neville was how ill he looked. Dark rings under his eyes, almost as if they'd been charcoaled. An awful pallor under the mottled red of his cheekbones. 'Would you like a starter?' he asked.

The waitress, who looked as if food never touched her lips, hovered beside their table. Elizabeth shook her head and smiled at Hubert. 'Not for me, thank you.' She had no desire to fleece the guy, no matter how deep his coffers. The bill waiting for him back at the office was steep enough already; and for precious little new evidence.

'Then I'll have the Normandy Chicken.'

'That sounds good. Me, too.'

'I'd like a progress report,' he had mumbled when ringing to make an appointment. 'Better meet in town this time. Better than here. You know what I mean. Would Saturday suit you? Let me buy you lunch. Book a table somewhere . . . wherever it suits you.'

She'd had the impression that he wanted to get out of the house. That he was searching for a way . . . any way . . . of filling in time. She had chosen the Rive Gauche. Plenty of comings and goings, lightish menu, ditto prices. He had listened to her report while knocking back two glasses of Beaujolais. 'I'd hoped you would have turned up more. Something more conclusive.'

'I'm sorry. It takes such a time, I know. Knocking on doors, asking questions, not always getting answers . . .'

An insolent fly was buzzing round the potted palm in the window. A July blue sky hung above the inhabited sculpture that was Argyle Street. On the pavement outside, a small group was gathering. Elizabeth kept an eye on them through the open door.

'You're doing your best, I'm sure. I just wish—' Silence descended on the table, broken only by the chatter of the other diners and, now and again, the tramp of lunchtime shoppers.

'You wish I could wave a magic wand?'

'Something like that. The boy is . . . was . . . a thread of my own life, Mrs Blair.' His words were getting slurred. 'Now that he's gone, something's been torn out of it. There's this hole. And it's turning into a chasm.'

Poor Hubert. The wine was doing him no good; making him maudlin. But he had cause, if anyone did.

'I need to know what kind of bastard killed him. The answer will be another form of torture. I know that. But it couldn't be worse than the hell of not knowing.'

His eyes were dry and burning and Elizabeth glanced away. Outside, the group was swelling. What on earth was it? The street wasn't usually so crowded.

'Do you believe in all that stuff, Mrs Blair? Hell and damnation?'

I believe you're going through it, Elizabeth thought.

A tour. That's what it was. The guide, a stocky woman with a giant clipboard, had assembled them on the pavement and was about to start her talk. *William Pulteney's plans for this area included a wide road lining the bridge to a Circus from which five other roads would lead off. This was abandoned as too costly. Only the bridge, named after Pulteney, was finished in his lifetime.*

Elizabeth turned her head – and her attention – back to Hubert. 'Several witnesses thought that Julian had money troubles. Do you know if that's true?'

He shifted in his seat. 'He'd run up the credit card occasionally. But at his age they all do.'

'And you bailed him out?'

'Occasionally.' Now it was his turn to look away. 'But I've got plenty. And he'd have grown out of it. I did—'

'Yes?'

'It doesn't matter. Doesn't signify.'

'Let me be the judge of that.'

'Well, I did refuse to pay it off for him . . . just before he . . . just before it happened.'

'How long before – exactly?'

'Two weeks. Maybe three. As a matter of fact, there was friction at home about it. The boy was mad at me. So was Diana. It was the first time I'd refused him money, you see.' Hubert was angry now, but whether at himself or his wife, it was impossible to tell. 'I told her I should have stopped years back. He had to learn the value of things. My wife disagreed, of course. She paid it off for him.'

'So how much did he owe?'

A silence. Then he said, 'Nearly two thousand.'

Serious money. Elizabeth wondered what it had been spent on.

Hubert didn't wish to say more on this topic. He skewed it to another angle. 'What about you? Are you able to put enough time to the case? Would it help if I paid you more? Because—'

'No. No – we're fine. It's not money. It's just the time it takes to work our way through the multiple layers of your son's friends and acquaintances.' Collecting stories. Looking for things that remain consistent and for the glaring inaccuracies and lies. And then putting it all into focus.

'Maybe Diana was right. Maybe I'm wasting your time and my money.' He seemed to be having trouble with his breathing and Elizabeth wondered uneasily if he'd brought his pills with him. 'Should have left the police to get on with it,' Hubert mumbled. 'Not being funny, but they are the professionals.'

'You know what I always tell people?'

'What's that?'

'Professionals built the Titanic. Amateurs the Ark.'

He smiled a little at that. Some of his colour was coming back. He wasn't going to flake out on her. 'Point taken. Here's your coffee.'

The tour guide raised her voice an octave. *A second scheme*

*was drawn up by Adam, but his patron died before it could
be realised. Pulteney's daughter, Henrietta, brought in a new
architect by the name of Baldwin, who kept Adam's scheme
for a wide street leading from Pulteney Bridge. Argyle Street,
Laura Place – named after another daughter – and Great
Pulteney Street were begun in 1788.*

'You haven't found anything out about the girl he was
with that night? The girl with dark hair?'

'Nothing at all. She's a missing piece in the jigsaw. No one
knows her, who she was, where she came from. Or if they do,
they're not saying. She may have been, well . . . someone he
picked up. Someone who picked him up.'

'And disappeared again?'

'Well, she certainly hasn't come forward. But then, would
you?'

'If I was innocent . . . yes.'

That was what bothered Elizabeth more than anything.
A voice in her head kept saying: Suppose he was killed by a
casual pick-up who will never be found? Suppose he took
her up to the allotments and tried to go too far too soon?
Tried to rape her, but she fought back? Such things
happened. And if he'd been drinking . . . But how could she
voice such concerns to a grieving father? It would be
inhuman.

There was a movement outside. The guide was moving
them on, her voice turning jocular. *Poor Henrietta couldn't
have picked a worse time to be taking on a grand building
project. Any idea why? Yes, you've guessed. The French
Revolution. Widespread financial panic. One by one, her
builders went bankrupt and work stopped. The large,
hexagonal pleasure gardens planned at the end of Pulteney
Street went to the wall. That building at the end – now The
Holburne Museum – see it? – was originally the spacious and
dignified Sydney Hotel, a lodging place, for many years, for
exiled French aristocrats.*

The dispossessed. The homeless. Elizabeth frowned, as if
searching through her memory.

'Something wrong?'

She only shrugged her shoulders and said, 'No . . . no. It's nothing.'

'Nice place,' said Max to Bernard Lucas, as he gazed through the open french windows at the garden. It tumbled down from the house through a series of stone terraces; two generous herbaceous borders blazed with poppies and delphiniums. The grass slopes seemed to swallow up all the afternoon traffic sounds from the world outside. There were beehives beyond the hand-beaten wrought iron bench and espaliered apple trees hiding the kitchen garden.

They talked horticulture for a few moments. At least, Max listened while Bernard talked. He was very knowledgeable. More relaxed and fluent than Elizabeth had suggested. But then, he was at home in his little castle. Everything calm and ordered. The air clearer and cooler up here under the speckled shade of the beechwoods. Soothing. Max still had a lingering headache. Alcohol had picked him up last night, but let him down hard this morning.

'Our sanctuary,' Lucas said. 'Well, my sanctuary. Wendy didn't want to come out here at first. Too isolated, she said. She's more sociable than I am. But I think she's come round to my way of thinking. The views are wonderful.'

Max had to agree. That great valley sweeping away westwards towards Bristol, deep woods running round every side of it. Three o'clock, blue-green shadows . . . almost sea blue . . . lying further out, in the great, hazy distance.

'Yes, I think she's happy here now. Of course, we both still miss the sea. We came up from Plymouth originally. We were only saying the other day, we belong in the West Country. Can't imagine living in London. I've no ambition to be a Whitehall whizzkid. Here at least, we can keep in touch with our roots. The sea's within reach.'

His eyes, battleship grey, gazed out over the wheatfields almost longingly. 'Not that we get down to the coast that often. You have kids and they soak up every bit of your spare time.'

'How many do you have?'

Lizbie Brown

'Just one boy. Tom. He's just been offered a place at Oxford.'

'That's great.'

'Well, yes.' The proud smile warmed his whole face. 'That's him on the wall over there. A quick sketch I did when he was five.'

The child's face – huge, blue eyes, fine golden skin – had been caught very touchingly. 'It's good.'

'Not really. I once had a pipe dream about going to art school, but I knew I wasn't good enough. Anyway, have a seat. Tell me what I can do for you.'

Max got down to the nitty-gritty and told him. Warren Rudd. Had Bernard ever bought anything from him? Sorry to waste valuable time on such trivia, but the only way to find out was to ask.

Lucas looked surprised. And a touch guilty. 'Yes. I bought that bench from him last summer. And a couple of other things. Plants and such. Why?'

'We're investigating a series of allotment thefts as well as this murder. There's a possibility – no more than that at the moment – that Warren might be implicated.'

'Oh, lord. I had no idea. It's a nice old bench . . . heavy . . . wrought-iron curlicues. And the plants . . . Oh, cripes. Will the police be involved?'

'Not at the moment. Anyway, you weren't to know. And you weren't the only one. Warren worked up quite a nice little market up at Draycott.' Max sat back in his seat. 'The other thing is, Warren said he spoke to you at the Toga disco. In the foyer, I believe?'

'Yes. Yes, he did. I couldn't get rid of him. He'd obviously been drinking. Very . . . fulsome. Tried to sell me some garden chairs to go with the bench. Last thing I needed, actually, a sales pitch, under the circumstances.'

'Circumstances?'

'Well, Dundy had just been thrown out and I was having to deal with the security people and there was a hell of a din coming from the stag do in the other room.' He shook his head. 'Of course, it's obvious that Warren's . . . shall we say,

202

not exactly pukka. Mick gets a bit embarrassed by him at times. But there are occasions when he's been extremely useful to us. Take the disco. We'd actually booked another venue, but they let us down. Double-booked. We wouldn't have got the Gabriel room if Warren hadn't known the manager and pulled a few strings. I remember thinking, thank God I won't have to sit through another one. It's always a pain.'

'You're leaving?'

'In a couple of months.' His face glowed with a sudden smile. 'Promotion. We're off to Livorno, all being well. My last posting before retirement.'

'Nice.'

'It is rather. I'm not fond of the heat – Wendy soaks it up – but it should be rather a cushy number.'

'What's a cushy number?'

Max looked around and saw that Wendy Lucas had entered the room. Crimson lipstick, but discontented lines around the mouth. On her face the same look of annoyance and suspicion as on that first day up at Draycott.

'For God's sake!' she said. 'Why can't you leave us alone?'

CHAPTER THIRTY-FOUR

'Pestering us at home as well as at the office!'

'It's all right, Wendy.'

'It's not all right. Invading our privacy—'

'He rang to ask if I could spare him five minutes. I couldn't see why not.' Bernard's grave good manners held out in spite of his obvious embarrassment.

'No, you wouldn't. Never do.' The words were more gently spoken, but her tone still retained an edge that was half mumsy, half bossy. The kind of voice you would use to an exasperating child. 'What's it about this time, if one may ask?'

'Nothing much. Warren Rudd. What was he doing at our disco?'

'Flogging over-priced goods and spinning a line, as per usual.' There was a sharp primness in her light blue eyes, but she had recovered her equilibrium.

'Yes . . . well. Did you get Tom's books?'

'They hadn't come in. Blasted shop. Quite useless.'

'Does he know?'

'No. You'd better do it now. Ask if he wants to try somewhere else.'

Bernard did as he was told. Disappeared out into the shining parquet hall. Wendy stood watching him with a curious expression on her face. As if it pleased her to exert pressure on him. As if an emotion that might have begun as tenderness was turning into . . . what? Some kind of irritation.

Odd couple, Max thought. He so stolid and she so fidgety and energetic. But you find that all over. Partners compensating for each other's little weaknesses.

At last, she turned back to Max. 'I could strangle him at times,' she said. 'He's so damned docile.' She seemed glad to have got him out of the way. Out of hearing. Wendy sighed deeply. 'I shouldn't say things like that. He's the best husband in the world. We're just two opposites. I'm too impatient. Always have been. Too late now to change.'

She glanced at herself in the mirror and smoothed back her bleached blonde hair. Not bad-looking, Max thought, for her age. But restive. Something coarse-fibred about the mouth. Discontented. And vain about her fading looks.

He shuffled in his head a pack of questions he wanted to ask her. Where to begin? Then he spotted a wedding photograph on the piano and asked, as if with casual interest, where she had met her husband. And surprisingly, now that they were alone, she seemed keen to chat. Gave him her life history.

She had met Bernard at a dance in Plymouth. They had been childhood sweethearts. Well, almost. Wendy was seventeen and Bernard nineteen when they started going out together. Her father had been a solicitor's clerk (she seemed proud of the fact); Bernard's a night security man in the naval offices in Devonport. Bernard had actually gone to sea for a while, while Wendy worked in an insurance office in town. After their marriage, she had encouraged him to study at night school and get a job with the civil service. Constant hard work led to promotion, a better house, a small measure of success.

'And now you're off to Livorno,' Max said.

'What? Oh, yes. Italy. Well, of course, it'll be a wrench. I've only just got used to this place. It's very quiet up here. Bernard loves it, but occasionally I'd enjoy a good gossip over the fence.'

'So who will take over from your husband when he leaves?'

She lit a cigarette, blew a long spiral of smoke out of her mouth. 'I don't think we can discuss that, do you? It's MoD business.'

'But just as a matter of interest. Off the record. Will it be someone from Draycott or will they appoint from outside?'

She wouldn't be drawn. 'I really have no idea.'

In spite of her apologetic smile, he thought her nervous and wondered why. 'Do you mind if I ask you something?' Max used his soft, faintly flattering voice. He wasn't above turning on his own blue-eyed charm when it might yield results. 'Something personal?'

'That depends.' Her eyes met his, then swept away again. But she's susceptible, Max thought. She had turned a bit flustered, girlish; something was getting through that abrupt exterior.

'What did you think of Julian Neville? Was he as bad as they make out?'

She moved over to the fireplace. Something faintly sneaky about the way she looked at you. 'My opinion of Julian? He was inconsiderate, spoiled, lazy, irritating. And yet there were times when you couldn't help liking him.'

'Only like?' Max's voice had taken on a measure of confidentiality.

'What do you mean by that?'

'Well . . .' Backtrack, Max, gently does it. 'We'd heard a rumour . . . and I'm sure it was only silly gossip . . . we'd heard some nonsense that there may have been something between you and Julian. Something more than just a working relationship.'

It happened in offices. That was how he'd met Jess. She'd worked for a while in the tacky little detective agency he'd started out at in Manchester. 'A right little bomber,' Frank Ackroyd had called her. Max made an effort to get his mind back to the present. Wendy's colour had risen.

'That's outrageous! But that's Draycott for you. They'll talk about anybody and anything, given a boring afternoon and a tea break. And what they don't know, they'll make up. It comes with the paper clips and the stewed tea.'

'So there was nothing in it?'

'Of course not.'

'You didn't . . . I'm sorry about this, but I have to ask . . . stay on working late, the two of you, in the evenings?'

'Occasionally we stayed late.' She adjusted the collar of

her blouse. 'But not often, I assure you. Julian didn't believe in hard work.' Her voice was now smooth and ironic. 'If I had to hazard a guess, I'd say it was Hilary you've been talking to. It doesn't matter. You don't have to tell me. It's just that she reads too many steamy romances.'

'I can imagine.'

'And she had a thing about Julian herself. He used to joke about it, but she could make a real nuisance of herself. I remember once, some girl rang up to speak to him and Hilary pretended he wasn't there.'

'Girl? When was this?'

'Oh . . . a couple of weeks before he . . . before the murder.'

'You don't know who she was? The girl?'

'Sorry. All I can tell you is that he was furious with Hilary. It actually seemed to matter to him and that was quite rare for Julian.'

Interesting, Max thought. Hilly forgot to tell us that. He moved on to a new subject. 'I did hear that you asked Julian to dance with you at the Toga Night. Is that true?'

With very ill grace, Wendy admitted that this was so. 'I'd had a couple too many. We all had. But isn't that what these functions are all about? Letting your hair down for an hour or two.'

Trying, with limited success, to introduce the next question tactfully, Max said, 'This is probably an exaggeration, but we also heard that you were dancing quite . . . intimately with him.'

'I told you, I'd had too much to drink. It was a stupid five minutes.'

'And what did your husband make of it?'

'Bernard was marvellous. He made me drink a lot of black coffee and got me back to normal. Look – I'm human,' she blurted out. 'I do stupid things like everybody else at times.'

And your marriage has turned out to be monotonous, Max thought.

He said, 'It must be difficult for you to be popular round the office . . . being married to the boss, I mean.'

'I'm not there to be popular. They'll probably tell you I

rule with a rod of iron . . . that I'm hard on them. Well, I am. The work wouldn't get done otherwise.'

'Do you tell tales to your husband about what goes on in the office?'

A little girl's smile. 'I may need to tell him things sometimes. Certainly. But not everything. Not all the tittle-tattle. He wouldn't be interested.'

'How do you get on with Morgan Dundy? Is that a difficult relationship?'

'There were several clashes between us, I admit. Morgan thinks she's better than she is. She's an uppity little madam, so I have to put her in her place occasionally.'

'But it's not personal?'

'Why would it be personal?'

'Let's say sexual rivalry. If you both fancied Julian . . .'

'That's absolute nonsense.'

'OK,' Max said with a smile. 'You've been very helpful. One last thing . . . the night Julian was murdered . . . could you tell me what you and your husband were doing?'

'That's easy. We were doing what we always do on Saturday nights. I cooked dinner. I watched television and Bernard got his books out, then made us a gin and tonic. I remember because Tom was away on an Outward Bound weekend. When we went to pick him up from the station on the Sunday afternoon, there were police cars all over the place and I asked someone what was happening.' She stared past Max's head at the jugs on the painted shelf. 'I couldn't believe it when they told me. It was just . . . surreal.'

'You were shocked?'

'What kind of question is that?' She gripped the front of her skirt as if she had a stomach ache. Her hands were broad, strong-looking, larger than the average. 'Of course I was. We all were. Stunned would be a better word.' She gave a shudder. 'I kept thinking, over and over, his body must have been out there all night in the wind and the rain.'

'Pretty gruesome end.'

'To a very young life.'

The conversation stopped. There was a moment's silence,

a curious stilling of time and mood as if – afterwards Max wondered if he had imagined it – almost as if a ghost had passed through the room. Then she said in a tone as dry as dust, 'It's in the newspapers every day. Violence, rape, murder. Why should we be surprised any more?'

'Yes, well.' Max got to his feet, held out his hand. 'Thanks again.'

Wendy's was clammy, damp almost. 'No problem. Let us know if there's anything else.'

'There is one thing.' Max remembered to ask about the missing photographs.

Which brought a frown to her face. 'I haven't seen them anywhere.' She thought for a moment. 'We did have holiday photographs around at the time. It may have got mixed up with the other pack. Hang on a minute. I'll have a look.'

But the holiday photographs weren't in the bureau where they ought to have been. 'Tom may have taken them to school,' she said. 'Tell me where your office is. If I find them, I'll post them to you.'

Max thanked her. It was only as he was on his way out that he thought to ask, more by way of an afterthought than anything else, 'Which school does your lad go to?'

'Beechen Cliff.' The voice rose a little as if in emphasis. 'Yes, I know it's a coincidence, but we lived in the catchment area when Tom was eleven. Masses of people do.'

Well, yes, Max thought. And it might mean nothing at all. But isn't it peculiar that all roads seem to lead back to that particular little square mile of the city?

The Chestnuts was a solid Edwardian semi-detached house on the Wells Road. A weeping willow in the centre of the front lawn, a garden table and chairs with a green parasol on the side one. There was a conservatory at the back. The bay windows were freshly painted.

Hilly's mother – had to be – opened the door. A tidy little woman. Something bird-like about her. Small bones, not a scrap of make-up.

'I'm sorry to trouble you, but I'm looking for Hilary Russell.'

'Hilary?' She looked surprised. 'May I have your name?'

'Elizabeth Blair. I'm a private detective. Your daughter and I have met.'

'Good heavens!'

'Briefly,' Elizabeth said, not wanting to give the woman a heart attack.

'May one ask where?'

'Up at Draycott. On a murder enquiry. Would Hilary be in?'

'I . . . think so.' She still stood rooted to the spot. 'She hasn't mentioned this at home.'

'I expect it slipped her mind. Actually, I did ask them all to be very discreet.'

'Who is it, Anne?' called a voice from along the hall.

'It's a . . . It's someone for Hilary.' Anne Russell said it as if under some pressure. She was plainly apprehensive. She said to Elizabeth, 'I'll just call her. If you'll excuse me for one moment.'

She disappeared upstairs. Elizabeth was left gazing at the large entrance hall with pink and grey Edwardian tiles. A grandfather clock, telling her that it was ten minutes past four. Pink flock wallpaper, smell of floor polish. All that was missing was the aspidistra. The house was silent for a moment. Then an elderly man appeared on the scene. Tall and greying in a tweed jacket. High colour, peremptory manner. 'Anne's looking after you, I take it?'

'Oh, yes. I'm being seen to. You must be Hilary's father?'

'For my sins. I don't think we've met.'

'No, I guess we haven't.'

'You're American.'

'For my sins.'

'Hilary doesn't know any Americans,' he said shortly.

'She knows this one. We met up at Draycott.'

'So it's work?'

'Not . . . quite.'

'Then what is it exactly?'

'I'd prefer to discuss the matter with your daughter, if you don't mind.'

'We don't have any secrets in this house—'

Elizabeth, smiling, said that any business she had with Hilary was a private matter.

He made a dismissive gesture, said with an air of annoyance, 'I don't want to insist—'

'Then don't,' Elizabeth told him. And that was the extent of the social niceties until footsteps came running down the staircase.

'Mrs Blair!' Hilly's round cheeks were flushed as red as a poppy.

'Well, hi there.'

'Hilary – who is this person?'

'It's nothing, Daddy. Just work. Just someone from the . . . from Personnel. She's new around the place. I said I'd fill her in on training procedures.'

'At this hour?'

'We thought we'd discuss it over a drink in town.' Hilly already had hold of Elizabeth's arm, was leading the way, desperately smiling, down the front path. 'I'll see you later. Shan't be late.'

CHAPTER THIRTY-FIVE

'How dare you come to my home like that? How dare you? If you wanted to talk to me, you could have phoned. You could have contacted me at work.'

Well, well, thought Elizabeth. What have we here? Fear. Panic. Why should Hilly respond so extravagantly to what had been a simple house call? There was the father, of course, a right old Victorian horror. Nevertheless . . .

She stopped on the pavement outside the house and gazed at Hilly curiously. 'Does your father always talk to your visitors like that?'

'Like what?'

'As if he owns you? As if you don't have a life of your own?'

'I don't think that's any of your business.'

'Possibly not. But it may be relevant.'

'To what? To one of your stupid little cases? What arrogance, if you don't mind me saying so. People may be used to you sticking your nose into their home life in Los Angeles or wherever it is that you come from. It's probably par for the course over there . . . but it's not how we do things here, I can assure you!' She didn't once pause for breath. She was standing all this time with her hands shoved hard into the pockets of her sloppy jacket, her chin at a belligerent angle, and her words came spilling out in an uninterrupted torrent. 'I think you've got a cheek. I really do. How would you like it if people kept bothering you at home?'

'I wouldn't mind. I've nothing to hide.'

'Neither have I.'

'No?'

'No.'

'I'm not exactly sure I believe you.'

'I don't care if you do or not. I don't have any guilty secrets.'

All this time, Hilly's face had been growing more and more flushed. She wasn't a good liar, that was for sure.

'I told you where I was that night and I've nothing more to say.'

'What night would that be?'

'The night Julian was killed. I was staying with a friend. A girlfriend. Zoe Phillips. I often spend the night there, when we go clubbing and such.'

'Yes, we checked with your friend. She confirmed that you spent the evening with her and that you stayed over.'

'Well, then?'

'Well, then.'

Elizabeth gazed at her with her shrewd, green eyes. 'I guess I should be satisfied,' she said without conviction.

The elderly maple above their heads shifted and sighed. A little ripple of wind turned up the pale underside of the leaves. A cooler breeze had begun to blow and every now and then a small cloud would go over the sun.

'So what did you do that evening at your friend's house?'

'We cooked supper and we played Scrabble and watched a video. We often do that on a Saturday night.'

'What did you watch on video?'

'*Persuasion*. Jane Austen. That's what we watched. It's one of our favourites.'

Didn't she realise that every prim new detail she trotted out was making the story less believable? Elizabeth jingled the keys between her fingers, kept turning them over and over, thinking hard.

'Tell me something. The night of the disco. You left at the same time as the Rudds. Ten-thirtyish. Surprisingly early. Most people stayed until it ended at midnight.'

'I was tired. That's all.'

'Tired? Any particular reason?'

'I . . . I'd been out a lot that week. I fancied an early night.'

'But the disco was your baby. You organised it. You were in charge. Funny you should leave that early.'

'Not really. Wendy said she'd clear the buffet and pay the DJ.'

'You know, it's a funny thing, but Julian left early as well. No one can remember seeing him after eleven. Now isn't that a coincidence?'

'Not really. They're a pain. Office parties. Boring as hell.'

'I'd hardly call this one boring. Not with Dundy bursting in.'

'No. Well, maybe Julian had had enough.'

'Of being attacked by jealous rivals?'

'Possibly. Why ask me? How should I know?'

'You were his . . . friend. I thought he might have told you.'

'No.'

'OK. So . . . how did you get home that night?'

'I . . . I got a cab.'

'Your father didn't fetch you?'

'No. Not that night.'

'But he mostly did. That's what I heard.'

'Well, he didn't that night.'

'Any particular reason?'

'It was late. He had a cold. So I told him I'd take a cab.'

'Which cab company did you use?'

'I can't remember.'

'You must know which you called?'

'No. I . . . There was one standing outside the pub. It had just dropped somebody off.'

'And you happened to come out at exactly the right time?'

'Yes.'

'Lucky.'

'Yes.'

The girl stared defiantly back at her.

Elizabeth said, 'No one would blame you for falling for Julian, you know. I understand how these things happen. You're shut in with each other all day long at the office. He's the biggest flirt on earth. Enormously good-looking. It's summer. One night, he says come out and have a drink. You weigh it all up – or maybe you don't – and you think, what the hell? Or maybe you're just past thinking.'

Hilly's cheeks were even redder. She spoke quickly, vehemently. 'I didn't. I didn't fall for him. We were just good friends.'

Elizabeth laughed and said, 'Oh, come on! Julian had a gift for stirring up women. He wouldn't know a platonic friendship if it drove up and parked next to him.'

'You're wrong.'

'Am I? I'll tell you what I think happened. He played around with you for a bit, just for a laugh and then he ditched you for the girl with long, dark hair, whoever she was. Maybe you can enlighten me. Maybe you spent some time watching them . . . hung round outside a certain flat he used for assignations. Maybe you bided your time until one night, when you couldn't stand it any more, you killed him.'

'No! It wasn't like that.'

'Of course, some might say – some have, actually – that he needed a good sorting out. That he deserved what he got.'

She wouldn't look up. Elizabeth said, 'I was hoping you'd be a sensible girl and tell me the truth. Just between the two of us. Mind you, I didn't check with your Mom and Pop. Perhaps they saw your cab arrive that night—'

'No. No, they didn't. They'd gone to bed.'

'At eleven o'clock on a Saturday night?'

'It might have been later.'

'Not if you left at the same time as the Rudds.' Elizabeth paused. 'Of course, there is one way to settle it. I could check with your parents. They lie awake, you know, waiting until they hear the door click. I used to with my kids. Couldn't sleep until I knew they were safely in. Especially these days. Yes, I think I'll slip back and ask them—'

'Don't you dare!'

Elizabeth fingered her car keys, looked back at the house. 'I didn't tell your father what I do for a living. The detective agency, I mean, not the patchwork. I'm sure he wouldn't object to the quilts, but as for the other . . .'

'That's blackmail,' Hilly said.

'Oh, I don't know. Persuasion by any other name.' Elizabeth turned on her heel. 'You know, I've got this feeling that your mother wouldn't have told him – I guess I'll just pop back in there—'

Hilly caught her arm even as she moved. 'Wait! Don't bother my father. All right – I'll tell you. I'll tell you everything.'

Elizabeth turned and came back. Hilly's face had now gone very pale, almost doughy, but her voice was clear and firm as she said, 'Drive us somewhere. Anywhere, so long as it's quiet and private. Anywhere away from here.'

CHAPTER THIRTY-SIX

She couldn't get it all out fast enough. Seemed relieved to get it off her chest. Elizabeth sat gazing out through the windscreen at Beechen Cliff as Hilly poured out her story.

'I wasn't with Zoe the night Julian was murdered. I was at my boyfriend's house. Well, manfriend. I'm not ashamed of it, if that's what you're thinking. It's just that Daddy doesn't approve. Ed – that's my friend's name – is divorced, you see, with three grown-up children. He's also . . . well, he's a plumber, if you must know. Daddy nearly hit the roof when I told him. And he made life so difficult that I pretended I'd broken off the relationship. I just don't tell him when I'm seeing Ed. I pretend I'm over at Zoe's and she covers for me.'

So clumsy, overweight Hilly was having a secret affair. Good for you, Elizabeth thought. Atta-girl.

'I don't like telling Daddy lies, but I can't stop seeing Ed. He means too much to me.'

'So where does your gentleman friend live?'

Hilly hesitated. 'Cedar Road. No.11. I went over there at about eight o'clock the night Julian died and Ed cooked dinner. He's a brilliant cook. And we had lots of wine and . . .'

'And you went to bed?'

'Yes. I left after breakfast on Sunday morning. I got back in time to help Mummy with the vegetables for lunch. And we heard about Julian on the local radio. I was so shocked that Mummy had to get me a brandy.'

After a pause, Elizabeth said, 'And you left the Toga Night early to meet your Ed? Am I right?'

'Yes. I stayed at the disco for a couple of hours. Long enough for people to say I was there. Then Ed picked me up in the car park at about a quarter to eleven and we went back to his place. Ed drove me home at about a quarter to one. Daddy thought I was at the disco and having coffee with friends afterwards.'

'His surname?' Elizabeth prompted gently. 'Ed who? I'll have to check with him.'

'Murdoch. Ed Murdoch.'

Elizabeth scribbled it down. She said to Hilly, 'So why don't you leave home if your father's such a tyrant? Go and live with Ed. You're old enough.'

'Easier said than done. He'd kick up such a fuss. And he'd give Mummy a bad time.'

'You can't stay there for ever.'

'That's what Ed says. And I want to be with him all the time. He knows that. It's all I ever dream about. But it's best that we hang on for a while. There'll be some way around it. I don't know what, but it'll work out in the end.'

Elizabeth wasn't convinced; she had seen the light of bigotry in Russell Senior's eyes. He was the kind of man who liked his womenfolk under his thumb. Still, only Hilly could sort out the problem. Stretch that octave between the dream and the deed. Who said that? Shakespeare . . . somewhere.

After a silence, Hilly said, 'I hope you catch whoever did that to Ju. He didn't deserve to die in that horrible way. Oh, he could be a pain. He was like a precocious child. But I still liked him. It was fun to watch him larking around, winding people up. I miss that a lot. I miss him. He had a nice side . . . you know?'

Elizabeth said, 'Really?'

'Really. The trouble was he liked acting a part.'

Theatrical I'll believe, Elizabeth thought.

'Lots of parts. You could never tell which was the real Ju. I sometimes wondered if he knew himself.'

Elizabeth had a sudden thought. 'That panto. Did it ever get put on?'

'Of course not. Julian never finished it. Too much like hard work.' Hilly shook her head, remembering him fondly.

'I don't suppose you found those photographs? Of the disco?'

'Yes, I did. Sorry, I forgot. I'll drop them in to you.'

Five-thirty. Larkhall. Elizabeth had just locked the car and was opening Glenda Dundy's front gate when a vehicle came down the street like a bat out of hell; parked askew, two doors down, with a back wheel on the pavement. Gerard Dundy slammed the driver's door hard without locking it. A wiry man in a dark green shirt . . . He had been drinking. You could smell it on him.

'You again?' he said when he saw Elizabeth standing there.

''Fraid so. Sorry to trouble you.'

But Dundy wasn't interested in any apologies. He came lurching towards her. 'I'm sick and tired of you people following me around. Do you hear me? Sick of having to explain myself. Sick of all the aggro—'

'Look – I only wanted—'

'I don't give a shit what you wanted—'

'OK. OK. Calm down.'

'Why should I? What's it got to do with you anyway, you nosy old bag?'

'Look – I'm sorry . . .'

He came towards her, pulling something out of his jacket pocket. A knife. The sort of knife you use to slit fish open. 'You will be, unless you get out of here fast.'

CHAPTER THIRTY-SEVEN

Elizabeth said, 'I'd put that away if I were you. Your neighbour's watching us. I bet she'd just love to call the police.'

Dundy swung round and saw the movement at Edith Pike's window. He made an obscene gesture in that direction. The lace curtain twitched, then dropped.

'Nosy old so-and-so, I quite agree.' The offhandedness of Elizabeth's voice was deceptive. She'd held her ground, but her knees were shaking. 'Puts out all sorts of lies, I shouldn't wonder. Actually the reason I called was to get your version of something she told me. Are you happy to talk here or would you rather go inside?'

'Here will do.' He'd shoved the knife away . . . thank God. 'OK.'

'So what's the old cow been saying?'

'Well . . . she says you appear to have a regular assignation with someone . . . a man . . . at your house on Friday nights, while your mother's out. Is that true?'

Dundy, his neck mottled with red, appeared to be trying to control his temper. 'Assignation? What's she on about?'

'You don't have a regular visitor on Friday nights?'

'Of course I don't. It's rubbish. She's lying.'

'So it's not true?'

'I said so, didn't I?'

'She described the man as fortyish . . . smart . . . drives a blue thing as big as a bus. It's a very precise lie.'

'She's like that.' His face was a slatey brown, his mouth small and tight. 'She's as mad as a hatter. Makes things up, because she's got nothing else to do.'

He was lying, of course. He couldn't look her in the face. But that in itself was significant. 'OK, Mr Dundy. Thanks for your time. I'll let you get on in.'

Her car was twenty yards or so down the road. Instead of driving off after she'd started the engine, Elizabeth did a three point turn, double parked and sat there for a few minutes watching Dundy's house. A window was shoved open in the front room. He didn't bother fastening it, but slumped into a chair, as limp as a dishrag. Then he picked up the phone.

She'd have given her eye teeth to know whom he was talking to.

It was six-thirty. Way past going home time, but as he had no idea what he was going to do with this restive Saturday night, Max was still hanging around the office and drinking coffee. The drifting scent of geraniums from the mews below reminded him of Ginger. He wouldn't have admitted it, but the office now seemed silent without her clattering away on the keyboard. And the window sill looked bare and empty and the stamp box was empty and the in-tray brimming over.

'You should have thought of that before you fired her,' said Elizabeth when she stumped upstairs with the shop takings. She sounded irritable. Could be flinty when she felt like it.

Like Jess last night. The night they'd spent together in his bed. The physical thing had been mind-blowing, as usual. But this morning, for the first time . . . well, it had seemed insubstantial. Standing there, waiting for her cab to come (she refused a lift back to the hotel); standing there with a crunchy feeling in his stomach, he had wished she would say something . . . warm. Comforting . . . instead of being vague about when he would see her again. When he'd asked, her clear, cold voice had said, 'Not now, Max. I can't think. I'll call you.' It was as if he'd said or done something to set her at a distance. But he had no idea what. He'd just been left there high and dry, without an anchor. Stranded, as if some tide had swept him out to sea, then back again to an uncomfortable, shingly shore.

Should he have been more forceful? Perhaps if he'd insisted? That wouldn't have been a good idea. Jess could be wilful. That hadn't changed. In fact . . . she was probably more so. He hadn't liked that distance in her voice. Coolness. Maybe he should do as Elizabeth advised and run some checks at her hotel. But he threw the idea out almost as soon as it arrived. It didn't seem right . . .

'. . . I still don't believe a word he's saying.' Elizabeth was looking at him as if she expected a reply.

'Who? Sorry?'

'Max, did you hear anything I said in the last five minutes?'

'About what?'

'About Hilary Russell. And Dundy.'

'What about them?'

'I give up!' Elizabeth wore an expression like a teacher who would like to make you stand on a chair in front of the class. 'I'm going home. I'm wasting my breath trying to fill you in on my afternoon.'

'Sorry. I was miles away.'

'That much is obvious. If you want my advice, you'll get your mind off your love life and back on the—'

The phone rang, saving him from having to listen to the rest of her lecture. Max swung sideways to pick up the receiver. The voice on the other end had a faint Norfolk twang. It didn't wait for him to answer, but plunged headlong into the message it wanted to deliver.

'Mrs Blair. It's Zeph Harris. I should have told you this before, but it would have got me into more hot water. I'm off now, so it doesn't matter any more. The Rudds were up at the allotments the night Julian Neville was killed. But don't tell Warren I tipped you off or you'll sign my death warrant.'

CHAPTER THIRTY-EIGHT

Elizabeth kept going back over Harris's phone call in her head, to make sure that she'd missed nothing. He'd gone on to say that the Rudds had been loading stuff into a van on the waste land at the top of the allotments on the night of the murder. He couldn't pin it down to an exact time. Tennish, maybe? It was dark. They were using torches. He'd seen Warren lifting things up there before. Had tried (pretty stupidly) to blackmail him and had got beaten up for his pains. There were two other things she might find interesting . . . just for the record. Zeph had known of a certain folder containing a fraudulent set of accounts prepared by Warren's dodgy accountant and had removed it from Warren's safe about a week ago. Some time soon, the folder would be winging its way to the police in Manvers Street. Once he'd got safely away, where Warren couldn't find him. In the meantime, the bastard could sweat. There was one last thing. Not one he was proud of, but he had to get it off his chest. He'd picked up Julian's wallet the morning after the murder. It had been lying in the bushes halfway along the alley that led down to the main road. He wasn't proud of this, but he'd taken £30 in cash and dumped the rest in the canal. Shouldn't have, he knew, but he was a bit tight that week. Terrible what life brought you to.

'What do you think?' Max asked. 'Is it the truth?'

'The whole truth?' Elizabeth thought about it. 'Probably.'

'So what do we do next?'

'Drop in on our not-so-naïve friend, Trev, and find out why he lied to us. I'll give you that pleasure. I'll call Mick Rudd and ask if he can spare ten minutes of his precious time? It'll be fun to hear what he has to say for himself.'

But the only thing she had the pleasure of addressing that day was Rudd's answerphone. Everybody had the damned things these days, Elizabeth thought. It gave you the hump.

She got home at seven and, having made herself a good, strong brew, took herself and the enamel coffee pot out into the garden to check over her notes on a lecture she was to give to the South Harptree Ladies' Circle. The typed sheets were spread out on the slatted table and she sat there with her reading glasses on the end of her nose, feeling a shade irritable, a touch bored.

The task should have taken her no more than five minutes, but the wind was getting up and the papers kept flapping and the Home Farm tractor, rattling round and round the field by the church, kept ploughing a furrow through her thoughts.

Those early travellers setting off on The Oregon Trail were advised to take plenty of cotton spreads . . . two or three quilts per person, as the least they would need. Yes, they were treasured possessions and cleverly stitched artefacts. But above all, they were an indispensable part of the baggage as these families set of into the great unknown. The second-best quilt would have been used as bedding, as protection for china, would provide comfort in moments of exhaustion, illness or even death.

Jim Junior had had an old Bear Paw that he called his poorly quilt. Said it made him feel better to curl up in it. Which was a godsend, because when that kid caught the measles, he would like you to think it was the plague.

He sure liked to tell you about his symptoms. Even long-distance. *Dear Mom*, he had once written from summer camp. *I cut my finger on an arrow. It was messy. This boy called Spud laughed. Your loving son, JJ.*

Still reading, she turned the page. *Comforts. We all need them. Those quilts insulated the wagon walls against storm blasts, rain and Indian attacks. They were used as burial shrouds, as a kind of reassurance, in the great wilderness, that the body was still linked to its family. The Ritter family buried three daughters, victims of the cholera epidemic of 1852, along the Platte River after placing them together in a wagon box covered in quilts.*

Jim Junior was still a hypochondriac. Worried that his hair was dying, the last time they had talked on the phone.

Listen, even as a boy you looked faded, she had told him.

That sandy hair, neither one colour nor the other. Greyish eyes, ditto.

She took a sip of coffee and read on. *But let's head on across the Missouri, over the greenish-grey of the endless plains . . . astronomical distances. We're going to cross the snowy ranges of The Rockies. Long's Peak, Gray's Peak, Pike's Peak . . . all nearly the height of Mont Blanc. And those women in sunbonnets are still running a needle and thread through squares of cotton. Still finding a heap of uses for a good quilt. They make privacy barriers in tents and one-room cabin homes. You give them as Christmas gifts when there's damn all else to give. You wrap your milk cow in a Nine Patch, to keep the flies off her abscesses. Oh, didn't I tell you? He got stung by a swarm of bees . . .*

Correction. *She got stung*. Better get that right.

Elizabeth's pen scored a line and she made the adjustment.

A voice rang out from the other side of the hedge. Dottie was talking to herself, or to the roses. 'Come along now, old girl. Get a grip. No use feeling sorry for yourself.'

Elizabeth shook her head. Hope I don't get like that.

Dottie's voice said, 'Getting a bit gaunt, aren't you? We can't have that.'

Was she finally going off her rocker? It seemed likely.

'Can't have you going off your grub.'

Oh, she was going round the bend all right. Elizabeth sat very still.

'Come along now. Have a lovely carrot.'

No need for the men in white coats. Dottie was talking to the calf in the field that ran along the bottom of the garden. A pretty little thing with a tail the colour of treacle toffee.

'That's better. That's my boy. Aren't you a little beauty?'

Elizabeth, pen in hand, sat staring at the tossed mass of

green down there in the woods. And something whirred at the back of her brain. 'Well, now,' she said softly to herself. 'We didn't think of that. It's a long shot, but . . . I wonder . . .'

She turned over the final sheet. It was more or less OK. She closed the folder, lifted her arms above her head in a long stretch. The rectory windows were glinting in the last of the day's sun. The church field blotched with violet at the edges where long shadows were forming. On the patio slabs, a scatter of creamy petals. The roses were getting ragged. I'll have to deadhead, Elizabeth thought. At the weekend. No time until then.

She did pull up a few weeds, however, before taking the coffee pot and all her bits and pieces back indoors. She dumped the coffee things in the sink and switched on the radio just in time to catch the eight o'clock news. Not the plummy Radio Four announcer, but a more local voice going on about Banes and the Dorothy House hospice. She glanced down at her watch. Damn! It's slow. I missed the headlines.

She was about to switch the thing off again . . . dull stuff . . . facts and figures about council estimates . . . when a name caught her attention.

A police search is being carried out for a missing woman. Morgan Dundy was reported missing by her sister when she failed to answer phone calls at her home in Larkhall or turn up for work. Morgan was a colleague of Julian Neville, who was found murdered on Beechen Cliff in April . . .

CHAPTER THIRTY-NINE

'So where does the sister live?' Elizabeth asked on Monday morning. They sat facing each other in the office amid the usual muddle of papers.

'South Wales. A little place called Ystwyth. Why?'

'Thought I might go visit her. How long would it take to drive over there?'

Max shrugged. 'Couple of hours? Andy says it's not her real sister. Morgan was adopted as a baby.'

That was old news. 'So where's Dundy? Did the police pick him up?'

'Not as yet. Not that I know of.'

'Then get round to the gym. Find out his reaction. And Max—'

'What?'

'Don't hang about.'

Dundy, at that moment, was leaning back in his mother's easy chair and rubbing one temple with shaking fingers.

He hated the idea of leaving without telling her. He wished he could stay until she got back from work. But he had no choice.

He couldn't stand the terrible humiliation of another night in a police cell. Just the thought of it made him sweat and shiver inside. So . . . getting out was the only way. He lit another cigarette. Turned his eyes, blue and absent, towards the marble clock, which went on ticking away with hypnotic slowness. She wound it every night at the same time, just before it struck six. Same as Grandad used to do. The nightly routine, year in and year out, generation after generation.

He hadn't intended to go there to meet Morgan. He'd thrown her note in the bin and set fire to it. But it had proved impossible to get the thing out of his mind. *There's something I have to tell you.* Gerry thought: Shouldn't have gone. Better I didn't know.

Better she hadn't laughed at me.

His mind felt tired and hazy.

The clock gave a click and struck the half hour. Dundy took a sip of whisky. He felt tempted to ring Mum for a quick word. It would have been comforting, but he knew he couldn't, because that would bring her rushing home.

It was important to get the timing right. Important to keep his nerve.

His thoughts kept coming back to Morgan, her arms flung out to each side, her hair in a wide, tangled arc around her face. He remembered that way she'd had of tossing it back over her shoulder. You could almost be moved by her waif-like beauty. Until she opened her mouth . . .

Until you heard her laugh.

Once he had loved her to distraction. Once she used to lie endlessly on his bed. In another lifetime. But she had pushed him aside. Always you had to surrender to them. At which point, they crushed you.

Morgan's voice, in his ear, said: *Serve you right. Never could stick up for yourself.* Hallucinations. His crazy imaginings or hers? Gerry didn't know any more.

His head felt hot as if he were going to cry.

Hopeless, she'd called him. Mummy's darling boy.

He picked up the package from the table. He who hesitates is lost. I'm lost already, Dundy thought. Always was.

He got to his feet and stood the package up against the clock. Thought for a minute, then went over to the sideboard. Out came a new bottle of whisky with the seal still intact. He wouldn't enjoy drinking it. It was now just a sad necessity.

He walked across to the door of his mother's living-room, opened and closed it behind him. Stood leaning against it. He felt drained, yet his brain was feverish, as if it had an infection.

'Her work,' he said aloud. 'Hers and Deborah's.'

Outside, the sun shone on the vegetable patch and the wire mesh fence.

Paula Jones was waiting to open the door of her ground-floor flat in an Edwardian villa in Branwen Road. She was a pretty, fair-haired girl of about thirty. She wore a long camisole dress with a white tee-shirt underneath.

Elizabeth had said on the telephone that she would be there at around noon and she was a little late. It was twenty past. 'I'm sorry,' she said now. 'Traffic on the bridge.'

'No problem. I'm not going to work today. Come in.'

Here was a girl whose calm, grey eyes were as calm as a mill pond. Her graceful surface only a little ruffled by the fact that her sister was missing. The flat was light and graceful, too, its tall sitting-room decorated with light chintzes and a basket of dried flowers in the hearth. Elizabeth made all the necessary explanations. 'It's good of you to see me at such short notice. I was wondering if you could tell me something about Morgan's childhood, Mrs Jones.'

'Lisa. Her real name was Lisa.'

'I'm sorry?'

'Lisa. That's what she was christened. But that wasn't good enough for her. She had to invent this ridiculous new name for herself. Call me Morgan, she announced at the breakfast table one morning. It sounds more interesting.'

Elizabeth said, 'I was going to ask you about her character. Anything that would give us a new slant on your sister.'

'Her character?' Paula looked down at her hands, which were clasped tightly in her lap. Then she said, 'You want the truth? She was a complete mess. She made my mother's life a misery. I tried not to hate her for it, but I'm afraid I failed.'

'Does your mother live in Ystwyth?'

'My mother is dead, Mrs Blair. Cancer. Three years ago. They say it's caused by stress, don't they? Well, Mam had her fill of that and most of it was caused by Lisa.'

'Your sister was a troublemaker?'

'All her life.' Paula shook her head and picked up a

snapshot that was lying on the table. 'I was going through the album – the police wanted something recent – and I came across this.'

She passed it across the table. Elizabeth gazed at the image of a slight child with a mop of dark, curly hair. One thin forearm stretched stiffly out like a ballerina.

'That's Lisa when she was nine. See the necklace she's wearing? It came from a Christmas cracker, but she didn't tell her friends that. You know what she said? That her real mother gave it to her when she was a baby . . . and her real mother came from foreign royalty. She was a liar even then. You wanted to laugh, she used to tell such whoppers. But she could be very convincing. She was very, very good at it. She'd invent all these tiny little details and gradually they would all believe her. Which would set her off all over again.

'She used to tell them that her real mother was an actress. That's how she made her living after she escaped from Romania. She played Juliet in the West End . . . that was one of Lisa's favourite stories. I can hear her now. "We lived in a dear little mews flat with window boxes. But my real mother couldn't look after me properly, what with all the tours and such. She finished up living in Paris. I don't blame her for abandoning me. She couldn't help it." '

The lies exposed the dreams. Elizabeth sat watching the tape go round and round in the machine, then she said, 'Did she ever try and trace her real family?'

'When she was eighteen. Yes, she did. But her birth mother didn't want to know. She'd gone over to America to start a new life. She was a university lecturer, she'd married and had a new family. I think she was scared Lisa would upset the apple-cart.'

'Sad.'

'But provident,' Paula said with a note of grim humour. 'They wouldn't have known what hit them.'

'So what happened after her real mother rejected her?'

'What do you think? The lies got bigger, her behaviour got more extreme. She turned down a university place and went to work in the biscuit factory.'

'She didn't go to India?'

'Is that what she told you?' A wry smile touched Paula's mouth. 'Typical. Romanticising everything. No, she didn't go to India. She stayed here in Ystwyth and gave my mother a hard time. Which was really unfair, because she had done everything in her power to make Lisa feel secure. She had so much love and attention . . . much more than she deserved . . . but she still went on living this dream life of hers. She was proud of how well and how easily she could lie.'

Elizabeth sat back in the easy chair, thoughtful and distracted.

'She wanted to be liked, Mrs Blair, so she'd tell whatever lies she thought necessary.'

'You must have resented that?'

'Of course. I hated it. God help me, I think I hated her.'

'But you still kept in touch? They said you rang her—'

'Every week . . . yes. Nick – that's my husband – said I was mad to bother. But Mam made me promise on her deathbed. I couldn't break that promise. Mam went on loving her, you see, in spite of everything.' She got up and walked over to the window. 'You want to know the truth? I hate her, but I also feel sorry for her, deep down. Mam used to try and explain it to me. Lisa told lies to build herself up, so as to be the same as other children, so that she would fit in. She lied to exaggerate her own worth.'

'So that she had control over what other people thought of her?'

'Exactly. She lied to inflate her self-esteem. And because she didn't know any other way. It amused her, but it became a habit, like alcohol or drugs. She couldn't stop doing it. Can you imagine what that must feel like? When you're on your own in your own room at night with this great blank inside you and there's no one to impress?' She shivered. 'Terrifying.'

'Tell me how she met Gerard Dundy.'

'She met him in a pub, I think. But I wasn't around at the time. I was away at college, so all I have to go on is what Mam told me when I rang home.'

'Which was what?'

'That Lisa had moved to Bath to be with him. That she seemed better at first. More settled. She'd even got a proper job at the MoD.'

'How well do you know Dundy?'

'I only met him once – at Mam's funeral. They got married in a registry office in Bath.'

'So what did you make of the marriage?'

'She gave him a hard time, like she gave all of us.' Paula shrugged. 'They might once have needed each other but the one time she brought him here to the funeral, well, Gerry had been drinking and Lisa was in a funny mood. You never knew what she was going to say, but that day . . . she was on a high of some sort. Affronted, my aunties were. Coming here and chit-chatting like it was some kind of party. Nick wondered if she was on something, but I said that was Lisa. Never fitted in. Glad if she could get herself noticed, even at her Mam's funeral.'

Elizabeth said, 'You probably can't answer this, but would you say she was emotionally involved with another man?'

'Emotionally involved? She wouldn't know the meaning of the words.'

'OK. I'll rephrase that. Do you think she might have been playing around with some other man? Did she ever mention anyone by name?'

'Dozens. She's always going on about her love life, but you take it with a pinch of salt, all of it. You just stop listening . . .'

'Did she ever mention a young man she worked with? Julian Neville?'

'The one who got bumped off? Yes. Funny, that. A couple of weeks back. She said . . . now let me get it right . . . she said he was paying for her holiday next year.'

'Paying for her holiday?'

'Yes. Funny, that. He's going to pay for my trip to the sun, she said. How can he do that, I said, if he's dead?'

But someone else might, Elizabeth thought. Some member of his family. Or a murderer whom she happened to be blackmailing.

CHAPTER FORTY

Dundy wasn't at the gym and Jason Lee couldn't (or wouldn't) say where he was. Running Mick Rudd to earth wasn't so simple either. He wasn't at work that day and the blasted answerphone was still on at his home. After leaving a terse message on it (*This is Max Shepard. It would be delightful if you could manage to call us back some time. It's quite easy. You just choose a finger and punch this number.*), Max decided to spoil Trevor Walsh's day off. Trev was cutting neat stripes into his already immaculate front lawn. When Max introduced himself and said he'd rung the office first, Trevor nearly had a fit. 'You didn't tell them who you were?'

'Any reason why I shouldn't?' Max gazed right back at him.

'Yes. You might get me into hot water. They might . . . They might think—'

'They might think what?' Max studied Trev's terrified expression. Like a rabbit, he thought, facing the farmer's shotgun. 'You know what I'm here for?'

'No.' Trev wasn't good at the game of bluff. His face had taken on a cheesy hue.

'Look – don't waste any more of our time. Or shoe leather. We know Rudd wasn't at that lecture with you on the night of the murder. I'd like the truth this time, if you don't mind.'

His whole face caved in. 'I didn't want to lie to you.'

'Then why did you?'

'It's difficult. Mick's my boss. And I helped him out once before and he sort of assumed I'd do it again.'

'You're on a slippery slope there, pal.'

'I know.' Trev looked at Max with large, rabbity eyes. 'It's

237

just that . . . well, Mick has this lady friend he sees now and again.'

'And you cover for him if Karen asks?'

'Mostly I don't have to. It's just if anything crops up.'

'Like a murder?'

'Mick didn't have anything to do with that.' Trev's cheekbones froze.

'How do you know?'

'I just do.' A flap of panic. Meltdown starting.

'How?'

'Well – he's an ordinary sort of a chap.'

'So are most murderers. Didn't anyone tell you? So did Rudd catch any of this lecture he was supposed to be at?'

'No. He just said if anyone asked . . .'

'. . . he was up to his ears in bandages. OK. So I need the name of this lady he was supposed to be seeing.'

'I can't tell you that. I don't know.' Trev was breaking out in a sweat.

'You're sure of that? You're not spinning me another line?'

'No. No, honestly. You'll have to ask Mick. He's the only one who can tell you.'

As she drove back across the bridge, across all that water, light-coloured in the early evening haze, Elizabeth's face wore a weary expression.

So all Morgan's stories – it was no good, she still couldn't think of her as Lisa – might have been a tissue of lies. The wife-beating. The affairs . . . particularly that with Julian Neville. What we have here, she thought, is a pathological liar with no self-identity. Someone who has been lying for so long, she doesn't know what the truth is any more. Most of us can lie on occasion, out of panic or to get ourselves out of a hole or to save a friend's feelings. But for Morgan, lying has become a driving force . . . a weapon in her armoury. A power trick. She gets a real thrill out of it. Imagine living on that treadmill. Imagine having to live one big lie because you hate your real self that much. Not even knowing who that self was.

Elizabeth thought, it's the liar, not the victim, who suffers most in the end. I mean, look where it's landed her. In a kind of limbo between two worlds; one real, one imagined.

And just look where it's landed us. Right back at square one. She had a niggling headache. Oh, God, she thought, we'll have to start again from the beginning.

'She had no idea where Morgan might be? No theories?' Max asked.

'None at all,' Elizabeth said, dropping the car keys on the desk.

'So what do you think?'

'Search me. The only thing that's certain is that she hasn't turned up yet. What about Dundy? Did you get hold of him?'

'Nope.'

'If he's not at the gym, he'll be at home.'

'I rang his mother's house from Draycott. There was no reply.'

'Then try again later. Better still, go round there.' Elizabeth dropped into a chair and sat there staring out of the window, without uttering a word.

'You all right?' Max asked.

'Whacked. All that driving. Max – can I try something out on you? A theory? Something that popped into my head the other day . . . ?'

'Go on.'

'The girl Julian was with the night he was killed . . .'

'Yes.'

'We couldn't find her.'

'So?'

'So let's pretend it's not a girl at all.'

'Don't follow.'

'Just bear with me. Something started me thinking about gender. What if it was a young man with dark hair that Julian was in a clinch with? From the back you couldn't necessarily tell the difference.'

'You mean Neville was gay? But he had a reputation with the women. Everybody says so.'

'They all fancied him, which is quite another matter. What if he was bisexual . . . playing games with both sexes?'

'Sounds far-fetched to me. What put that into your head?'

'Don't ask. It's not at all logical. The gay thing keeps cropping up, that's all. Those two running The Trout. Gerry and his mate making regular visits. The gay bar at The Princess Amelia—'

'Where the staff knew Toby Perrin.' Max had a peculiar look on his face. 'Julian Neville was certainly very pretty.'

'And Morgan was telling her husband – and us – a pack of lies.' She brought him up to date on her Welsh trip. Elizabeth sat there skimming through it all in her mind. Ideas all mixed blurrily, the pattern non-existent. All you could do was follow one thread and hope it led to another.

'It's a thought, I suppose.' But then he dismissed it. 'Nah! Doesn't feel right.'

So that was that. 'Did you get hold of Mick Rudd?' she asked.

'Nope. I rang him twice more, but it seems he's playing hard to get. All you get is the answerphone. I checked with Warren's secretary, while we're on the subject. She still insists Warren couldn't have been up there. They were stocktaking all evening.'

Elizabeth shook her head. He's a hard nut, she thought. We won't get far up there. But his brother was another matter; by far the weaker character. And he wasn't going to elude her for much longer.

Ten past six. Max parked the car just down the road from Glenda Dundy's house. Thunder was rumbling somewhere over the distant hills. There was change in the air; the wind had moved round to the west and it was cooler.

He pushed open the creaky metal gate and walked up the path.

The door was ajar. Funny. They were usually locked and double-locked.

Max rang the bell, but no one came.

'Anyone at home?' he called out.

Apparently not. He pushed the door open and entered. There was no movement in the house, no radio, no television talking. All lay silent. There was an odd smell in the passageway. Brandy? Or was it whisky? Gerry was back, then. Better be careful, thought Max. If he's been drinking . . . better not do anything in a rush. He continued down the hall, walking without a sound.

The door to the kitchen was ajar and he caught sight of an arm resting on the breakfast bar. A woman's arm. Not Gerry, then.

But Glenda . . . stinking of the stuff?

'Hello? I hope you don't mind. I let myself in.'

Glenda Dundy looked up from the glass in front of her. She was shivering. Her eyes red-rimmed in a puffed and tear-stained face.

'What is it? What's happened?' Max asked.

'My son is— He's—'

'OK. It's OK. Take your time.'

'He's . . . dead. He killed himself. They found his body this afternoon . . . slumped over the wheel of his car.'

CHAPTER FORTY-ONE

'They found him parked up in the woods.' Glenda stared at Max with sightless eyes. The phone began to ring out in the hall. 'Leave it. Take it off the hook.'

Max did as he was told. When he came back into the kitchen Glenda was sitting in the corner by the fridge as if paralysed.

He took the glass from Glenda's hand and poured the dregs down the sink. Searched around for the kettle. 'Coffee,' he said. 'Hot and strong. That's what you need.'

Glenda's puddingy face was stiff with shock and disbelief. 'I feel sick.'

'Of course you do. Anyone would.' He remembered when his Grandad had died. You couldn't grasp the significance. You looked at people and they all seemed so . . . ineffectual.

Glenda got up and pushed away the stool. With hypnotic slowness, she turned her eyes towards the shopping basket on the work-top. Margarine, sugar, washing-up liquid remained unpacked. She must have come in with them just before the police arrived.

The kettle was beginning to hiss. Max found a jar of coffee and two mugs, then raided the drawer for a teaspoon. He said, 'Lots of sugar. It's good for shock. Or would you rather have tea?'

'Yes.' A single tear rolled down Glenda's face. She looked pathetic. Like a cabbage-patch doll that somebody had sat on.

'They shouldn't have left you here alone.'

'I didn't want anybody.'

'Nevertheless.'

Glenda moved, as if in slow motion, and started to unpack the groceries. 'There isn't anybody.'

'No family?'

'My sister's away on holiday.'

'A friend, then?'

Glenda shrugged, then picked up a carton of yoghurt from the basket.

'Leave that. It won't hurt.'

He wasn't getting through. Glenda stood staring at the yoghurt as if transfixed. Then she lifted her eyes to Max's. 'He'd had so much hassle. He couldn't take any more.'

'Hassle? Who from?'

'Everybody. Both his wives. The police. The bastards who made anonymous phone calls.'

'Recently?'

'This last few weeks, it's got worse.'

'Tell me about them. What did this caller say?'

'I don't know. He wouldn't tell me. But it was poison. You could tell by the look on his face. Then there was the note he got through the post.'

'When?'

'Just last week.'

'Can I see it?'

She went into the other room, came back with an envelope and a slip of paper. 'Here.' She thrust it at him.

The note read: *I thought we might meet tonight. Usual place? Nine o'clock? J.*

'It's *his* writing,' Glenda said. 'The one that got his head bashed in.'

'Julian Neville?'

'That's the one.'

'So—' Max was befuddled. 'Who was the note intended for?'

'Her, of course. Morgan.' Glenda wiped her eyes. 'Who hated my boy so much that they wanted to torment him with that? I ask you?'

'I've no idea.'

'Neither have I.'

'So . . . what did he do about the note? Did he report it to the police?'

'He hated the police. What was the point? He went round to see her. Challenged her about it, but she just laughed. And . . .'

'And?'

'He hit her. Just the once. But he was provoked. He was upset about it when he got home.'

'You should have reported all this to the police.'

'I know. But—' She shot him a wary look. A shade of something crossed her face. She hesitated, then said, quite abruptly, 'There's something else.'

Max wondered what was coming. 'What's that?'

Silence.

'Mrs Dundy, I'm trying to help.'

She shot him another look, then said, 'He left a tape for me.'

Max put down the coffee jar, wondering if he had heard correctly. 'A tape?'

'In an envelope behind the clock. I didn't tell the police. They'd say it was proof that he'd done something to Morgan.'

Very carefully, Max said, 'Why? What was on the tape?'

Silence.

'Mrs Dundy?'

Silence.

'Was it anything to do with Morgan's disappearance?'

'He wanted to say goodbye to me.' She spoke in a thin, tired voice.

'But that's not all?' He felt pity for the woman, but his mind was already on a more practical tack. He realised that evidence couldn't be suppressed. 'So what did you do with the tape?'

'I hid it. He wasn't thinking straight. He didn't mean what he said. He was sick.'

The kettle was coming up to the boil.

Max said, 'Where did you hide it?'

The kettle bubbled to a frenzy, then clicked off.

'Look – there's no need for the police to know.' Cross your

fingers, he thought. Not yet, anyway. 'Maybe there's some clue on the tape that will help us find Morgan.'

'No!' Her hand jerked at a bag of flour.

'What did he say? Can you remember any of it?'

Glenda dumped the flour on the work-top. Her lip trembled.

'I really do want to help.'

Glenda looked away from him, shook her head; and then her hand took itself back to the groceries.

'Mrs Dundy . . . if I don't know, I can't help.'

She reached into the very bottom of the basket. Pulled out a box of tissues, two packets of tea and then . . . a square, white envelope with something inside it.

Tape-sized.

'May I?' Max held out his hand. Held his breath.

'The radio's over there.'

Glory be, Max thought.

The tape was rambling, incoherent at times, but of a devastating and incriminating honesty.

'Mum . . .' Dundy said in a clear, hoarse voice. '*Try and think the best of me, no matter what happens. I know what I've done is wrong. But she broke my heart . . .*'

Glenda's face wore a stricken, appalled expression. She doesn't want to believe it, thought Max, but he must have done something to Morgan.

'*I didn't want to hurt her. I wanted to stop, but she couldn't leave me alone.*' He sounded furious now. Beside himself with grief and anger. '*She wanted me to . . . wanted to play games with me. We'll put things right, she said. I'm sorry, she said. I wasn't going to go there . . . but then I kept thinking that maybe she meant it. Maybe this time she'll mean what she says. But she was lying, as usual . . .*'

'I hate her. I don't care what's happened to her. She destroyed him.' Glenda hid her face in her hands. There was a maimed look about her. That's what loss does to you, Max thought. It breaks bits off. Bits that matter. Ease of mind, trust, spontaneity. Bits that might never grow back on again.

'*Playing with me, she was. Pretending to be surprised that I'd turned up. Said what the hell was I doing there? Always on the outside looking in, that's me. Like when I used to clean the windows for you when I was a kid. Remember? Right into the corners, young man. And don't be using dirty water.*'

A sound like a sob, followed by a click. He switched the machine on again, had another try. The voice this time was shaky, but determined. '*Don't miss me. I wasn't much of a son. Well, maybe you did find something to love in me, but not the rest of them. What's wrong with them, Mum? Women these days? She wanted to break me ... And I wanted to break her. So I went for her. I showed her—*'

A pause.

'*Meaningless, all of it. Oh, God, I'm so tired.*' In a softened croak, he added, '*Mum. Light a candle for me somewhere ...*'

There followed a mumbled sentence that Max couldn't make out. He asked Glenda to interpret.

'He asked me to kiss David for him.'

'David?'

'The baby. His son. If I ever got to meet him.' Glenda made a weary gesture. 'Some hope—'

Max didn't want to ask the next question. Hated to add to the woman's misery, but it had to be done. 'I'm sorry to have to ask this at such a time, but ... your son wasn't ... well, he couldn't have been gay, by any chance?'

'Gay?' She stared at him with blank eyes.

'Homosexual?'

'Gerry? One of those?' Her face had gone white. 'Never! No way. What makes you ask?'

'Just a track we got led along. Don't worry about it,' he said gently. 'One last question. You don't know anything about a visitor your son had on Friday nights when you were out of the house? A man?'

'His fishing friend comes now and again.'

'Joe Grenfell? On a Friday night?'

'You'll have to ask him. Gerry can't tell you.'

Before he left, Max got the number of one of Glenda's

workmates and made sure she would come round. It was the least you could do.

He was about to get into his car when the phone bleeped. Elizabeth's voice sounded urgent.

'Max? I thought you'd better know. Hubert Neville had a heart attack. He's been rushed off to hospital. It made the front page of *The Chronicle*.'

'How bad is it?'

'Critical.'

Poor old Hubert. They were going down like ninepins. He told her about Dundy.

Elizabeth said, 'I'm sorry to hear that. So where'd he leave Morgan? That's the question.'

'And in what state? I'll have to pass this on to Andy.'

'Sure.' Elizabeth sounded abstracted. 'Listen – pop round to the hospital and see how Hubert is. I'd like to know.'

'OK. What's on your programme?'

'Mick Rudd,' Elizabeth said grimly.

'If you can find him.'

'I'll find him, don't you worry.'

'Well, be careful.' Max climbed into the car, thinking as he slammed the door that there was no such thing as an unconnected action. Had Hubert heard about Morgan's disappearance? Or Gerry's death. Was that what set off the heart attack?

We're all links in the human chain, he thought. No act so small that it doesn't affect someone else further down the line. It started with Julian's murder and it's still being passed down, God help us.

Half an hour later, Elizabeth parked the Citroën outside Mick Rudd's semi-detached. The house seemed to be deserted. No sign of life anywhere at the front – but his car was in the garage. She could see the front end of it under the half-closed door.

She climbed out of her own car and locked it. Slipped in through the gate and round the side of the house. The back door was unlocked. There was someone in the kitchen.

'Mr Rudd! I'm so glad I found you in! You're a hard man to catch up with. We've been trying to get hold of you for days.'

CHAPTER FORTY-TWO

'Zeph who?' Rudd said, when she told him about Harris's phone call.

'You know who I mean. The busker who got beaten up by the allotments.'

'That down-and-out?' He attempted a laugh. 'The man's a beggar. A crusty. Why the hell would you believe him?'

'Because he has a few interesting things to say about your brother's shady dealings,' Elizabeth said, looking him straight in the eye. 'So which one of you knocked him about? Or was it a joint effort?'

Rudd glared at her darkly. 'That's ridiculous.'

'Is it? I don't think so. I think you were trying to shut him up. I think he saw you kill Julian Neville.'

'Now look here—'

'No, you look here, Mr Rudd. I've got a phone number for Zeph Harris . . .' (Fingers crossed behind her back.) '. . . and he says he's willing to testify against you. Think what that would do to your career with the oh-so-stuffy Ministry of Defence.'

'You're bluffing,' said Rudd, but with less conviction. His face had blanched.

'Try me and see. I've got nothing to lose. Whereas you . . .' She let her eyes rove around the expensively fitted kitchen.

Rudd looked at Elizabeth. He seemed to be reflecting rapidly.

'I don't want to call the police, but—'

He finally caved in. 'OK. So I told a few fibs.'

'A few hundred, more like. It would be most interesting to know why you forced Trevor Walsh to give you a false alibi for the night Neville was murdered.'

'All right. All right.' Rudd sounded sullen. 'I'll tell you what really happened, but I had nothing to do with any murder. There's this woman I've been seeing . . .'

'Behind your wife's back?'

'Well, I'm hardly likely to tell her about it, am I? I got Trev to say I was at the lecture, but I spent the night with Suzy.'

'Not all of it. Harris saw you up at the allotments.'

'Warren asked me to nip up there for half an hour to help load up some stuff. It was to do with his business.'

Funny business, thought Elizabeth. 'What kind of stuff?'

'A couple of stone urns and some old railings.'

One piece of which they'd left behind, lying on the grass; the length that had later been used as the murder weapon.

'I was just doing Warren a favour. He trusts me. He knows I won't go blabbing about it. And in return . . . well, he gives me a share of the profits.'

'So where exactly were you parked?'

'At the very end of Lyncombe Terrace by the allotments.'

'Pretty near the spot where the body was found?'

'Yes. But that was later. Much later.'

'So what time were you up there?'

'Not sure. It was dark. Nine-thirtyish, perhaps.'

'OK. So you were up there thieving—'

'I can't deny the fact. Some of Warren's business is a bit dodgy. He's on the shady side of the law at times. But it's nothing big. I mean, nothing that really matters.'

'GBH isn't big? Murder?'

'We didn't have anything to do with that, I tell you! I was back with Suzy by ten. You can ask her. Or her kids.'

So he was probably telling the truth this time. Elizabeth felt the familiar sinking feeling, the looming up of a cul-de-sac. 'So does your wife know you help Warren out with his shady deals?'

'No. She doesn't like me being involved. But how else do I pay the bills? Karen never got on with Warren. He upset her once. Tried it on with her one night while I was away on a course. She's never forgiven him.'

'But you did?' Elizabeth found that curious.

'Listen, he's my brother. She probably took it the wrong way. Read it wrong. Old Warren likes a laugh. He's all right . . . underneath.'

'And he's very generous?'

Rudd shifted uneasily. 'Listen, I've got four kids and a wife who likes to spend. And once you've started . . .' He shrugged. 'You get used to the extra.'

And principles aren't always remunerative. 'Do you also get used to the violence?' Elizabeth asked carefully.

'I told you. We had nothing to do with that murder.'

'I wasn't talking about the murder. I was talking about Zeph Harris.' Elizabeth gazed at him carefully and thought she saw something approaching guilt in the blue eyes.

'He turned up at Warren's office one night demanding money. We had to put the frighteners on him. Warren gave him the once-over, but he doesn't know his own strength. It went too far. That was a mistake.'

You're right there, thought Elizabeth. The biggest he ever made. And one that he might regret before long. When the police caught up with him . . .

'By the way,' she said, as she was about to leave. 'Trevor said he lent you some photographs he took at the Toga Night. Is that right?'

'He stuck them on my desk at work. Yes.'

'There are two missing. Would you happen to have them here? Or the negatives?'

'I didn't even look at them. I was up to my ears that week. They sat on my desk for a day or two, then he grabbed them back.'

Max walked down the corridor, hearing the soles of his shoes squeak rhythmically on the hospital floor. Bartlett Ward. Cardiac. There it was on the door to his left. Appropriate, he thought; just what I need. The heart ward. Someone to hook me up to a machine and get it back to a normal state.

He had seldom felt so jumpy inside. So disorientated. Jess again. What does she want from me? At dinner the other night . . . she had never been so deliberate. Eyes flashing out all sorts of messages, fingers resting on my face, my thigh. Familiar, yet unfamiliar. Oh, God. How I wanted her. And she knew it. He stood back as a girl in a white coat rushed through the swing doors with her phone madly bleeping. And, of course, the inevitable happened. She turned me on. We finished up in the sack. All I ever dreamed of. So why do I feel this sense of vague unease? This . . . banality? Like we're playing parts in a play and the plot's somehow wrong. Or the script. Too many clichés. Or was it the set? Maybe. That bloody awful flash restaurant that someone had recommended. Someone with crap taste.

Someone with a lot of money. Max winced as he remembered the size of the bill.

He found Diana Neville in the day room and introduced himself. 'Mrs Neville? Max Shepard. Mrs Blair asked me to pass on her very best wishes. How is your husband?'

'Very poorly.' She sat heavily on one of the easy chairs by the window.

'But he'll be OK?'

'God knows. I suppose.' There was a harshness in her voice which was somehow shocking.

He said the usual. Clichés again. 'If there's anything we can do . . .'

'Yes. There is. Call off your damned investigation. Forget it. Just forget he ever called you.'

'But—'

'I've had enough. We've had enough. We're at the end of our tether.'

Late in the afternoon, the phone shrilled. Elizabeth picked it up as she was passing Max's desk. Didn't recognise the voice at first. Scholarly, upper class, but that was par for the course in this part of the world.

'Is that the . . . Damn it, I can't read the thing . . . Is that The Sherborne Agency?'

'Shepard.'

'Shepard. I do beg your pardon. Well, then, is this the lady who called on me the other day. American. Took my papers and didn't return them . . . ?'

'Papers?' For a moment, she sat frowning. Then it came to her. 'Mr Griffith? The buddleia—'

'Indeed.'

'I'm so sorry. Didn't I send them back? I'll do it right this minute. They'll be in the post tonight.'

'Good enough. There's one other thing. I want to pick your brain. Do you know anything about planning permission? How to repeal it?'

'I think, perhaps, you should call the Council.'

'I already did. They're hopeless. I spoke to this female and she said he did apply for it, so it was all legal and above board. And I said to her, well, I'm jolly well not going to let the next owner get away with all that banging. I've already spoken to the estate agent . . . well, a boy in a suit . . . and put him in the picture. Forewarned is forearmed, I told him. I'm blessed if I'm going to—'

'Excuse me, but are we talking about the shop next door to you?'

'What else? I thought I'd made that clear.'

'You mean it's for sale? Toby Perrin is moving?'

'Has moved. To Marlborough, it seems. And good riddance to him.'

'The place is empty?'

'Thankfully, for the time being. They're asking a lot of money for it. Were you interested?'

'No. Not really.' She didn't want to buy the joint. But she found the fact that Toby Perrin had scarpered most interesting . . . Plus the fact that the flat was sitting there empty.

Elizabeth felt a prickle of anticipation. 'But you could tell me the name of the estate agent. You never know . . . it might be useful.'

On his way back from the hospital, Max dropped in at Angola House. The job was all but over. Not much to show for it, but the Council's brief thought there was probably enough evidence on the last video to nail the case. All that remained was to remove the equipment and send in his expenses sheet.

He parked well down the road and legged it up to the flats. The dreary Sixties building hadn't changed since his last visit, except that there was a new layer of graffiti on the poster advertising a meeting of the Watch Committee. The stairwell was still being used as a lavatory, to judge by the smell, and half a dozen disaffected teenagers still sprawled, three floors below, against the ugly breeze block wall that served as a meeting place.

He let himself into the empty flat on the third floor and went to check the camera, peering out through the hole he'd drilled in the wall and into a door frame on the landing. His back was pressed against the thin, chipboard panel that separated him from the bleak-windowed bedroom.

The circular image with its fuzzy edge revealed two boys walking along the passage, one long and bony in split jeans, the other stumpy in a black baseball cap. The bony one stopped in front of the peeling, green door of No. 47. Max's finger curled around the camera. A glint of light. Stumpy had lit a cigarette. They moved on.

Max found a piece of fudge in his pocket and started to unwrap it. He'd give it five minutes more before packing the stuff up. Time for a can of coke from the pack in the corner. He stretched his long legs as far as he could in front of him, opened the can. It fizzed lightly in the silence and bubbled down again.

A door banged.

Five minutes later came an old woman with a string bag. The lift wasn't working, so she crept down the stairs.

Max sat staring into space. Almost dropped off. But then he heard a sound. Pssst!

A boy with a spray can. Max clicked with one finger. It was something. The slogan, still wet on the wall, said: BIN THE SLUTT.

The boy had gone by the time Max shut the door of the flat behind him, leaving the equipment packed in a rucksack to be collected some other time. There was no one around as he slipped down the stairs. It was as he reached the bottom of the stairwell that he heard a sound.

From behind, not in front.

He turned, but too late.

It was just a dark shape that hit him. A shape wearing a balaclava on its head. Then flying atoms. Pain. A thick, fierce darkness.

CHAPTER FORTY-THREE

——◆◆◆◆——

Elizabeth let herself doze until she heard the post plop through the front door. Until there was something to get up for. Then she heaved herself out of bed and drew back the curtains. Glory be! A pale morning, for once. Cooler. Mist out over Reuben's field. A bit of a shock, after such a summer.

Some gulls had come to visit. A whole crowd of them, mewling and shrieking, tearing the morning apart out over the valley. Did that mean there were storms out at sea? She wrapped herself in her dressing-gown, pottered down the narrow staircase and bent down to pick up the letters. She took them into the kitchen, picked up a blue pottery mug and filled it with orange juice, then put the kettle on and went to find her spectacles.

No bills today. That was a blessing. No brown envelopes.

But what was this? Something long and square. Feels like . . . yes . . . photographs in a brashly coloured folder. A stick-it note on the outside: *I almost forgot these. Can't see that they'll be much help. Let me know when you've finished with them and I'll collect them from your office. Hilary.*

While waiting for the kettle to boil, she spread them out on the old pine table.

Twenty-seven photographs, all neatly numbered on the back, left-hand corner. (Civil servants, she thought. When did *you* ever number anything?) Most of them were pretty silly. Mick Rudd dressed as Nero. (Why else would he be playing the fiddle?) Hilly, draped in somebody's red velvet curtains and waving a curly wig over her head. Trev posing with a javelin and dustbin lid.

And there was Warren, leaning against the bar, in his shirt-sleeves.

Her eyes caught something else in the background. A splash of blue, further along the bar. Julian. No mistaking him. Julian in his blue bath-towel, bare, brown legs stretched out in front of the bar stool . . . smiling at some other young guy in a waiter's uniform. Italian . . . or Greek. Long, dark hair.

Ice exploded in her stomach.

A dark mane. Shiny, dark hair falling halfway down his back. Yes, definitely *his*. Male.

Of course, they might just be mates chatting over a pint. No, thought Elizabeth. Not mates. You could sense it even from a small, dog-eared snapshot.

A star-struck smile on Julian's face The smile of a fallen angel. Dazzled . . . definitely. A look of euphoria.

So . . . let's see the others. The next showed, in the background, Julian still at the bar. After the draw had taken place . . . had to be. The prizes had gone from the table in the corner. Julian grooming his hair with one hand while the young waiter made him laugh.

Next?

Same scene, almost. But he wasn't there any more. That's odd. They'd vanished.

Elizabeth studied the last but one. Ah . . . there he was, surely, on the other side of the glass doors that led to the back staircase. Obscured by the glass panels, but . . . there was a streak of blue. It had to be him.

Or was she imagining it?

What she needed was a magnifying glass. More and more these days, Lord help us. Let's see now. Where did I put it?

She tried the basket next to the telephone directory (where it was most used); her sewing box; the table next to her bed. (Midnight reading.)

Nowhere.

Now she remembered. She'd been studying the seed catalogue. She stood on a chair and rummaged in the overhead cupboard above the hob. Had to be here . . . just a question of where. Too many things up here she ought to get

rid of. Jim's fishing flies. French francs in an old tin box . . .
Aha!

She could see now with more clarity. There was a bit of
fuzz around the edges, but . . . but . . . but . . . Yes. It was
Julian. She felt a thrill of recognition.

A bottle of wine in one hand, his arm round the other
guy's shoulders. Mates? In a pig's eye! OK, so young men did
drape themselves round each other when they'd had a skinful,
but this was different.

Elizabeth's gaze passed to the last photograph. Same scene,
same people. (Odd how people do that.) Cheryl in the
foreground, sipping a gin and tonic. The crowd behind. And
someone, at the very edge of it . . . a face in half profile.
Someone whose gaze was firmly fixed on the glass doors. Or
what was going on behind them.

Someone Elizabeth knew. Someone she still had doubts
about—

Thoughtfully, she stacked the photos back into a neat pile.
Shoved them into the folder and was about to make the
coffee, when the door bell shrilled.

'Not Dottie—' she muttered. 'Please not . . . at this hour.'

The prayer was answered. It wasn't Dottie on the doorstep,
but a young man in police uniform. Max's friend, Andy. 'It's
all right,' he said, seeing her face. 'Nothing to worry about.
Well, not much. Your phone's not working. Did you know?'

'No. I didn't. What do you mean? Not much?'

'Max spent the night in hospital. We've been trying to get
hold of you.'

'He's lucky it wasn't worse,' Elizabeth told Ginger a couple
of hours later. She stood on the stairs that led up to the office.
Ginger leaned against the wooden handrail in the deep bend
two steps lower. 'The caretaker found him staggering around
the alley beside the dustbins and the generator room.'

'So what did they smack him with?'

'Well, it wasn't a bunch of bananas. The Doc reckoned it
was lucky he turned so that it caught the side of his head and
not the back. Oh – and they threw paint over him when he

was out cold. Lucky it wasn't in his face or he might have been blinded.'

'Any idea who?' Ginger asked, shocked.

'Your guess is as good as mine. They took his wallet and credit cards, so I'm hoping it was just a casual mugging.'

'Hoping?'

'If it's someone trying to put the frighteners on, they may try again.'

'Good God!'

Elizabeth smiled grimly. 'Dangerous occupation, this. I'll show you the figures some time. Detectives who have mysterious accidents. Anyway, thanks for coming in at short notice. Can you hold the fort for a while, do you think?'

'No problem.'

'I'm really grateful. You were the only one I could think of. I'll relieve you at lunchtime, if that's OK.'

'Take your time. I've nothing on. So is Max still in hospital?'

'No. They discharged him. He's resting up at home. I'll go round there later. But in the meantime, I've got an appointment with a boy in a suit.'

Whose name was Marcus Way, from Lister, Goddard and Way of Quiet Street; fair and mustard-keen, with admirably polished shoes and a great desire to show off his expertise. He flashed her a hundred dollar grin as he escorted her up the stairs from the side entrance to the flat above what had once been Toby Perrin's shop.

'The premises are really remarkably spacious, consisting of two reception, three bedrooms and a kitchen of some character.' They clumped up the last few stairs, the boy inserted a key into a lock and the door creaked open. 'As you can see, we have all the original fireplaces, newly exposed beams and from that window, over there, an absolutely splendid view down over the city to the Abbey. Well, if you stand in the very corner.'

So, OK, he was right, if you stood on tiptoe and leaned

sideways. Craned your neck to peer round the trees and over the railway bridge . . .

'The property is in good repair. Full central heating . . . gas. Roof completely renovated and refelted. Gutters and downspouts all clear. New bathroom fittings—' He was like a wind-up mechanical toy that went round and round and said exactly what he had been told.

'Not like my place then.' Martha Washington could do with a good overhaul, but it wouldn't be this year.

'Sorry?'

'I have a shop in Pierrepont Mews. Doesn't need antiquing.'

The boy in the suit looked puzzled. 'So you're opening a second shop? Expanding?'

Don't I wish? 'Business rates are high in the centre of town,' she told him. Which was true. No need for further elaboration. What am I doing here? she asked herself, when I have no intention of buying the joint and no idea of what I'm looking for. Like a lot of things in Elizabeth's life, there was no logic involved. Decisions got themselves made on a hunch and a prayer. She turned from the window and gazed slowly around the empty room. Bare ceiling, bare white walls, bare boards. It was very empty and very clean. Someone had certainly scrubbed the place out. Was that what the smell was? Heavy-duty Ajax? Metal cleaner? Carbolic? Or just heavy, stale air?

The boy showed her round the bedrooms, the bathroom and, last of all, the kitchen. 'The last owner had a butcher's block right here in the middle. Fashionable now. Looks superb in a place with this ambience. Better than a boring old pine table.' He steered her once more towards the window. 'There's a cobbled yard down below . . . perfect for garden furniture . . . you could eat out there in this weather. And a bijou garden with a fig tree. And even a footpath that leads right down to the Kennet and Avon. That's the wonderful thing about these town houses. The nooks and crannies, the sheltered corners, the sheer neighbourliness . . .'

Edward Griffith hadn't thought so.

'It has great charm, don't you think? Can't you just imagine

it filled with rustic furniture . . . gingham curtains and a jug
or two of wild flowers?'

Blessed are the inarticulate, Elizabeth thought, for they
shall inherit the earth. If I have anything to do with it. 'So
why is he selling,' she asked, 'if it's so very charming?'

'Not sure. Found a rural property, I think. Better for his
image.'

'Which was?'

'Hand-made artefacts. Furniture with an individual
touch . . .' He was running out of sales patter. 'Tell you what,'
he said. 'Take five minutes to look round by yourself. Feel
the ambience.'

Smell the ambience, more like, Elizabeth thought. 'Is there
a problem with the drains?' she asked.

'There is something,' he conceded. 'Perhaps it's coming
from outside.' He opened the window and stuck his head
out. Sniffed hard.

'It's definitely in here,' Elizabeth told him.

He closed the window again. 'I think you're right,' he said,
as the salesman's smile began to fade.

'Something left in the garbage can, maybe?'

He opened the door under the sink, but found nothing.

'Perhaps something crawled in and died,' Elizabeth said. A
mouse? A rat? They'd had an invasion in the cottage in the
Fall, when a little man had come round with his van and laid
poison.

'It's stronger over there,' Elizabeth said. 'It seems to be . . .'
She stopped and sniffed. 'Yes . . . it seems to be coming from
the other corner.'

'The walk-in pantry,' the boy said. He strode over, trying
to look purposeful. The cupboard was locked.

'That's odd,' he said. 'It was open the last time I was here.'

'You're sure of that?'

'Positive.'

'So when was that?'

'Last . . . let me see. Last Wednesday.'

Five days ago. Business obviously wasn't brisk. He went to
fetch his briefcase (almost bigger than him) from the other

room. Got out a large bunch of keys; but none of them fitted. 'I remember now. There was a key in the door.'

'So where's it gone?'

'You tell me.' He looked baffled.

'There's glass at the top there.' At some time or other, a small window had been inserted above the pantry door. 'Why don't we take a look? Stand on the packing case,' she said. 'Over there, by the door.'

He hauled the box out and dragged it over to the pantry door. Climbed on it, stretched up . . . But it was no good. 'I need at least another foot,' he said.

'Pity the furniture's gone,' Elizabeth said. Then, 'Hang on a minute. I'll go next door.' She had left the room before he could protest. Five minutes later, she came puffing back upstairs, carrying an aluminium stepladder.

'I know the old guy,' she explained, hauling it across the room. 'Met him through business. This will do fine. There you go . . .'

Marcus Way laid down his bunch of keys and shook the ladder to make quite sure it was safe. Gingerly, he ascended first one step, then another. He doesn't like heights, Elizabeth thought. That's shut him up. He stood on the top rung but one, holding on hard, stretching his neck upwards in order to peer in through the narrow window. Then, 'Oh, my God!'

He was down the ladder faster than he had gone up. And shaking like a leaf.

'What is it?' Elizabeth asked. 'What's the matter?'

He was very nearly out of the room by now and making for the outer door. 'Someone in there,' he yelled back over his shoulder. 'A body.'

Elizabeth climbed the stepladder herself. She had been warned of what she would find when she took a look, that someone was lying dead in there. What she hadn't reckoned with was the identity of the body.

Someone small and thin. Like a stick insect, in fact. Morgan Dundy.

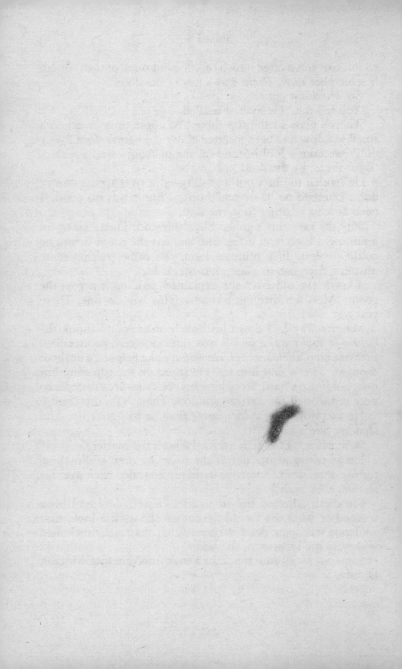

CHAPTER FORTY-FOUR

Max lay on the striped sofa in his basement flat in Edward Street. He had just turned off the afternoon film. His head hurt, his eyes stung. He felt as if a brick wall had fallen on him. So when the doorbell rang, at ten minutes past four, he decided to ignore it. But it was persistent, so he manoeuvred himself, swearing silently, off the sofa and went to answer it.

'Not a pretty sight,' said Ginger when he opened the door.

'What the hell are you doing here?'

'Nice to see you too,' Ginger said. 'Elizabeth sent me with some letters for you to sign.'

'What happened to the other job? The Water Board?'

'Boring.' She shoved a bunch of roses into his spare hand. 'These are for you. They're from Elizabeth. She said to tell you she's returning the compliment. Does that make any sense?' She didn't wait for a reply. 'So . . . you've been in the wars?'

Fran, his oldest sister, used to say that to him. As the reflection from the whitewashed wall hit him, he felt weak suddenly. His legs threatened to give way.

'Careful.' She half led, half supported him back to the sofa. 'God, they didn't half give you a crack. That dressing looks a bit manky. Want me to change it?'

'It's OK,' Max said, sinking back against the cushions.

'It's not OK. But if you want it to turn septic—'

'OK. OK. Do what you like.'

He must have sworn a bit as she got the thing off, because she shook her head, but sort of anonymously, as if he were a lost cause. Ginger fetched water and a new dressing from the packet she'd found lying on the coffee table. Her freckled nose was very close to his as she dabbed at the wound. A snub nose, except for the little tilt at the end. 'Hold still,' she said, 'or it'll hurt even more!'

'Don't worry about it. I always go white when I'm having fun.' She was not pretty, he thought. Nobody could say that. But unusual looking. Attractive . . . almost. The thought surprised him. 'Where did you learn to change dressings?'

'My mother's a nurse. It probably rubbed off.' She secured the sticking-plaster with neat fingers and stepped back to survey her handiwork. 'You'll survive.'

'I'm not so sure of that.' He sat there wincing.

Her left eyebrow (very neat and the colour of dark marmalade) carefully lifted. 'Absolute torture, I expect?' She stood gazing down at him through wide, seemingly innocent grey eyes.

That was what was different about her. 'You're not wearing your glasses,' he said through the pain.

'I decided to try contact lenses. Want a coffee?'

She stood out in the kitchen waiting for the kettle to boil. Slim and lithe, Max noted automatically through half-closed eyes. Not a bad figure. She made no attempt to clear the mountain of dishes in the sink. Funny that. Most women would have been attacking it and reading him a moral lecture.

'How long have you lived here?' she asked, as she ferreted for the last two clean mugs in the cupboard.

'Five years. Were there any calls for me? Personal, I mean?' He'd asked Elizabeth to ring Jess's hotel and explain what had happened. She might have rung back by now.

'Nothing.' Ginger heaped coffee into a mug from the cupboard. 'Are you hungry?'

'Not really.'

'Because if you are . . .'

'No. I'm fine.' She was being too nice, much too accommodating. Max felt suspicious. 'You'd better get back to the office. You haven't got time to cook.'

She looked aghast. 'I didn't intend to. I meant I'd ring for a take-away.'

'I can do that. If I need to.' He couldn't have faced anything at the moment. He felt sick and the headache was getting worse. 'Thanks anyway,' he said offhandedly.

'Don't mention it. Elizabeth cancelled your credit cards, by the way.'

'Right.'

'Did you lose much? From your wallet?'

'Absolutely zilch. And I'm over my credit card limits . . .' The dinner with Jess had seen to that. 'So they won't get much there.'

'There's one more thing I'm supposed to tell you. But gently. It's about Morgan Dundy.'

Max sat up hard halfway through her account, but the pain knocked him back down again. He thought perhaps that Ginger would find it funny, her voice was surprisingly gentle. 'Headache bad?'

'Mmn.' His eyes were closed.

'Taken aspirin?'

He nodded.

'They checked you for concussion?'

'Yes. Look – could you please go now? It's good of you and all that, but—'

She was gone before he knew what was happening.

CHAPTER FORTY-FIVE

The buzzer on the door woke him with two business-like, sharp blasts. Max sat up, then winced as the pain hit him. Duller than before, but still uncomfortable.

'Bloody hell!' said Andy, gazing at him from the doorstep. 'What number bus was it?'

'What?'

'That you had an argument with?'

'What time is it?' Max asked, not having the energy to quip back. He was the colour of cold spaghetti. There was a bright red weal across one side of his forehead. A dozen or so stitches, and his left eye was practically shut.

'Seven o'clock. Get back to your sickbed. I'll put the kettle on. I was going to bring a beer or two, but they tell me you're not allowed alcohol.'

Max heard him clattering around in the kitchen, washing up, presumably. That was what domestic bliss did for you. He remembered a time (not so long ago, either) when wild horses wouldn't have got Andy's hands into soapsuds. But since he'd bought a little terraced house with Lyn . . . well, it was pathetic really. He'd even taken to filling flower pots on a Sunday morning.

'Remember who hit you yet?' Andy asked when he brought in the coffee.

'Nothing. Just being slammed against the wall.' Max's voice seemed to be coming out in a thin bleat. 'And the balaclava.'

'General description then. Tall or short? Black or white? Voice . . . accent?'

'Tallish. White, I think, but he wore gloves. Didn't say anything. Just thumped me.'

'I'll bring over some mugshots. We're doing a door to door on the estate.'

Max took a sip of coffee, then lay back against the crumpled cushions. 'Waste of time,' he said.

'Nevertheless . . .' A pause and then, 'Did you hear about Morgan Dundy?'

'Yeah. Ginger came round. And Elizabeth rang.' It's like Waterloo Station, Max thought. But Elizabeth hadn't kept him long. She'd been in a funny mood; abstracted, not very talkative (which was almost unknown), restless. Maybe he should have asked what was on her mind, but quite frankly, he hadn't felt up to case analysis.

'She didn't tell you she was going to Perrin's flat?'

'No. My partner is a law unto herself.' A woman with a very strong will and a powerful amount of energy.

'One day she'll bite off more than she can chew. You should keep her on a tighter rein.'

Easier said than done, Max thought. You try it.

Andy said, 'We pulled Perrin in.'

'You think he killed her?'

'He had a key to the place. How else could she have got in there?'

'Perhaps she had one cut when she was meeting Neville there.' *If* she was meeting him; if it wasn't all a parcel of lies. But the old man . . . what's-his-name . . . Edward Griffith . . . had seen her there. Max stopped thinking, at that point. It hurt too much. He asked a simple question. 'What's Perrin saying?'

'He's never been near the place since he moved out. But he would say that, wouldn't he?'

'DNA tests?'

'Being done. We searched the flat and talked to the neighbours.'

'And?'

'The old man next door heard raised voices . . . male and female . . . in the kitchen of the flat at about nine o'clock last Thursday evening. He thought it funny, under the circumstances, and nearly called the police. But then it quietened down, so he persuaded himself that it was the estate agent showing somebody around. He kept an eye out and saw Gerard Dundy leave the place at nine-thirty.'

'He's sure it was Dundy?'

'Yes. He took the number of the car. Definitely Dundy's.' Silence for a while. Max sat there with his mug of coffee; Andy helped himself to another custard cream. 'And Dundy's prints were all over the flat.'

'That's it, then. He must have killed her. But what was she doing in Perrin's flat? That's what I don't understand.'

'You've got me there.' Andy sat staring out of the window. An occasional pair of legs went by at street level. 'We'll keep on plugging away at Perrin. He's got to be involved somewhere along the line.'

'You know he's gay?'

'So you said. But does it lead anywhere?'

Not that Max could see. 'What about the neighbours on the other side? Did they hear anything?'

'No. 1 Fosse Terrace. Just round the corner. Family called Rowley. They had the telly on loud and the son had his music on the go upstairs. Dad thought he might have seen someone leave the side entrance to Perrin's shop at around ten-thirty that evening . . . but couldn't be sure. It was dark by then. Might just have been someone walking a dog. So . . . where does that leave us?'

'God knows.' Max heaved himself upright, put the mug down.

'You look like death.'

'I feel like death,' muttered Max.

CHAPTER FORTY-SIX

When Ginger called again at eleven o'clock the following morning, Max was still brassed off.

'I brought you some supplies,' she said, holding out two Waitrose bags stuffed with groceries.

'Thanks. But you shouldn't have bothered.'

'I didn't. I'm only the carrier. Elizabeth bought them.' Ginger dumped the bags in the kitchen. Came back to survey him as he lay despondently on the sofa in a tee-shirt that had seen better days and baggy old shorts. 'Why don't you get dressed?' she said. 'You'll feel better.'

No, he wouldn't, Max thought. Today the old Ginger was back. Brusque with him. No more sympathy. Perhaps he'd imagined the other, gentler girl. But then, women did that to you all the time. Changed . . . metamorphosed. You never knew where you were with them. Which took him neatly back to the reason for his ill-humour.

Jess. Why hadn't she contacted him? Didn't she care at all?

The phone shrilled. Max raised himself expectantly.

'I'll get it,' said Ginger.

'No – it's OK.'

But she'd already picked up the receiver. 'It's your sister,' she said, after listening for a moment.

Max slumped back again. 'Which one?'

'How many have you got?'

'Three.'

'Good God! Well, it's Fran.'

'Who was that?' Fran asked when he got himself to the phone.

'That?'

'The girl.'

'Oh . . . just someone from the office.' Aware vaguely, as he said it, that it sounded churlish.

'Well, she's not at the office now,' Fran said meaningfully.

'No, well, she came round with some stuff.' He heard a clattering sound from the kitchen. Like dishes being crashed down.

'What happened to Jess, then?'

'Nothing. She's still around. Somewhere.'

'Pity. I thought you'd have come to your senses by now.' Her voice sounded kind but bossy. Fran all over.

'Look – I can't talk now. Can I ring you back?'

'Suit yourself,' said Fran. 'I only rang to ask how you were.'

'I'm OK. Sore, but it doesn't hurt so much.'

'Well, just watch yourself in future. Silly devil.'

'Look – I've got to go. There's someone at the door.'

'Convenient,' said Fran. 'I'll speak to you later.'

He put the phone down. The conversation – and the shrilling doorbell – had brought back his headache. Perhaps he'd take an aspirin. The doorbell went on and on. Somebody had their finger stuck permanently to the button.

Someone impatient. Where the hell was Ginger?

'Don't bother yourself,' he said sarcastically. 'I'll get there . . . somehow.' He staggered to open the door.

Jess was standing on the area steps. 'I'm afraid I can't stay,' she announced at once. 'But I brought you these.' She held out an expensively Cellophaned bunch of hothouse blooms.

Max looked up from the flowers to Jess's face. Her smile was sympathetic and disturbing. 'You poor lamb. Just look at you. You should be more careful . . . you know?'

She took a half step backwards and hesitated. Her shiny eyes focused on the pansies in the window box. 'Sweetie, I'm so sorry I didn't get around before, but you've no idea how hard they've been working us. Talk about slave labour . . . Trouble is, if you turn a job down, they won't look at you again, so there's nothing for it but to work until you drop. I'm afraid I'm flying straight off to Paris,' she said, still hovering. 'In a couple of hours. Tony got me this amazing catwalk job with Givenchy. I mean, I didn't believe it when he told me. Givenchy, for God's sake! And then we're off to New York for a month. There's no rest for the wicked. So . . . I'm glad you're on the mend. Honestly, I nearly died when they told me you were in hospital.'

'That was two days ago,' Max said pointedly.

'I know. But I had to go back to London, briefly. I'd have been here if I could. You know that.'

Do I? Max thought.

'Anyway, I must fly. I'll pop in and see you again when I can. OK? In the meantime, you take care. That's an order.'

Max watched her sway back up the steps. Stood there, stiffly, in the doorway for a minute or two, before, eventually, taking himself back into the sitting-room. Ginger stood in the kitchen doorway with her rucksack in her hand.

'I was about to leg it,' she explained. 'I heard her voice. Thought I'd use the back door.'

'No need,' Max said heavily. 'She couldn't stay.'

'Right. Nice flowers,' she said, smiling in such a way that she could almost have meant it.

Max gave them a stare, before dumping them abruptly on top of the bookshelf.

'Tropical?' Ginger went on with unnatural animation. 'What are they?'

Max neither knew nor cared. Bright orange things – lilies? – with sharp points to the petals. Ever after, he would associate them with wounded emotions.

'Do they smell?' asked Ginger brightly.

Only of Jess's exotic . . . primitive . . . perfume. It hung in the air . . . all over him . . . heavy, like incense in church or something you drank on foreign holidays.

'There's something . . .' She was no longer looking at the flowers. Her attention had shifted to the window, or rather what she could see through it. 'I think she's dropped something on the steps. A scarf?'

Max went with wooden legs to investigate. Yes, there was a wisp of yellow silk on the top step. He stared at it, thinking. If you hurry, you'll catch her. Am I capable of it? Do I want to? Yes and no. Why should I put myself out? Chase after her?

Nevertheless, he did. He struggled up the steps to street level. Picked up the scarf and set off in the direction of Pulteney Street. That's the way she would take back into town . . . He felt it, that little burst of activity. It made his stitches throb, as if they were going to split apart.

Don't run. You haven't the strength.

He walked steadily down to Duke's Hotel and turned the corner. He was sure to catch sight of her now. She would be halfway down Pulteney Street, within shouting distance.

She was. And just a bit further down the street was a flash car, with a flash bloke standing next to it. The specimen he'd met that day in her hotel room. Numbly, Max stood there and watched as Jess covered the last few yards, said something to the crappy sod (pale blue trousers, silk shirt and cK shades) and gave a sudden spring forward to drape herself all over him.

Max looked at them carefully before setting off towards them, as if he wanted to be sure that the picture he was registering was quite in focus. His eyes were black and blue, but they could see straight.

Perhaps for the first time, as far as Jess was concerned.

Your big mistake, he told himself (apart from ever getting mixed up with her in the first place) was not applying work routines to your own situation. First rule of the game. Check your witness's statement and then double-check. You could have asked the hotel receptionist. Excuse me, but did they book one room or two? But basically, you're just the same as all the other punters on the books. You don't want to believe anything unpalatable until it's shoved down your throat.

Vanity, he thought. That's what brought her back. All that pretence about caring about me. Wanting to see me again. All she ever thought of was herself. All she ever wanted was sex and plenty of it. And to pull strings.

He felt sick, disillusioned, angry. But mostly at himself. So, it was time he told her. Turned the tables.

'You forgot this,' he said casually when he was a yard away.

She spun round, her eyes widening as they took him in.

Max didn't find it necessary to waste words. Just one would do. 'Slag.' He dropped the scarf in the gutter at her feet.

'Max – wait—'

'Sorry,' he flung back over his shoulder. 'More important things to do.'

Ginger was still there, still clutching her rucksack. She must have read his face, because she said, 'Trouble?'

He even thought about pouring it all out. But only for a few seconds. Even the new, watered-down Ginger would make wisecracks and he wasn't up to that. So he told her his head was splitting (which it was) and left it at that.

He woke next morning without the headache, but with a sour feeling that something had gone badly wrong. It wasn't until he turned over, burrowing his head back under the duvet, that he remembered everything and wanted to lose himself in sleep again. But it was too light and bright (the Indian bedspread hooked over the window had come away at one end). He'd have to get up and make coffee. Stick the radio on. Anything to fill the immeasurable emptiness of this blanker than blank morning. With an effort, he hauled himself out of bed and into the bathroom; had a shower and cleaned his teeth with moody concentration. Threw a couple of slices of bread into the toaster and was forcing himself to consider going into the office when the phone rang.

It was Elizabeth. 'Hi! How are you, this fine morning?'

'How do you expect?' he asked irritably. Elizabeth sounded cheery but distant. There was a briskness in her voice which didn't make his heart feel any lighter. More lumpen, in fact, as he remembered that she hadn't visited him once since his troubles had started, which felt to Max very much like neglect. Like not caring. Oh, she'd sent Ginger round, but hadn't been near the place herself, except to phone. Which wasn't at all the same thing. Hell, he might have died and all Elizabeth cared about was running her folksy quilt shop.

'My, we're grouchy.'

'So would you be if you'd got a lump on your head the size of a duck egg.'

'Listen – I was just talking to Andy. The forensic results came back on Morgan. She was strangled with a length of flex. No sign of a struggle, so she was probably taken by surprise. No signs of sexual attack. The pathologist thinks she died at around tennish, which almost fits in with the time Dundy left.'

'DNA tests come up with anything?' Max asked, interested now, in spite of himself.

'Nothing, I'm afraid. But there's one other thing. She was pregnant when she died. Three months . . . which takes us into a whole new ball game.'

'Neville's baby?' asked Max, trying to calculate backwards and finding it too much.

'Could just have been. If for once in her life she happened to be telling the truth and they did have an affair.'

'Unless it was his. Gerry's. She arranged to meet him to tell him about it. But why Perrin's flat? And she hated Gerry. So why would she tell him?'

'Money?' Elizabeth suggested. 'Babies are expensive items. She'd want maintenance. And he'd probably want to help, provided—'

'Provided the child was his. But suppose she told him somebody else was the father?'

'Then he'd blow a gasket.'

Max, at that moment, had another thought. *I didn't want to hurt my baby*. 'Suppose she wanted him to pay for an abortion? But, of course, technically it's no business of ours any more.'

'How come?'

Max told her about Diana taking them off the case. 'So that's that.'

'Perhaps,' said Elizabeth. 'Perhaps.'

Max didn't like the sound of that. 'Look – if she's not going to pay the bills, it's no use wasting our time on it.'

Silence at the other end.

'Elizabeth? You there?'

'I'm here.' But she sounded all distant again. As if no longer listening.

'Get on with the other stuff. The Burgess case. The woman who wants her husband followed. Look – I've got to have my dressing changed. I'll be in this afternoon. Can you manage on your own till then?'

'If I can't, I can always call the Squadron-Leader.'

'Jones the Onion?'

'The same. He rang yesterday and offered us his services.'

'Work for us, you mean?'

'Thought we might want the advantage of his sharp brain.'

Max almost grinned. 'So what did you say?'

'I told him to bugger off. Oh, and I set him on to Warren Rudd. I told him he was behind the allotment thefts.'

'You didn't?'

'Give the Squadron-Leader someone else to pester, I thought. Look – I've got to go. Lots to do.'

'So you'll call the Burgess woman?'

'Yes, yes,' she said hurriedly. ''Bye, Max. See you.'

Sitting in her car, on the slope of the lane looking down over Bath, Elizabeth watched a grainy greyness sink over the city. A rain smell stirred the heat. There was colour still in the billowing green of the chestnuts, in the ruffled hedgerows down below in the valley, but the light was growing pale and glazed. She lifted her wrist, noted the time. Three minutes to seven. Getting on for eight hours since her conversation with Max. And since she had nipped upstairs to give extra precise instructions to Ginger. Send these faxes to these numbers. Do it from the little print shop in town, not the machine in here. Do it now, while I mind the office. Don't be long. And don't say a word about this to anyone, not even Max. No, I don't expect any replies. And I'll be unavailable all day.

'In the shop?' Ginger had asked, scanning the letter she'd just printed out.

'No. Elsewhere.'

'And if he wants to know where, exactly?'

There was a long pause. 'Tell him I had to drop everything

and go off for the day. Yes, that's vague enough. That ought to keep him quiet.'

Ginger looked up and said conversationally, 'This isn't dangerous, is it? You're not going to get yourself bonked on the head like somebody else I know?'

'Shouldn't think so,' Elizabeth said. 'But don't worry. I'll ring for the cavalry if I need them.'

'OK,' said Ginger. She did not sound concerned or even interested. Just matter of fact. By eleven, Elizabeth had been out of the place and climbing into her car in an alley behind Henrietta Street. She drove herself up Lansdown Hill and into the car park of The Angel Gabriel, an anonymous enough place, enough comings and goings that one more car wouldn't be noticed – the pub was open all day, after all, busy with local custom – and then, at tea-time, back to her cottage in South Harptree to make a quick phone call, take a shower and change her clothes. Calm and relaxed, by then, because at last, no question about it, she knew the identity of the murderer. The plan had worked. Her brain had got it all sorted.

Now, all that was left to do was wrap it all up, finally, by doing a little coaxing. Elizabeth reached into her pocket for a bar of chocolate and tore off the silver wrapper. She was dimly aware of a tension running through her, a spark of unease. If she handled this the right way, if inspiration came to her as she went along . . . if she didn't get too clever-clever . . . it shouldn't be too risky. She preferred not to think about what might happen if things went wrong.

CHAPTER FORTY-SEVEN

It was five minutes past seven by the clock on the mantelpiece. Wendy Lucas was aware, obscurely, that the Blair woman was late. She was not able, and this was what puzzled Wendy, scared her under the circumstances, to keep her mind fixed in the present. She needed all her wits about her, but they would keep flying back, escaping into the past. Am I going mad? It's so irrational, she thought. Feeling that those days were real and this isn't. She lit yet another cigarette. Caught a glimpse of herself in the mirror as she did so. She felt herself lifted to a state of even higher detachment as she studied the blonde woman in the blue frock. Remote eyes, painted face. I don't think I like you much. I'd rather be the old Wendy, which, of course, meant the young Wendy. The simpleton. The lonely teenager who had fallen, hook, line and sinker (splendid naval image) for Bernard in a grubby little dance hall in a grubby little Plymouth suburb.

Bernard. Where is he? They said he couldn't be contacted. He had left the building.

These days, we might be walking in different worlds for all the real contact we have with each other. These days, we're like old friends with nothing much to say to each other.

The old Bernard . . . no, the young Bernard . . . well, I just liked the colour of his eyes. That greyish blue, the colour of the sea in winter. I chased him until he caught me.

I liked him because he looked lonely, too. Neither of us had anybody else. And he was good-looking and sweetly shy. Nicer than the other boys . . . kind and sensitive. Terribly correct, of course, even then; never tried to take liberties like all the others; but that was because of the way he'd been brought up. Because of that awful, religious mother of his, directing every aspect of his life. I wanted to liberate him, change his life, make him happy. Dear God, how naïve. Why do we always want to change them? Why can't we see that some things are impossible?

A click – like a domino falling – out in the hall. Wendy turned from the mirror. *Bernard? Thank God. Is that you?* But it was only the cat flap. She relaxed again. Not true. Perhaps she never would be able to relax again. She went back to her reflections. It was only in the past that her mind found a kind of balm.

The young Bernard – nineteen years old – had taken her to the pictures once or twice and then invited her home to tea. She'd accepted with breathless pleasure. He'd met her on the corner by the old Gaumont (knocked down now, like a lot of things) and they'd walked from there. How cold it was that day, but she'd felt cosy to the fingertips, hanging on to his tweed-clad arm, belonging.

Their honeymoon had been a bit of a disaster. They had taken a room in The Temperance Hotel in Plymouth. No money to go further afield. Yes, the sex had been a disappointment, but that, quite frankly, was the norm in those days . . . before the pill. Nerves, tension, ignorance. No real sex before marriage (not unless you were the reckless sort or knew more than was good for you). Too scared you'd get pregnant.

I was far too young, she thought. We were both too young. How little we knew of the mechanics of it all. How pitifully little. If we'd only had a hundredth part of the freedom they have now. The pill, the openness, the savvy. Wendy often found herself envying the youngsters in the office. Even that gormless Hilly had found herself a lover.

A car crunched to a halt on the gravel outside the window, but Wendy seemed hardly to notice it. She was still in the past. Infidelity. Did it matter? Only if you got found out, it seemed. Wendy drew on her cigarette and contemplated the row of family photographs lined up on the piano.

Yes, Bernard had been good to her; generous, attentive, a

perfect husband in all but one area. Their sex life had never been brilliant. On the indifferent side, as a matter of fact. Oh, they did it; they'd produced Tom; but there had always seemed to be something wanting. Excitement, true sexual fulfilment.

For a long time she'd thought, no use grumbling or grousing and longing for things you don't have. That possibly others don't have either. Multi-orgasms and exotic positions. We're all right as we are. But then, when Julian had turned up at Draycott. Oh, God, the twitch of the flesh . . . the body wanting things it didn't get at home.

Why the hell did he ever have to choose Draycott? Why couldn't we have gone on meandering along quietly as we were? Everything might have been all right, damn it.

Might still be all right now, if you keep your nerve. That's why Wendy had to see the detective woman, why she hadn't tried to put her off when she had received the fax. Even though Bernard wasn't here. Even though she would have to manage on her own, cobble up some sort of story as she went along . . .

She couldn't risk losing it all now. Home. Status. Tom. All she had to do was hang on for another few weeks. Then they'd be off to Italy. The whole nightmare would go away.

'Mrs Lucas?'

Standing there outside the open patio door was the Blair woman, her keen face tanned and golden above the cream linen of her workmanlike shirt. 'I didn't hear you arrive,' Wendy said tonelessly.

'You were miles away.'

'I was thinking how that chintz had faded.'

She leaned forward and straightened a cushion on the sofa. Smiled with a touch of . . . not contempt exactly. More a kind of cynicism. She pushed a stray end of blonde hair back behind one ear, tried to cobble her disturbed thoughts back in one piece, shake them into some sort of form and structure. For Tom's sake, she told herself. For that if nothing else. Tom still needs me . . .

* * *

Wendy Lucas waved Elizabeth to a chair and said, 'Is there something we can help you with? You didn't quite say, on the phone . . .'

'I didn't, did I?' Elizabeth could feel the tension in the room. The flavour of fear. Something fragile in the air, though Wendy Lucas had this ceremonial smile on her face; like she was reading the menu and couldn't quite decide what she wanted. Chicken, duck or something more audacious. Something you would dive right into and maybe regret later.

'Can I get you something? A drink?'

'I'm fine,' Elizabeth said. She threw a casual glance around the room. 'Is it just the two of us? Is your son around?'

'No. He went to a friend's house.'

'And your husband?'

'He's not back yet. He's probably in a meeting.'

'This late?'

'It happens sometimes.'

'Did you tell him I was coming?'

'No. I couldn't get through to him. Why? Did you want to see him?'

Elizabeth leaned back in the sofa. 'That depends.'

'On what?'

'On what you have to tell me, I suppose.' The room had books and pictures and cushions galore, but all ranged in rows. Nothing haphazard. The result was a place that was too tidy to be pretty.

'But I told you all I know about Julian Neville.'

'Is that right?'

'Are you calling me a liar?' Wendy's eyes penetrated. Her voice went all dramatic. It was a great performance.

'I rather think so. Yes.' Elizabeth shed the veneer of politeness.

Wendy said she'd never been so insulted in her life. She said if Elizabeth was going to be like that, she could jolly well leave, as it was unpleasant to have someone tell you, bold as brass in your own house, that they didn't believe you.

Elizabeth said lies were lies, wherever they were told.

Wendy turned her indignation up another notch. 'Do you

do this all the time? I mean, is this what your job consists of, walking into people's homes and abusing them? I really do think you've got a cheek!'

Elizabeth didn't say a word. She gave Wendy a faint, pitying smile as if to say, I can sit here for hours, you know. I'm in no hurry. I can wait.

'Are you listening to me? Did you hear what I said?'

No reply. Just an ironical lift of the eyebrow.

Wendy's voice was querulous now, as she stubbed out her cigarette in an ashtray on the sideboard. 'I've had enough of this play-acting. Perhaps you think it amusing to try and make someone feel guilty when they're not. I've got nothing on my conscience, I can assure you. If you're expecting some sort of confession, well, you're going to be disappointed. I've got nothing to hide. Nothing at all.'

She appeared to be working herself up into a rare old state, and when somebody gets going, Elizabeth thought, then you oughtn't to stop them.

'And if I had, I don't see what business it is of yours. I mean, Hubert Neville's gone, poor thing, so he won't care now whether you find the boy's murderer or not—'

'Hubert's dead?' Elizabeth found her own voice (thin and shocked) in an instant.

'Yes. I heard it on the six o'clock local news.'

'I'm real sorry to hear that.' Elizabeth meant it. She remembered Hubert's beautifully clear, slightly harsh voice. The old-fashioned integrity of the man. Wondered if he had been glad to get out of it all, wondered if he would recover his self-sufficiency in the next world.

If there was one.

Elizabeth said, 'His wife must be devastated.'

'She's tough.' Wendy spoke quickly, impatiently. 'She'll survive.'

'You know Mrs Neville then?' Elizabeth was studying the other woman with a curious expression in her eyes.

'No. No, not really.' She was desperately trying to back-track. 'Only through what Julian used to say. I mean, in odd remarks at the office.'

'Oh, yes?'

Wendy Lucas reached for another cigarette. She took her time lighting it, but her fingers were shaking. 'I think she rather ruled the roost at home. That's all I meant.'

'The boy was scared of her?'

'I wouldn't say that. But you couldn't help noticing.'

There was a brief pause, then Elizabeth, going in obliquely, changing tack, hoping to disorientate, said, 'What else was there to notice? Did you know much about the Dundys' home life? Morgan and Gerard?'

'Only that their marriage seemed to be a disaster.'

'You heard that he killed himself?'

'Yes. Yes, I did.'

'And were you aware that Gerard Dundy asked his mother to light a candle for him?'

'A candle?' she said in a high-pitched voice. 'Where?'

'In church, one presumes. It was one of his last wishes. You see, he made a tape for her just before he poisoned himself in his car. Rather like a suicide note, but more . . . vivid.'

Wendy wasn't prepared for this. Her skin went china pale. One hand held tight on to the table edge. 'What's that to do with me?'

'Well, there were some very interesting things on it,' Elizabeth said. 'Some very interesting revelations.'

Wendy's head shot round and her lips parted. She was thoroughly rattled.

'Apparently his wife was a blackmailer. Did you know that?' Elizabeth didn't exactly say that this was on the tape. Just implied it. Well, that was OK. For Hubert's sake . . . in his memory . . . she was prepared to bend the rules a little.

'How could I?' Strain was written all over Wendy's face and her eyes seemed glazed. She watched Elizabeth like a mouse watches a cat, with great wariness and not a little terror. 'I always thought her underhand,' she said. 'A bit of a bitch. No one liked her.'

Elizabeth thought about Morgan and the school-marmy Wendy and wondered at what stage the employee had got the upper hand over the office supervisor. What kind of taste that would have left in the mouth. 'I rather gathered that.' A short pause. 'Don't you want to know who she was blackmailing?'

She mumbled, 'Not particularly. Why should I?'

'Oh, come on, Mrs Lucas. Don't waste my time. I have it on tape. Would you like to hear it?'

A shake of the head. Pretty vehement.

'Because I can play it to you, if you like. If you'd care to hear a dead man's voice . . .'

Elizabeth was praying that Mrs Lucas wouldn't call her bluff, because, first of all, she didn't have the tape and, more important, there was nothing on it to prove Wendy to be a blackmail victim. But it was the only way she could think of to get the truth out into the open. You made do with what you had. The quilter's motto. And the trick worked. A small shiver ran right through Wendy's body. Her voice, when it finally emerged, was a ghost of its former self. 'No. I don't want to hear it. It was me she was blackmailing.'

'I rather thought so. Would you care to tell me about it?'

'I . . . she found out something—' Drawing deeply on her cigarette. 'She found out that I'd got a crush on Julian. He asked me over to this flat he borrowed from a friend and . . . and we had sex. Just a couple of times and then he didn't want to know. It was just a laugh to him. I was mortified when I came to my senses.'

'So what happened next?'

'What happened next? Morgan Dundy found out. How I'm not sure. Maybe Julian told her. Anyhow, she threatened to tell Bernard. And I couldn't face that. I'd been so stupid. It was a nightmare. Too late, I found out that I valued my marriage after all. After twenty-seven years, well, it had seemed pretty hollow. Well, you've seen Bernard. He's hardly a bundle of fun . . .'

'But suddenly you found that he had virtues? He could give you things that Julian couldn't? Like this house, your son, a comfortable life-style? You were shelling out to Morgan in order to preserve all that?'

Suddenly Wendy was going to pieces, letting it all out. She no longer hid her feelings behind a hard mask. She let rip, hesitantly at first, but then with more and more venom. Morgan had put her through hell. And Julian had been too arrogant and too shallow to give a damn.

'He was rotten to the core,' she said. Her eyes were hard and hot and the red lipstick stood out sharply from the pallor of her skin. 'People fell for him and didn't think about the morality of it until it was too late. But they can't lock you up for having an affair, can they? I didn't kill him and I didn't kill Morgan.'

'But you wanted to?'

'Oh, I wanted to, believe me. And I'm not sorry she came to a sticky end, because she enjoyed hauling you over hot coals. She was a real little psychopath.'

There was a pause. The sky outside was opaque and slate grey; there were cloud shadows in the valley. 'So just out of interest,' Elizabeth said, 'for the process of elimination . . . where were you the night Morgan was killed?'

'I . . . we were down in Plymouth for the night. My mother died recently and we were clearing her bungalow.'

'Was Tom with you?'

'Tom? No. He was off for the weekend with a friend. I wouldn't want him burdened with that kind of thing. It's a foul job. Quite depressing.'

'Well, that's all very interesting,' Elizabeth said. The shadows had reached the outskirts of the city. They skimmed the long terraces, washing over each in turn, swallowing them up. 'And quite a coincidence. You say that Morgan was blackmailing you?'

'Yes. She was.' There was a rising note in Wendy's voice, the sound of tension approaching a cracking point.

'That's most odd. Because it wasn't you that Dundy mentioned on his tape—'

Silence. Then Wendy's voice said faintly, 'I don't understand. Who—'

'Your husband. I understood that it was your husband who was being blackmailed.'

CHAPTER FORTY-EIGHT

—————◆►◄◆—————

'Bernard? But I don't understand—'

'Oh, I think you do, Mrs Lucas. I think you're playing games with me.'

Elizabeth saw that the other woman was suddenly shaking all over. She was losing control of her limbs. She had to grasp the chair back to support herself. The shadows engulfing the city had reached the Abbey. And when that was blotted out, the rain would start to fall. Hurtling down with the sound of a breaking wave.

Elizabeth said quietly, 'It was your husband who had the affair with Julian Neville. Isn't that right?'

'Absolute rubbish.'

'I don't think so. When did you find out that your Bernard had gay leanings? Or was he bisexual, like his young lover?'

'I won't take any more of this . . . this filth!' Wendy forced herself to let go of the chair, desperately trying to get a hold on herself. Trying to assert herself in face of the enemy advancing. 'Get out of my house, before I call the police.'

'You wouldn't dare. You wouldn't want them to hear how your husband left two hundred pounds in cash in a waste-paper bin this afternoon.'

'What waste-paper bin? Where?'

'The one in the lay-by just down the road from The Angel Gabriel.'

'You're mad. Why would he do that?'

'Because he received a typed note asking him to . . . this morning at about eleven o'clock. Quite a polite little note, but it seemed to have the required result. I watched him deliver the goods at two sharp.' Elizabeth fished deep into her pocket for a padded brown envelope and dropped it on to the table in front of Wendy. 'Two hundred pounds, all intact. You'd better count it. I wouldn't want to get done for theft, not at my time of life.'

The shadows were now a greenish blue, filtered with mauve. A deep rumble of thunder rolled, now and again, over the woods. And in between, a dangerous stillness.

'It was you!' said a voice from behind them. Bernard Lucas stood framed by the doorway. Elizabeth turned to look at him. Their eyes met. From the outside, she thought, he resembles a stolid, eighteenth-century parson. Grey flecks in his brown hair; weighty face. But the eyes give him away. Shadowless grey eyes. Clear, but oddly cold, like the sea on a winter's afternoon.

'Who did you think it was?' Elizabeth asked. 'Morgan, back from the dead?'

He shook his head slowly. His disgust was as much with himself as with her.

'You're sorry you fell for it. Well, I don't blame you, but at least we know where we stand.'

Before he could answer, Wendy's voice interrupted, gritty with anger. 'Don't say anything, Bernard. The money's here. She can't prove anything. There are no witnesses.'

'There's an employee of mine who delivered the note to the receptionist at Draycott. And I have photographs of your husband dropping the money in the lay-by.'

'Bernard – get her bag.'

'Oh, I wasn't stupid enough to bring the camera with me. It's in a very safe place, I can assure you.' Elizabeth looked at Bernard. Picked her words carefully. 'I bet you wanted to die when you saw Julian slope off with that Italian waiter?'

'What are you talking about?' Wendy's voice was harsh, gritty with anger.

'At the Toga Night.' Her gaze was still on Bernard Lucas. 'You saw them disappear through the glass doors into the staff quarters. From the look on your face, I'd say you were devastated.'

'But you weren't there—' Wendy's face was as white as parchment.

'It was captured on one of Hilary's photographs. One you missed. One that you didn't manage to destroy. So . . . I'll ask the question again. At what stage did you find out about your husband's affair with our friend, Julian?'

'He didn't. It's not true—'

'That's enough, Wendy. It's no use.' Bernard spoke wearily. Mechanically, as if enormously tired. 'I fell in love with him,' he said heavily. 'I didn't want to. He made me.'

'For God's sake, Bernard—'

But he ignored his wife. Correction. The truth was that he seemed to have forgotten that she was there. Eyes vague, he stared at Elizabeth, then took another couple of steps into the room. If he's with us, she thought, then it's on a parallel plane. On auto-pilot. His expression was – well, weird. Confiding but secretive.

He went on, 'Julian reminded me of someone . . . a boy . . . I had a crush on as a teenager. It brought back my first real love affair. My first experience of raw sex. I couldn't stop thinking about him. He was so . . . beautiful. I kept wanting to touch him.'

Wendy said, 'I'm going to be sick.' And rushed out of the room.

Bernard went on talking, as if in his sleep. 'His skin so bronzed. He'd spent the summer on a Greek island. The one where the gays go. He used to laugh when I looked shocked at things like that. But when I was his age, well, you had to keep it all under wraps. You got married and hoped those feelings would all go away.'

'You didn't tell your wife, before you married her?'

'What do you think?'

'You didn't. Was that fair to her?'

A shrug. 'Perhaps not. But I needed someone to share things with. A home. My career. The MoD is very stuffy. I'd never have got so far if I'd . . . what do they call it? Outed myself.' He grimaced. 'Dreadful term.'

'And your wife never guessed?'

'Not until I told her Morgan was blackmailing me. I became expert at hiding it. You have to be in this job. Long ago I learned to shut my feelings out of my everyday life. Except for . . . well, the lurid times. Once or twice a year, I'd nip down to Plymouth – ostensibly to see my parents – and pick up a one-night stand in some tacky gay bar. That's all I ever allowed myself . . . until Julian came along. He was an aberration – but a luscious one.'

His eyes met Elizabeth's. She caught a disquieting glimpse, suddenly, of something else going on underneath. Hard to tell what. Contempt? Disdain? Mockery?

'Absolutely bloody stupid, of course, the whole thing. A summer folly. But I'd never felt such a see-sawing of emotions. I couldn't believe that this was at last happening to me. The thunderbolt. A massive electrical charge. But he knew. Julian. One day he just smiled at me and there we were, the two of us, pulled together irresistibly like a pair of magnets.'

Elizabeth heard Dottie's voice in her head. *The blind boy. Unrequited love. Cause of most of the world's crimes.*

After a pause, Lucas said, 'We weren't at all alike. Maybe that was the attraction. He made me a bit less boring. My old-fashioned embarrassment amused him. He used to tease me, you know. You're a babe, he would say, and laugh. And it did seem funny at first . . . and touching. Other guys look at me, he'd say, but you're the one I want. You won't believe this, but it was a very tender relationship. We'll just lie here, he'd say, and you can tell me how it was when you were my age. I could open up to him . . . you know? Be myself, for perhaps the first time in my whole life.'

'How long did it last?'

'Just a few months. But I was so crazily addicted that I wanted to see him all the time. Life is on the wire, Bernie, he used to say. And for a few short weeks, I chose to live on the edge, like he did.' His eyes were no longer vague, but fierce. Full of longing.

'You used to meet at Toby Perrin's flat? Is that right?'

'Yes. After dark. How was your day? he'd ask, as soon as I got inside the door. And if it had been a bad one, he always made it seem better. His love-making.'

'Tell me something, did his father know that he was gay?'

'Bisexual. He used to mess around with women too. No. Julian kept it from his father. He was afraid Hubert would cut his allowance. And he worried about his father's heart condition.'

'But his mother found out?' Which was why, Elizabeth thought, Diana had cleared all the evidence from his room. Why she was so scared when we started to dig around. Terrified of the truth leaking to the police and the press.

'Only when that little bitch . . . Morgan . . . started to blackmail her, after Julian's . . . after he died.'

Diana, too. Elizabeth wasn't surprised. Morgan had been very greedy and utterly ruthless. 'So . . . everything was hunky-dory between you and Julian. Then what happened?'

'I told you. He had to go chasing after some greasy little Italian waiter he met in the bar at The Gabriel.'

Elizabeth nodded. 'A guy with long, dark hair. And you spotted them leaving together?'

'Yes. Gerry Dundy had jumped on him. After they threw him out, I went out to the foyer to see if Julian was OK. Stupid. Dangerous. I shouldn't have . . . but it was fine, I told myself. I could act the part of the concerned employer. They'd just think I was doing my job. Solid old Bernard. But I wasn't solid underneath, I can tell you. I was a shivering mess. Blazing mad . . . worried sick about him.'

He looked round the room as if to remind himself of where he was. Carried on with the story in a dazed manner. 'So . . . I went out to see if he was OK and this Italian boy was chatting him up. "Have a drink. It's on the house. You need something after that lot." And Julian was enjoying it, playing up to him. You could see that. I watched them from the alcove.'

'And when they disappeared through the glass doors?'

'I followed them. At a discreet distance, of course. They went down to the staff quarters and shut the door behind them.'

'And?'

Silence.

'What did you do next?'

Lucas said, and there seemed to be no more blood in his veins, no more feelings, no more anything, 'I didn't do anything that night. I was too stunned. But I tackled him about it next day. Of course, he spun me some yarn about meeting this old friend and going back to his room to watch the footie. A complete load of lies.' He laughed harshly. ' "I'm a babe," he used to say. "They all look at me, but I only want you." Well, that was a lie because I caught them at it.'

'On the night you killed him?'

'Bastard!'

'You were down at The Bargepole,' said Elizabeth.

'I left my car in the station car park. In a dark corner. It was deserted at that time of night. I knew he was going to this party, so I waited outside for him to come out. He'd been avoiding me and I wanted to talk to him. Anyway, I saw him in a clinch—' His body convulsed with an involuntary shudder. 'I saw him kissing the Italian waiter. I followed them along the canal path. I watched them at it down in the grass under the bridge. I watched them separate and I followed him all the way up the hill. When he took the short-cut by the allotments, I caught him up. I asked what the hell he thought he'd been doing. And do you know what he said? How charmingly he put it? He said he'd had a quick shag. A bit of rough . . . so what? Well, I saw red. I asked what about our relationship? He said what relationship? He didn't want a relationship, he was far too young. He just stood there mocking me and it was as if I'd just really seen him for the first time. You're nothing but a bloody rent boy, I said.'

Lucas rubbed his eyes with one hand. He was definitely coming unhooked . . . losing whatever moorings he'd managed to hang on to until now. 'And he started to laugh. He was laughing at me. I couldn't stand that. Not after all I'd been through. All the pain and the anguish. That was when I saw red.'

'You hit him?'

'I went to thump him and I tripped over this length of

railing that was lying on the grass. And something inside me snapped. I bent down and picked it up . . . a great iron thing with a knob on the end . . . and he was still laughing . . . laughing at me and I couldn't stand it . . . so I lashed out at him with it. Once I'd started, I couldn't stop. He went down and then he got up again and swore at me, so I hit him again. And again. And again. I couldn't stop. There was blood everywhere, but I didn't care.'

Loud rain falling outside the open windows. Great plops of it on the stone slabs. Great splats, like in a tropical rainstorm. 'Blood all over your clothes,' Elizabeth said. 'How did you get rid of it?'

'I peeled it off as soon as I got back to the car. The rain was lashing down. There was nobody about. There was a black poly bag in the boot. I peeled everything off and shoved it in there. I wrapped myself in an old rug we kept on the back seat and I drove home. I hid the bag in the garden shed, crept into the house by the back door and sneaked upstairs to get some clean clothes. Wendy was asleep in front of the television when I came down. She didn't suspect anything. Next morning, I burnt the bag with the clothes in. Luckily, the week before, I'd built this great pyre of hedge trimmings. I just added the poly bag, poured petrol on and set fire to it.'

'And that would have been the end of it, if Morgan hadn't found out? But she started to ask for money. So you had to kill her too?'

'She was taking every last penny I had. But that wasn't the worst of it. She threatened to tell the MoD about Julian and me.'

'And that wouldn't have gone down well?'

'Too right. They would have said it exposed me to blackmail attempts. You've seen how gays get treated in the services. And I was about to get my plum posting to Italy. The peak of my career. My swansong. I couldn't let her ruin it all.'

CHAPTER FORTY-NINE

In the garden, chill green and blue shadows, filtered with mauve. The rain went on pouring down as if it would never end. Indoors, too, once the dam had burst, it seemed there was no stopping it. Bernard's words came flooding out in a great gush.

'No one came to pick me up. Life went on. I was perfectly safe, it seemed. Miserable, terrified . . . unable to eat or sleep – but on the outside, the same boring old Bernard.' He was reliving it all. His face had the heaviness of a felled oak.

'Until?'

'Until I heard this radio talk, about a month after I . . . after Julian died. Write away your problems. Write a letter to the people who are stuck inside your brain. I'd have tried anything at that particular moment. It was liberating. But it was madness, because I did it at work. Wrote a letter to Julian. One day when I was screaming inside, when I couldn't concentrate . . . when it all got too much.'

'And Morgan found the letter?'

'Yes. One afternoon, there I was writing away, under cover of doing this report. And there's an almighty bang outside in the road. Everyone rushed out. There was a tanker on fire at the crossroads. All hell breaking loose. I went out to see what was happening. Everyone did . . . except Morgan. I'd shoved the letter I was writing underneath the blotter, but not far enough. She went in and started nosing round and she found it.'

'So what did she say?'

'Nothing, at first.'

'She didn't tell you?'

'No. She took a photo-copy and shoved it in her pocket. And then she bided her time. Waited until she worked out exactly what she wanted. A regular payment, in cash, every month on the dot. And extra cash if something caught her eye that she couldn't afford. What could I do? If she'd told the powers-that-be, I'd have been out on my ear. I'd have lost everything . . . my promotion, my pension rights. Not to mention the disgrace of it all if my family found out.'

'But they found out in the end? Your wife, I mean?'

'I had to tell her. She wanted to know where all the money was going. And I blurted it out.' His mouth twisted into a grimace. 'If I hadn't written that stupid letter, I'd have been safe.'

Elizabeth said, 'Actually, I don't think the letter mattered much, one way or the other.'

That surprised him. He turned his head abruptly. 'What do you mean? Of course it mattered.'

'OK, so it gave her positive proof. But I think Morgan knew about you and Julian all along.'

'She couldn't have. She didn't say.'

'No. But as you told me, she was good at biding her time. It amused her to watch and wait.' She was thinking about Morgan quarrelling with Julian at the flat; the last visit, particularly, when the brick went through the window. 'I can't prove it, but I rather think she'd spotted what was going on. Maybe Julian dropped a hint, before he knew how dangerous she was. He certainly liked living on the edge . . . and Morgan knew about him using the flat. Maybe she watched you going in there. Anyway, I'm pretty sure her first blackmail victim was Julian. That's why he was always borrowing money from people. If he didn't pay up, she would tell Hubert about what was going on, with, perhaps, disastrous consequences. And Julian loved his father.' Hubert was probably the only person in the world the boy had truly loved, apart from Diana. 'He couldn't risk anything setting off another heart attack.'

It was clear, now, in her mind. Julian had called Morgan's bluff on the night the brick went through the shop window. When she had bled him dry. When there was no more money he could lay his hands on. And after Julian's death, the little blood-sucker had moved in on Diana as well as Bernard. No wonder she could afford to buy a nice little house up by The Assembly Rooms.

If man is only a little lower than the angels, Elizabeth thought, then maybe the angels should reform.

'She certainly made a pile out of me. She loved the feeling of power . . . having a goose that laid golden eggs. Sometimes I despaired. Once or twice, I thought about walking into the police station myself, just to thwart her. But I couldn't bring myself to do it. There was Tom to think of. And Wendy. I had to stick it out.'

'Even though she was practically bankrupting you?'

'Greedy bitch.' The words slipped out with unaccustomed savagery. 'She knew Tom would need my financial support at Oxford, but she didn't care. She laughed. "You'll find it somewhere," she said. "Let him get a job like all the other poor students." '

Outside the windows, parched grass was soaking up the rain. Elizabeth said, 'So then you had this idea how to get her off your back? You'd kill her and make it look as if Gerry had done it?'

Lucas didn't answer.

'You thought, may as well be hanged for a sheep as a lamb?'

Slowly, Lucas looked up. 'It didn't come to me right away. At first, I just thought, if only I could pay somebody to get rid of her. It'd be cheaper in the long run. And then I thought, but there is somebody . . . and he might not need paying. Dundy was obviously unstable. He wouldn't take much pushing over the edge. The more I thought about it, the simpler it seemed.'

'Fire him up a bit and who knows? So you started a campaign?'

'Start off small, I thought.'

'You made a few anonymous phone calls?'

'I knew it would wind him up.'

'And then you sent him the note in Julian's handwriting?'

'It was one Julian had written to me, but you couldn't

tell. *I thought we might meet tonight. Usual place? Nine o'clock? J.*' A shade of cunning crossed his face. 'Rather clever, I thought. And it had the desired effect. She came in with a black eye the following morning. People noticed.'

Elizabeth remembered the rough edge in Dundy's voice the last time they had met. His tortured expression. You poor sucker, she thought.

'I didn't plan for him to kill himself.'

I bet you didn't.

'I didn't even think he'd get much of a prison sentence. You know how it is these days. A good lawyer would play up all the lies she'd told him . . . the unhappy first marriage . . . losing the baby. I thought, a jury will feel sorry for him. He'll do a year or so and then be out again. They might even treat his depression . . . straighten him out.'

Big of you, thought Elizabeth. Playing God with another man's life, exulting in your own strength. You can go to hell and back, Dundy, I'm all right. The coldness in his eyes made her feel chill suddenly. 'So . . .' she said, '. . . the night you killed Morgan. How did you get Gerry . . . and Morgan, for that matter . . . up to Perrin's flat?'

'The flat?' he said almost indifferently. 'That was a bit of a brainwave. I still had a key, you see, from when I used to meet Julian there. I couldn't risk being seen anywhere near Morgan's house. So I arranged to meet her at Perrin's flat at nine that evening. She'd been demanding an extra thousand pounds. I said I hadn't got it. I said we had to talk at a neutral venue. Anyway, she agreed to meet me there. I wasn't sure she'd turn up, but she did. She loved all the intrigue, you see. She was addicted to it. That, in the end, was her downfall.

'I got to the flat at a quarter to nine . . . prudently disguised in a baseball cap and an old tracksuit. I left my car at the bottom of the hill and took the footpath that runs up from the canal to the field at the back of Perrin's garden. I slipped up the back stairs to the flat. I opened the door, left it ajar, went down again and hid in the small broom cupboard at the bottom of the stairs.'

'Until they both arrived? Morgan and Dundy. How did you get him there, by the way?'

'I sent an e-mail to the gym from Morgan's machine at work. Meet me at this address at nine sharp. I've got something to tell you.'

'Which was?'

'No idea. It didn't matter as long as he turned up. Planted a few fingerprints. Had an argument that the neighbours might hear.' His tone became ironic, almost humorous. 'But as it happens, she did give him a bit of news, in the course of their conversation.'

'She told him she was expecting a baby.'

'You're ahead of me.'

'Whose baby?'

'His, apparently. Dundy's. The product of a last night together just before she left him.' A wry twist of the lips. 'She told him she was going to get rid of it . . . have an abortion, which made him very, very angry. I couldn't have arranged it better if I'd tried. He went mad—'

'Knocked her around?'

'Left her on the floor unconscious.' The grey eyes regarded her cryptically. You're a cold fish, Elizabeth thought with a shiver.

'And then he left?'

'And then he left and I finished her off.'

'You strangled her with a length of flex?'

'It was easy.' There was no expression at all on his face now. He looked at her as if from a great distance. As if he had forgotten that she existed. It was quite a shock, therefore, when he reached out a hand, slid out the drawer of the desk in front of him and produced a small handgun, which he proceeded to point in her direction.

'Bernard – no!' There was a movement behind them. Wendy had reappeared. In an undertone, she was pleading with her husband.

'Not here, certainly.' He was waving Elizabeth towards the patio doors.

'Tom won't be long.'

'I know.' He stood, curiously rigid, facing Elizabeth. 'Get her car keys.'

'Bernard – you can't.'

'I've no choice.' A decisive, peremptory, emphatic way of speaking. 'Another body? So what? Your body is God's holy temple, my mother used to say. Remember that, Bernard. Do not defile. Well, I had the sin of disobedience inside me. I defiled and I'll go on defiling. Can't stop. Won't stop. It's too late for me now, but I can save Tom. Stop his life going down the chute. He won't suffer—'

From the corner of her eye, Elizabeth caught the terror on his wife's face.

'Where are you taking her?' Wendy asked.

'The further away the better. Somewhere wooded.' He was thinking hard. 'Somewhere isolated. I want you to follow with the Fiesta. I'll need a lift back.' Thinking on his feet. 'Don't worry. I'll write Tom a note to say we've gone out for an hour. Get the car keys. And hurry. I want her and her car out of here before he gets back.'

'But you can't—'

'Don't argue. Just do it.' No more fear. Just despatching. 'You're wondering if I have the nerve to do it, Mrs Blair. I can assure you that I do. My mother made me very hard inside. She used to try and beat the sin out of me. Great power in her wrists, that woman.'

My God, he's barking, Elizabeth thought. Lucas's expression was quite calm, but seriously alarming. He was looking at her as if she was already dead.

'Wendy. The keys.'

The wait seemed endless, but at last she moved. Lucas stood gazing at Elizabeth as his wife edged nearer. Divide and rule, Elizabeth thought. And above all, delay. 'You're prepared to stick with him, in spite of everything?' she asked Wendy. 'Is that wise?'

Wendy said, 'We've travelled a long way together. And there's Tom.'

'You think the boy—'

'Shut up!' Lucas told her. 'Slide your bag across the floor to my wife.'

'I really don't think I should.'

'I'm not playing games,' he warned.

'Neither am I.'

'The bag. Or I fire.'

'Oh, I don't think so, do you? Not just here. How would you explain all that gore to your son?' She gazed back at him with more self-control than she felt.

Lucas hesitated.

'It's one thing to kill up on Beechen Cliff in a blind rage—'

His mouth tightened.

'Or in a deserted flat, when your victim's out for the count.'

He was circling round her; had placed himself at an angle between her and the windows.

'But in your own home, with your wife watching and—'

Her eyes moved behind him to the garden path.

Wendy's eyes went there, too. A look of horror filled her face.

Lucas tried not to look, but it was a losing battle. And as soon as he turned his head, just a fraction, Elizabeth launched herself at him . . . chopped the edge of her hand against his right elbow.

The gun went off, Bernard gave a yelp of pain, but it was the head of a Staffordshire figure that got blown clean off, not Elizabeth's. Not Wendy's. Nor that of Max, who was at this moment coming in through the double doors, closely followed by the uniformed figure of Andy.

'What kept you?' she asked, as she retrieved the gun from under the dining-room table.

'What made you think I'd find you? Bloody stupid, going off without telling anybody where. If Ginger hadn't been worried about you—'

Elizabeth interrupted to tell Andy he had his double murderer. 'He was good enough to confess.' She patted her pocket. 'I've got it on tape.'

She gave herself the satisfaction of noting Bernard Lucas's reaction. His eyes seemed to go dead; the man behind the face gave up, too. It was Wendy who let out all her feelings of resentment and bitterness. 'I hope you're satisfied,' she bit back at Elizabeth. 'I hope you can live with what you've done to my son.'

A lurch deep in her stomach. Elizabeth hoped so, too. But it didn't do to dwell on it. She watched Andy arrest the pair of them and reflected that life, at times, was a messy and unsatisfactory business.

CHAPTER FIFTY

There was a wind blowing. Exquisite. Elizabeth shoved the office window up as far as it would go, stuck her head out and breathed in all that freshness. The air had been rinsed clean. Behind her, in the far corner of the office, Max was running his fingers slowly over the keys of the piano, which meant that he was thinking. And stalling for time, but he'd had plenty and she was about to get a grip on him.

'So we're going to make her permanent?' Elizabeth said. 'You agree?'

'Who?' Max pretended he didn't know what she was talking about.

'Ginger. We should take her on permanently. She's very efficient.'

He picked out a lazy arpeggio; only one duff note. 'Can we afford her?'

'Can we afford not to? You've seen the monthly figures. Never been healthier, thanks to the cheques she chased up.'

'Yeah . . . well.'

'Is that a positive?'

Max raised one shoulder into a hunch. He supposed it would have to be.

'Then I can ask her?' Elizabeth had heard Ginger's footsteps coming up the stairs.

'I suppose so.' Just a note or two more, then he stopped.

'Hi!' Ginger said as she came through the door. 'How's the head?'

'Still sore.' Max turned on the piano stool.

'I've been meaning to ask for ages . . . What's a piano doing in an office?'

'Came up the stairs, but wouldn't go down,' Max told her.

'Rumoured to belong to a piano teacher who lived up here thirty years ago,' Elizabeth said. 'By the way, thanks for sending in the cavalry the other night.'

Ginger dumped her bag on the desk. 'I hear they got there in the nick of time?'

'She was lucky,' Max said. 'If Grenfell had kept me another quarter of an hour—'

'Grenfell?' Elizabeth said.

'We went round to call on him. Andy put the frighteners on. Know why Grenfell was visiting Dundy on Friday nights?'

'No idea.'

'He was supplying the gym with drugs. Muscle enhancing steroids to be sold under the counter. Imported cheap from the States and sold at a huge profit.'

'So how did you work out where I was?' Elizabeth asked.

'Process of elimination. Ginger was certain you were tailing one of them. And she was worried about you. The Lucases were the last on our list. What made you suspect Bernard, for God's sake?'

'A photograph that Hilly sent me. The expression that it caught on Bernard's face when he saw Julian disappearing with this other young guy. And when I asked myself who Morgan was fleecing, where she was getting all her money from . . . Well, it made sense. Who had most in the bank to give? And who had most to lose? The man at the top. Lucas.' After that, piecing all the bits hadn't been difficult. Matching up the colours until it felt right.

Max said, 'Poor old Bernie. You've got to feel sorry for him in a way. All his life as cautious as hell, frightened to dip his toe in. And the first time he decides to lose sight of the shore . . . opt for a little adventure . . . look what happens.'

Elizabeth said, 'It's the son I feel sorry for.' It's always the kids that suffer, she told herself. Sins of the fathers and all that. She leant back against the window sill and said, 'Perrin must have known Julian was bisexual. But he never let on. Scared he might get incriminated. By the way, Warren has been charged with theft and receiving stolen goods. The

Squadron-Leader rang me at crack of dawn. He's mightily pleased with himself. Thinks it was all his doing. He even renewed his offer to join us. Which reminds me . . .' she said to Ginger, '. . . how would you like to work for us permanently?'

Ginger's eyebrows went up. 'Is this a joint decision?'

'It is.'

'You're kidding me? You don't object?' she said to Max.

But she didn't strike any sparks. 'Why should I?' he asked airily.

'Because it's only a couple of weeks since you sacked me.'

'That was because you over-stepped the mark.'

'No. It was because you lost your rag.'

Elizabeth deliberately took the conversation back to Draycott. 'It's clear that they all had an interest in stressing that Julian was heterosexual. In throwing us off the track. Wendy actually did have a crush on him and used the fact, when desperate, to stop us guessing the truth about her husband. Morgan invented an affair with Julian because she was a compulsive liar. She only visited him at the flat once . . . the night he told her he wasn't going to give her any more money. The night she put the brick through the window.' But Morgan finally got her come-uppance, thought Elizabeth. And he that dies, pays all debts.

'And finally, there's Diana Neville, who was horrified when Hubert called us in, petrified of what we might uncover. So what did she do? Tried to put us off the scent by chatting on about Julian's multitude of girlfriends. She also cleared his room of anything that might have suggested a gay relationship. Incidentally, it was Diana who ransacked the office and sent us the rabbit's head, in the hope that it would frighten us off.'

She remembered what Julian's mother had said to her at the house in Beechen Grove, the previous evening. 'I lost all sense of proportion. I was devastated to be told my son was a sexual deviant. Terrified the papers might splash it all over their front pages.'

'Your son was himself. If the Lord made him bisexual,

who are we to argue? At least he deserves praise for trying to spare your husband pain.'

'That's what I'm hanging on to.' Bleak grey eyes stared at Elizabeth.

'I was so sorry to hear that Hubert had died.'

'I'm not.' There was no hedging, no skirting of the plain truth. 'He'll never know now. About Julian, I mean. I shan't have to see his pain every day. Easier to bear on your own . . .'

Was that why some of the stress had gone from her face? Was that why she seemed less . . . chill?

'So was it Mrs Neville who clobbered Max at the flats?' Ginger asked.

'No. I'd guess it was one of the residents of Angola House. Someone who didn't like him sniffing around.' Something nipped at her mind. 'Damn! I forgot something. Be back in a sec.'

'Disorganised,' said Max, as she vanished on to the landing.

'She solved your case for you.'

'And damned near got herself into deep trouble.'

'Never mind. You got her out of it and that gives you the edge. What more could a man ask?' Ginger stood there, a little smile twitching at the corner of her mouth, hugging her ribs with thin, freckled arms. Waiting for him to come back at her. And for that reason, I won't, Max thought. He was beginning to get a bearing on her. Lose his rag? No chance.

Actually, he was beginning to enjoy the cut and thrust. At least you knew where you were with her. An argument with Ginger . . . well, it wasn't at all like when Jess cut up rough. There was an undercurrent of humour underneath the goading. Perversity, maybe, but no snares, nothing to find yourself tangled in afterwards. Nothing to drag you down deep among the dead men.

Which is where he'd been with Jess. 'Hoo-bloody-rah!' Fran had said when he'd called her last night to say that she had been right all along. 'You found your brains. She was bad news, Max. Not worth the hassle. You didn't have a thing in common.'

'You're thinking about *her*,' Ginger's voice said lightly. 'Jess.'

No point in denying it.

'She was very beautiful,' Ginger said, sounding as if she meant it.

'That's a change of tune.'

'I never said she wasn't beautiful. I didn't like what she did to herself.'

Well, yes, thought Max. There was artifice. I can't deny that. I seem to have changed since I came south. Must have done. I've got used to different things. A different kind of woman. His eyes took in Ginger's tanned face and grey eyes. Her grey-blue silk trousers and slate-coloured top. All very understated. Clean-looking, he thought suddenly, for no reason at all. Clear all the way through, like a mountain stream. Oh, come on, Max! That's pathetic.

'Jess was a very beautiful liar,' he said, as if to no one at all.

Ginger said, 'Brave of you to admit it.'

'I thought you'd say "I told you so." '

'Can't hit a man while he's down,' said Ginger. 'Anyway, it happened to me a couple of years back.'

'What did?'

'I fell for a complete prat. He dumped me. Why do you think I moved back to Bath?'

'I never thought.' It explained a lot of things, Max told himself. Her attitude. Her stroppiness ... which he quite liked, now he came to think of it. Now that he knew how to handle her.

'Why should you?'

'Right. That's that done,' Elizabeth said, as she came bouncing back in through the door. She plonked a bulging carrier bag on the chair.

'What's what done?'

'The picnic.'

'What picnic?'

'The one I'm going on this afternoon.'

'Anywhere in particular?' Max asked.

'I thought I'd go sniff the ocean. Caroline will mind things down below.' Outside, there was a blue sky with clouds. 'We had a result, didn't we? I deserve a half-day off.' She needed to leap out of it all. The lies, the sleaze, the tragedy. There were times when it got to you. Times when you imagined it might turn infectious. And then you needed to clear the mind, unfog the brain. You needed little churches, Mendip stone cottages, a wheel of gulls, waves and breakers.

'Couldn't we all go?' asked Max. 'Shut up shop?'

'If you want to. Of course.'

Ginger looked surprised, but not displeased.

Breaking out, Elizabeth thought. We'll untether ourselves for an hour or two. From down below in the mews came a clamour of voices. She picked up the office keys and felt the afternoon swing towards her, open and unclouded.